'. . . Once we have begun our operations there can be no turning back, but if you agree to join me I have no single doubt as to our success. What is your answer?'

Hinckman stood up – his great chin jutted out and he threw his massive shoulders back as he replied:

'I guess this is the biggest proposition that's ever been put up, Lord Fortescue – but I'm your man!'

Lord Gavin took his hand, a sudden fire leapt into his strange, cold eyes. 'Within a year,' he said softly, 'you and I will be the richest and most powerful men in the world.'

BY DENNIS WHEATLEY

NOVELS

The Launching of Roger Brook
The Shadow of Tyburn Tree
The Rising Storm
The Man Who Killed the King
The Dark Secret of Josephine
The Rape of Venice
The Sultan's Daughter
The Wanton Princess
Evil in a Mask
The Ravishing of Lady
  Mary Ware

The Scarlet Impostor
Faked Passports
The Black Baroness
V for Vengeance
Come Into My Parlour
Traitors' Gate
They Used Dark Forces

The Prisoner in the Mask
The Second Seal
Vendetta in Spain
Three Inquisitive People
The Forbidden Territory
The Devil Rides Out
The Golden Spaniard
Strange Conflict
Codeword—Golden Fleece

Dangerous Inheritance
Gateway to Hell
The Quest of Julian Day
The Sword of Fate
Bill for the Use of a Body

Black August
Contraband
The Island Where Time Stands Still
The White Witch of the South Seas

To the Devil—a Daughter
The Satanist

The Eunuch of Stamboul
The Secret War
The Fabulous Valley
Sixty Days to Live
Such Power is Dangerous
Uncharted Seas
The Man Who Missed the War
The Haunting of Toby Jugg
Star of Ill-Omen
They Found Atlantis
The Ka of Gifford Hillary
Curtain of Fear
Mayhem in Greece
Unholy Crusade
The Strange Story of Linda Lee

SHORT STORIES

Mediterranean Nights

Gunmen, Gallants and Ghosts

HISTORICAL

A Private Life of Charles II (*Illustrated by Frank C. Papé*)
Red Eagle (*The Story of the Russian Revolution*)

AUTOBIOGRAPHICAL

Stranger than Fiction (*War Papers for the Joint Planning Staff*)
Saturdays with Bricks

SATANISM

The Devil and all his Works (*Illustrated in colour*)

Dennis Wheatley

SUCH POWER
IS DANGEROUS

ARROW BOOKS

ARROW BOOKS LTD
3 Fitzroy Square, London W1

An imprint of the Hutchinson Publishing **Group**

London Melbourne Sydney Auckland
Wellington Johannesburg Cape Town
and agencies throughout the world

First published by
Hutchinson & Co (Publishers) Ltd **1933**
Arrow edition 1962
Second impression 1964
Third impression 1965
Fourth impression 1973
This edition 1975

Made and printed in Great Britain
by The Anchor Press Ltd,
Tiptree, Essex

ISBN 0 09 907370 6

To

J.G.L.

In memory of an expedition
across a marsh and of a
thousand hospitalities

AUTHOR'S NOTE

All the characters in this story are entirely fictitious; the finances—ambitions—and situations of the Corporations described have no relation to those of any film business in real life, and this story is . . . as the fortune-tellers say . . . for amusement only.

D.W.

Contents

PART ONE

THE WAR IN AMERICA

1

A Plot to Dominate the World

'How do you know that?'

'Because, my dear Ronnie, having decided to take an interest in the film world I took some little trouble to find out.' Lord Gavin Fortescue's austere, lined face broke into the semblance of a smile. There was just a hint of pleased vanity in his quiet voice as he watched the evident surprise of the young man before him.

Ronnie Sheringham was puzzled. This was by no means the first time in their short acquaintance that Lord Gavin had shown himself possessed of important information about the affairs of people whom he did not know. He voiced his thought as he stretched out a brown hand for the gin sling beside his chair.

'How the devil do you get to know these things—you've never met any of these chaps, you haven't even been outside the hotel since we got to Hollywood.'

'I studied the situation so carefully before I left England that the scraps of information which you furnish often enable me to form much more important conclusions than you might suppose.'

'Yes, I thought as much.' Ronnie shot a quick glance at the strange little figure in the arm-chair. Lord Gavin Fortescue was not a dwarf, yet he was curiously ill-proportioned; his body frail and childlike, his head massive and powerful with a shock of silver hair. His rat-trap mouth and hard determined chin belied the mildness of his pale blue eyes; those eyes, set wide in the pale face, that could go so cold and soulless on occasions. A man of great charm, great personality, great intellect, but dangerous—oh, how dangerous, thought Ronnie, as he added casually: 'You would be a bit handicapped without me, though!'

Lord Gavin smiled, but into his eyes there crept that sudden hardness. 'It was fortunate,' he said quietly, 'that we should have met on the boat and that you should have been coming out to Hollywood to try your luck. As I must of necessity spend a certain portion of my time in the company of anyone who acts on my behalf, I naturally prefer that my agent should possess *savoir faire* and good breeding—but you can rest assured, my dear Ronnie, that I could have found a hundred people to perform the small services which I require with equal efficiency, if not with your charm of manner!'

'Anyway, I've fixed the big boy of Trans-Continental Electric for you—he'll be here any minute now, it's nearly three.'

'And it is your opinion that this man Hinckman will agree to my suggestion?'

Ronnie ran a hand through his brown wavy hair and nodded quickly, 'I'd put every writ I've got on it!'

'Good—when he arrives you will leave us, of course, he may not be willing to speak freely before a third person.'

'Just as you like.' Ronnie stood up and stretched himself, he strolled over to the open window and out onto the balcony.

The fierce sunshine of the early afternoon shone with almost dazzling brilliance on the palm trees and cactus in the hotel garden. Every leaf and spear showed with a distinctness almost startling to the eye—but Ronnie's strong blue eyes seemed impervious to the glare, he was a true child of the sunshine.

Others burnt and blistered if they were tempted to brave the Californian beach without due precautions—Ronnie's sturdy limbs only turned a shade more golden brown. He would love to have spent days on end baking in the heat, lazing about doing nothing—and he would have, had it not been for a question of money. After all, one had to live, and life is usually a problem for the youngest son of a youngest son brought up in the habits and luxury of England's ruling classes.

Ronnie was nearly thirty—already his contemporaries at Eton were succeeding to family places, or soundly established as junior partners in big businesses over which their fathers had control—while he was jobless, and his prospects almost nil. Since he had left Oxford he had had a dozen openings, many of them good ones, too. His amazing general knowledge, quick grasp of facts, and great personal charm endeared him immediately to new acquaintances. He won the confidence of elderly magnates with surprising facility, and lured them into offering him positions, *but* he lost that confidence with almost the same rapidity. He was incurably lazy and detested all routine. Money slipped through his fingers with disconcerting ease, and every few months he would find himself penniless once more. His partners or employers cut their losses, turning him adrift—yet such was his personal charm that they never blamed him and always remained his friends.

Lord Gavin was admiring Ronnie's broad shoulders and slim hips. The younger man was not tall, though taller than he looked. The square, broad head and deep chest robbed him of something of his height, yet he was a striking figure in the loose well-cut clothes he always wore. His bright shirts and socks gave him a distinction which would have been vulgarity in any man lacking his flair for clothes.

Even at his present age Lord Gavin had not completely conquered the bitter envy which filled his heart at the sight of others' fine physique in comparison with his own puny form. He was watching Ronnie's back with something of that envy now.

Ronnie turned suddenly and came into the room. 'It wasn't easy to get at Hinckman—he's got a whole army of secretaries and hangers-on.'

Lord Gavin smiled. 'Does that mean that you would like some money on account?'

'Well, I had to weigh out quite a bit.'

'I see—then how much shall we say?'

Ronnie shrugged, his hands deep in his trouser pockets. 'Oh, man's time, you know—I've been about a fortnight on the job.' He was far too clever to name a sum, and his remark had all the delightful casualness which implied an utter indifference to money.

Lord Gavin drew out his pocket-book. 'It is expensive here, I know—I trust a thousand dollars will meet the case?'

'Thanks, that'll do to carry on.' Ronnie took the note and thrust it into his trouser pocket as if it was of no more interest to him than the coupon in a packet of cigarettes, although actually at that moment he knew his hotel bill was nearly four hundred dollars and his funds were reduced to less than fifty. 'That'll be Hinckman, I expect,' he added, as a sharp rap came on the door of the sitting-room.

Hinckman it proved to be, a tall, broad-shouldered man of middle age dressed in a neat grey suit. A cigar protruded from the corner of his mouth—a soft hat slightly tilted off his forehead remained upon his head, his movements were abrupt and purposeful, his grey eyes quick with an authority which befitted the man who controlled the destinies of the great Trans-Continental Electric Corporation.

He nodded to Ronnie and then glanced swiftly at the man he had come to meet. Lord Gavin raised himself to his feet and leaned, a small bent figure, on his stick; it almost seemed that his powerful head was too heavy for his body—his pale eyes were searching his visitor's face.

Ronnie Sheringham stepped between them. With a wave of his brown hand he gave a casual introduction. 'Glad you were able to come, Hinckman—this is Fortescue.'

'Glad to know you.' Hinckman took Lord Gavin's small, plump fingers in his own big hand. 'Our friend here has been telling me quite a piece about you, Lord Fortescue.'

Lord Gavin gave a little bow, he waved his visitor to a seat and sank back in his arm-chair.

'I have been anxious to meet you for some time, Mr. Hinckman, and I know you to be a very busy man. I am most sensible of the honour you do to me in coming here, and I feel confident that I shall not waste your valuable time.'

'Is that so? Waal, it's mighty unusual fer me to go around seein' folks on business—they come to me, but I'm told you figure to go into motion pictures in a big way and I'm a business man.' With a flick of his tongue Hinckman transferred his cigar from one corner of his mouth to the other.

'Well, so long chaps. . . . I've got a date at the Plaza.' With an airy wave of the hand Ronnie picked up his hat and left them.

Lord Gavin leaned forward. He spoke clearly and impressively, his voice was soft and musical, he never raised it in any circumstances—yet his orders were always instantly obeyed; at times that very softness gave it a peculiarly sinister quality.

'I will not waste your time, Mr. Hinckman, by beating about the bush. I have, in the last few months, gone very thoroughly into the present state of the film industry in America, England, and Germany Many of the smaller concerns are definitely in financial difficulties—even the biggest are finding it no easy matter to continue the enormous outlay necessary to support their chains of theatres and pay their stars during this period of world depression. I have come to the conclusion that conditions at the present time offer a remarkably favourable opportunity for the formation of a combine which will control the film industry of the entire world.'

Hinckman, who had been listening attentively, gave a sudden guffaw of laughter. 'Say now,' he protested, 'you can't be serious?'

'I am—perfectly serious.'

'Then you certainly don't know what you're up against—the motion picture business is no pop-corn industry that you can corner with a few thousand grand.'

'I think I have already mentioned, Mr. Hinckman, that I have given very considerable thought to the problem. I am conversant with the affairs of the principal companies, their share capital, their assets, their liabilities, their directorates, and contracts with producers or famous stars. I will confine myself for the moment to a frank enquiry as to how you would view such a combine suggesting that it was possible to carry it into effect?'

The American spread out his knobbly hands. 'I'll certainly say it's a great idea; in fact, before the business became so immense I had views that way myself, but in those days I weren't in the same position I occupy today.'

'Exactly, but you agree in theory—providing that you were the active head of such a concern?'

'Sure. Look at the money we'd save if we could eliminate

15

competition. Stars' and directors' salaries could be cut in half! We could fix our own terms if there was no rival outfit for them to go to—though stars would still have to have big money, must have—to keep them in the public eye. Don't matter what trash you give the public—they pay to see the star. We'd all be finished if we scrapped the star system—all the same, we'd save big money!'

'Undoubtedly.' Lord Gavin nodded slowly. 'Moreover, a combine would smash all the smaller concerns, and by concentrating their studios and offices would save a huge figure in overheads.'

'Right again. They'd be able to fix the exhibitor, too—he wouldn't be able to get no films from other corporations. I figure he'd become a sort of agent only—the Combine would make the big profits here, there, and all the time, with a guaranteed market for every production.'

'Entirely my view, Mr. Hinckman. The wealth and power of such an organisation would be almost beyond the limits of imagination.'

'It certainly would, but as far as I can see imagination's just about as far as it will get, Lord Fortescue—there ain't no practical way to set about it—unless you happen to have found another King Solomon's Mine!'

'Hardly that—but I am fortunate in having a very considerable sum at my disposal. You see, I have been concerned in transactions—not perhaps on quite such a vast scale—but of a similar nature, on previous occasions, and a certain European syndicate which has benefited by my abilities before is prepared to back me in this present venture.'

Hinckman looked doubtful. 'It 'ud need the Bank of England and then some to buy up the motion picture business.'

'Not quite,' Lord Gavin smiled. 'I think I am correct in saying that you control Trans-Continental Electric, but you certainly do not own all the shares. It should be possible to purchase blocks of shares, options, and the goodwill of influential persons in hostile companies for a comparatively small amount compared to the actual capital of those companies. By such means control could be secured during a period long enough for us to effect our coup.'

'It's a mighty big proposition—let's hear how you figure to set about it?' Hinckman sat forward with sudden interest, his hard grey eyes fixed on Lord Gavin's pale face.

For thirty years he had striven with relentless energy for power and position. From a penniless lad in a Western Mining Camp he had risen to the control of the greatest film company in the world; but these last few years he had been dissatisfied. It seemed that he could go no farther—and now this small, quiet man before him was opening up new vistas to satiate his inordinate ambition.

'This is my idea,' said Lord Gavin slowly, 'you are recognised as the greatest force in the film industry today, Mr. Hinckman. It is for that reason that I have approached you— a lesser man could not carry this thing through. There are in America only eight or ten corporations of real magnitude—the others we can afford to neglect, the Combine will smash them later at its leisure. The ones we have to deal with are—afer the T.C.E., which you control—Pacific Players, Star Artists, Klein Brothers, Alpha Talkies, World Wide Pictures, Ubiquitous Films, Mozarts Ltd., Reno Films, and Stillman Comedies.

'Most of these have one big personality to whom his co-directors are subservient. It should not be difficult for a man in your position to arrange a meeting with these key directors. Put this suggestion of a combine before them with all its immense advantages. Those who do not feel absolutely secure on their ground will welcome the suggestion; others may do so also if they have wisdom and foresight.

'Those who come in with us at the beginning will be fortunate in the end, since when the Combine is actually formed they will receive the benefit of their support by full allotment in the Combine of their shareholding in the old companies.'

'Yeah.' Hinckman twirled his cigar restlessly. 'So far so good, but they're a jealous lot—we don't throw no bouquets when we meet. How about the guys that won't play? We'd have to get seven out of those ten if we're to be strong enough to break the

17

other three and the small folks as well. They'll sure fight like hell!'

'I agree—but if you can get, say, three or four of those ten with you in the beginning, we should be able to select three or four more amongst the weakest of our opponents, and with the funds at my disposal secure a controlling interest in their concerns. That would bring our total up to the seven you suggest as necessary.'

'That's no practical proposition to my mind—you'd have to re-sell at top figure to the Combine to get your money back. With every share you bought, their share 'ud be raised on you, you'd sure land the Combine with the baby 'fore you'd done.'

Lord Gavin placed the tips of his small pudgy fingers together as he lay back in his low chair. 'My dear Mr. Hinckman'—he shook his head with a mildly reproving look—'I fear you underrate my poor intelligence. I can assure you that by the time I came to purchase those shares they would be offered freely and at a very heavy discount. None but those who support the Combine in its inception can be allowed to benefit to the full by its creation.'

'Go right on, Lord Fortescue—it 'ud be mighty interesting to hear how you figure to bring *that* about.'

'In this way. You will agree, I think, that the prosperity of every business is dependent on the few vital personalities who are its brains and executive. Should these be removed or disappear it is a very serious thing and the larger the business the greater repercussions of such a shock. The shares of the concern begin to fall at once.'

Hinckman nodded thoughtfully. 'That's so,' he said. 'but how do you reckon to accomplish that?'

Lord Gavin's voice sank to a lower note. 'There are two methods. The first, I trust, will prove sufficient for our needs. It is that we should offer attractive forward contracts to such key-stars, producers, camera-men, etc., whom the Combine would anyhow have to employ later on. I mean, of course, those employed by the corporations that we decide to force into joining us after your meeting. The publication of the fact that their principal executives were leaving would destroy public confidence and lower the value of the shares. If possible we should induce these people to break their present contracts in addition—indemnify them for so doing, and create legal delays to postpone an action in the courts. By such means we could ruin the value of many films at present in preparation. Get me four companies willingly, Hinckman, and I will force the other three.'

A sudden gleam of enthusiasm showed in Hinckman's eyes. Such methods were no new thing to him. When he first began the grim struggle that he had waged for thirty years, he had found it essential to put any scruples about fair dealing behind him—results were all that mattered.

'It'll take no little handling,' he said thoughtfully, 'but I guess it could be done. There's complications, though, lots of 'em. Take Barton Druce, of Pacific Players—he'd never come in, not with me. We're about the biggest of the bunch, just about neck to neck. He'd fight us, and Percy Piplin—we'd never get him; what's he got to gain?—he and the Marybanks crowd have got their own show in Star Artists . . . they're producers, directors, and stars themselves, all rolled into one. Besides, star buying on forward contracts is a game that two can play—once we start the others'll be at it—it'll sure become a competition. We'll have a big pull if you're willing to finance the game, but let's hear about your other method.'

For a moment Lord Gavin did not reply, then he said slowly, 'I wonder, Mr. Hinckman, if you realise the magnitude of my conception. The world control of the *entire* film industry. Our revenues would be greater than the budget of any but a first-class state. The wealth of Ford and Rockefeller would not compare with ours. Again, our sphere of influence would be unbounded. By the type of film which we chose to produce we could influence the mass psychology of nations. Fashions, morals, customs, could be propagated by our will—we should even be able if it suited us to fill a whole people with a mad desire to make war on their neighbour—or if we considered that a universal language would lead to world peace we could induce the children of all nations to learn English, by a decision that our talking pictures should be made in no other tongue.

We should have power to do either endless good . . . or boundless evil. No king or emperor would ever have had such power in the world before!'

Hinckman drew a sharp breath at the amazing vision which this frail elderly man spread out before him in his soft, melodious voice.

'You're right.' he said thickly, 'you're right—the President of the United States himself would be small fry compared to us—I guess it's dangerous to think just how precisely powerful we'd be'

Lord Gavin nodded. His pale eyes glittered in his broad white face. His glance was filled with the tremendous power of the fanatic, but the grim lines round his mouth belied the saintly look lent to his face by the crown of silver hair.

'Then for such a tremendous project,' he went on, with sudden intensity. 'I think you will agree that unusual measures are justified—should they become necessary. In Europe during the last century we have become effete, we set too high a value on the continuance in our midst of individuals who are often useless. Such cowardice has been forced upon us by a slavish multitude—and we pay the penalty in that great conceptions are sometimes thwarted or brought to naught by this stupid overvaluation of the sacredness of human life. Today it is only in the younger nations that one can find those virile natures who continue to observe a reasonable standard of proportion; men who are prepared to take great risks to attain great ends. Sometimes it is even necessary for them to ensure their own protection.' Lord Gavin paused, but he continued to hold Hinckman with his eyes. Then, with a suden change of tone, he asked casually, 'By the bye, they tell me that you keep two gunmen yourself—is that rumour true?'

Hinckman grinned. 'That's so, Lord Fortescue—if you're a rich man it's best to in this country—a good few people do, especially since the Lindbergh baby case—I keep 'em as a sort of insurance against a hold-up.'

'Exactly,' Lord Gavin smiled; ' do you consider that these men are to be trusted—if, for example, it became necessary to carry the war into the enemy's camp?'

20

'I guess so—and that's your second method, eh?'

'A method that I would not for one moment suggest we should employ, my dear Mr. Hinckman—but of course we shall offer every possible inducement for the heads of other corporations to come into our scheme—why should they refuse?'

'But just supposing one or two big boys stood right out—people who'd just make all the difference between complete success and the Combine blowing up—I guess that's what you're meaning?'

Lord Gavin waved a deprecating hand. 'Mr. Hinckman, I have an unfortunate but rooted objection to dotting my "i's" and crossing my "t's". I have laid certain proposals before you —I have pointed out that certain eventualities may arise. This child of my imagination will need money, time, patience, skilful negotiation, and an inflexible determination to override all obstacles if it is to grow into actual life. Once we have begun our operations there can be no turning back, but if you agree to join me I have no single doubt as to our ultimate success. What is your answer?'

Hinckman stood up—his great chin jutted out and he threw his massive shoulders back as he replied:

'I guess this is the biggest proposition that's ever been put up, Lord Fortescue—but I'm your man!'

Lord Gavin took his hand, a sudden fire leapt into his strange, cold eyes. 'Within a year,' he said softly, 'you and I will be the richest and most powerful men in the world.'

2

So this is Hollywood!

Avril Bamborough sat in a basket-chair under the cool shade of a eucalyptus tree in Clair de la Lune's garden. She looked very graceful there, and she knew it! For one thing she was a very graceful girl, for another she had been trained since she was a tiny child to be graceful in movement and repose.

Avril came of a great theatrical family, her grand-father, her father, and her uncles had for many years been lords of the British stage, and it was their hope that she would follow in the great tradition. At sixteen they had feared that she would be a failure, she was then a tall gawky girl, her pale narrow face surrounded by dank locks of dark hair, her big eyes staring with apparent vacancy—as she sat, solemn and pre-occupied whenever she was among older people. 'The girl is clever in a queer, hostile way,' they had said, 'she may succeed in certain Shakespearian roles or true drama, but she'll never get over with the modern plays.'

To their surprise the ugly duckling had become a swan. Her face broadened and took on colour, the dark hair, properly dressed and sweeping back from her forehead, was fine and lustrous. Her mouth was a trifle wide and her chin a little long, but they spoke of generosity and determination. Above all, the big, dark, violet eyes gave her real beauty, and by the time she was twenty her youthful shyness had disappeared.

She knew her Shakespeare backwards—and an enormous repertoire of stock plays besides. She had played minor parts for years, but only minor parts, that she might not spoil herself or her future public. Then the grind of two years in the Provinces and a tour in South Africa—after that the lead in two London plays, neither a raging success and neither a great play—but each a sound, satisfactory performance. Avril Bamborough, the critics said, had come—and come to stay.

It was then that she had decided to try the new medium of the films. Amongst the older members of her family there had been opposition—but John Bamborough, the rebel of the clan, had seen the future of the screen many years before. 'Uncle John' was now a power in the film world, his studios at Hatfield were renowned. He swept aside the protests of the elders, and welcomed Avril with open arms. She trained once more, and made a thorough study of the new techniques. Titchcock directed her and she starred in two of his big films.

Then came the German-American producer, Hugo Schultzer

—the big man of Ubiquitous. He offered her a Hollywood contract. Uncle John was loth to let her go. but he knew that the
experience would be good for her, and make her an even more
accomplished artist. That was an all-important factor to a
Bamborough; money came second—and so, a week before her
twenty-fourth birthday. Avril Bamborough had sailed upon the
great adventure. Only the day before, she had stepped off the
train at Hollywood.

Hugo Schultzer stood beside her chair. He was a nice old
homely German, fat and jolly. With a frank pleasure that gave
the lie direct to any suggestion of triumphing over his rivals,
he produced this new star from whom he hoped so much.
Social occasions were usually avoided by him, and in other circumstances he would have fought shy of Clare's garden party,
where a galaxy of stars would be certain to forgather, but today Hugo Schultzer was quite happy to face the film world
for the pleasure of presenting his new leading lady.

It pleased him greatly that Avril was easy to talk to and un-
affected. So many girls lost their heads when they reached stardom, and poor old Hugo had no idea how to cope with them
when they behaved like fractious children. He had dreaded that
with Avril, but he need not have worried. Fame was an attri-
bute of her family, and she considered that a star's contract
was only her rightful portion after all the years of grinding
work she had gone through.

A multitude of people strolled about the lovely garden, the
women in bright colours, the men in flannels. Here and there
she saw a face vaguely familiar, and yet so different from its
prototype on the screen that she hesitated to recognise it—but
most of the people about her stirred no chord of recognition
in her mind. She turned to Schultzer. 'Do tell me all about these
exciting people, please.'

He smiled. 'Most of them haf names you would not know—
some stars are here, yet also many who make for broduction.
Engineer, scene artist exberts of every kind. When imbortant
beoples arrive, I bresent them to you—Ach, here now is "Uncle
Andy".'

Avril saw a fine stalwart old gentleman approaching. Set at

a jaunty angle on his white hair he wore a rakish panama. 'Uncle Andy?' she repeated. 'I'm afraid I'm terribly ignorant, but do you know I haven't an idea who he is.'

'He is the Grand Old Man of Hollywood, he is here since nineteen eight, and is now World Wide Pictures. Uncle Andy —come here—I wish to bresent to you my new star—Miss Avril Bamborough.'

Uncle Andy removed his panama with a flourish. 'I'm sure delighted to make your acquaintance, Miss Bamborough. It certainly is a great victory that Hugo's scored—taking you off the English screen—it's a real pleasure to meet an actress of your quality here in Hollywood.'

Avril thought him charming. 'I feel very small fry here,' she smiled, 'but it cheers me up tremendously to hear you say such nice things.'

'I mean it—every word,' he assured her. 'I saw your uncle— or would it be your grandad now—way back in eighty-eight, and I've seen your folks act a hundred times since then. You're not the girl to go back on your family—even an old man like me can see that by the tilt of your chin! Hugo's a lucky fellow to have signed you up.'

'It won't be for want of trying, if I let him down,' Avril's violet eyes became very earnest.

He waved the suggestion aside with a sweep of his hat. 'You don't need to tell me that, Miss Bamborough—and I'm no poacher, but if Hugo isn't satisfied—World Wide Pictures'll take over your contract every time. I saw your last film when I was over on the other side—it certainly was great stuff . . . why, say—here's Issey.'

Uncle Andy beckoned to a little Jew who was passing at the moment. A tiny man with quick, bright eyes, and a flamboyant tie that cursed his socks. He paused, flashing them a smile which displayed two rows of enormous teeth—four of which were gold.

Uncle Andy laid a hand on the little man's shoulder. 'Issey my boy, I want to introduce you to Miss Avril Bamborough— Miss Bamborough, meet Mr. Issidor Vandelstein—he's Mozarts.'

24

The gold teeth flashed again. 'Ai'm sure pleased ter meet yer, Miss Bamborough. Vos you come to vork in Hollywood?'

'Mr. Schultzer has been kind enough to give me a contract.' Avril smiled.

'Now ain't dat fine, and vos you vorkin' on der screen 'afore?' Uncle Andy slapped him on the back. 'Miss Bamborough is one of *the* Bamboroughs, Issey—you sure know that name, they bin big folk in the theatre for generations.'

Mr. Vandelstein looked doubtful. 'Ai don't know no Bamboroughs,' he said, ' 'cept some fellah vot makes British Talkies.'

'What you need is education, Issey.' Uncle Andy shook his head.

'Vot vould Ai vant with education, ven Ai make motion pictures?' Mr. Vandelstein wanted to know. Avril's dark eyes twinkled.

'I made two pictures for Mr. Titchcock,' she said.

'Now ain't that fine! Vell, Ai vish you all the luck in der vorld, Miss Bamborough,' and with another flash of the amazing teeth Mr. Vandelstein passed on.

Hugo Schultzer had seen a friend that he wished to speak to, so for the moment Avril was alone with Uncle Andy. The handsome old man sank into a chair beside her.

'You'll certainly find us a queer lot, Miss Bamborough—there's all sorts gets to Hollywood. Good 'uns and bad 'uns—but there's a whole heap of good even in the worst of 'em, if you just go looking for it. And believe you me, half the evil that's talked ain't true—no—not by a long chalk.'

Avril thought the Grand Old Man a dear. She was anxious to learn all that she could about this new world she had come to live in, and she found him a bottomless well of information, interlarded with kindly, humorous anecdote.

'I'm terribly anxious to meet some of the real stars,' she said after a while. 'Do you think many of them will be here this afternoon?'

'Sure—there's Lila Dalmatia over there in the green hat—she's talking to Hustler Beaton at the moment. Then the dark chap in the open shirt is Pritchard Tix.'

'Is Piplin here—or either of the Marybanks?'

'No, they don't go places—they prefer to live quiet, and I guess they're big enough to please themselves. Rita Ravo was the same, and so's the English colony—Warren Hastings Rook, Jeremiah Mustard, an' all that bunch. Maybe since you're a Bamborough they'll take you up—if so you'll be fixed for the quiet life, too, and I'll not say there's anything against it for the serious artist. It sure means better work on the set. Say now—there's Carlo Green an' Handsome Harry. Howdo, Handsome—come right over here.'

'Miss Bamborough,' Uncle Andy flourished his panama once more, 'I want you to meet Mr. Carlo Green, whose name I reckon you'll know as well as your own, and Mr. Harry Honeydew—the big noise of Reno Films Ltd., and a star in his own right into the bargain. Boys—Miss Bamborough's signed up with Hugo Schultzer, and she's sure going to make a picture that'll be good to see.'

Avril looked at Carlo Green with interest. It was difficult to imagine that this six-foot-three of quiet, charming gentleman could once have been the down-and-out labourer that D. Y. Gritter had found inciting his brother workmen to strike for an extra dollar a day. In Handsome Harry she was not interested —she knew his name but only vaguely, though he seemed to know all about her, and with a smile which he firmly believed to be irresistible, began at once to talk to her of London and the people he had met there.

'Carlo, my boy—I want two words with you.' Uncle Andy took the famous star by the arm. 'See yer later, Miss Bamborough.'

'Have you see the rock garden, Miss Bamborough?' Handsome Harry enquired with a smile. Avril shook her head. 'Then you certainly should—I'll take you right along.'

The rock garden proved to be well worth seeing. It was stocked with every kind of cactus, from prickly giants to tiny midgets, and a thousand varieties of little flowering plants. The paths twisted in and out between huge boulders, and here and there rustic bridges spanned the cool trickle of a waterfall.

In all the shady corners comfortable seats were set, the occupants being sheltered from view except by the casual passer-by.

Many of the nooks were already taken, but Handsome Harry found a vacant place and they sat down.

He stretched out his long legs, and leant an arm along the back of Avril's chair, an arrangement that she did not care about, but the gesture was so natural that she did not wish to look foolish by asking him to move it.

Handsome Harry proved a friendly, good-natured person, but a bore. He sat there with his hat tilted over his eyes and talked continuously of motion pictures—their past, their present, and their future. Avril would not have minded that, but unfortunately, in his view, motion pictures and the activities of Handsome Harry were synonymous. It seemed that he had been in Hollywood since the early days. Somewhere in the dark ages of 1920, when Avril had been a little girl at school, he had been a star. He was still a star—but Avril felt certain that he would have passed from public favour long ago, had it not been that he held a controlling interest in Reno Films; and the company had to allow him to direct his own pictures whether they liked it or not.

His mentality had not advanced since the days when his films were world famous. Those were the days before the coming of the German influence, and the talkies—when real talent was scarce on the screen, and Hollywood still a small town with dusty back lots on its main boulevard.

Avril let him run on but ceased to listen. Snatches of conversation came to her from the seat just round the corner—it was her own name that caught her ear.

'Bamborough? Oh, yes. I know John Bamborough well—his second boy was in Pop when I was at Eton.'

The voice was quiet and lazy—it was an English voice, and despite its laziness there was something clipped about the words. It had that curious intonation that has been substituted by modern youth for the old Oxford drawl. Avril wondered vaguely who the man could be.

The voice went on, 'Oh, when the Combine starts to function, they'll give her a contract—she's pretty certain of a job.'

'An' you reckon it's a certainty that Hinckman'll put this Combine over?' an American voice enquired.

'Yes, rather, I'd put my last writ on it!'

'They'll need big money—we're all half broke in this darn town.'

'That end is all right—I've known the chap whose financing it for years—Gavin Fortescue—he's worth millions.'

'Would that be Lord Fortescue?'

'Yes, Dorrington's brother—Gavin would have been the Duke if he'd been born two hours earlier. They were twins, you know—rotten luck for him—people say he tried to do his brother in when he was about ten, anyhow, his jealousy turned his brain a bit—he's a queer eccentric bird.'

'Well, now—you don't say! And are you acquainted with the Duke?'

'I've stayed at Wenchworth now and again—lovely place, it had three hundred and sixty-five windows—one for every day in the year . . . at least—no, that's Blenheim—I'm confusing the two. When you come over to England I must take you down, they're both worth seeing if you like that sort of thing.'

'I'd appreciate that, Mr. Sheringham.'

'Oh, not a bit—I can easily arrange it by dropping a line to Uncle Bill.'

'And this Lord Fortescue—he really means to see Hinckman through?'

'Yes, you needn't worry about that.'

'What d'you figure the Combine'll be floated for?'

'It isn't settled yet—I favour a hundred million—pounds, not dollars—I don't see how we can do with less.'

'That's a pretty tidy sum, but I guess you're right. When'll the flotation take place?'

'All depends. Once we've got the interests we want secured, we shall go ahead. Of course, that's where people like yourself and Hinckman come in, everybody who's in on the ground floor of a thing like this is certain to make a packet, owners, producers, and stars as well. Those who are stupid enough to get left will find themselves out of a job. The biggest star would be chicken food in a year if their publicity was cut off—they'll have to come over.'

'That's mighty true, Mr. Sheringham—and it's to be a world concern, you say?'

'Yes, I'm pretty well in with most of the English crowd; in fact, I've got the biggest concern more or less in my pocket already—so there won't be any serious opposition there.'

Avril lost the remainder of their interesting conversation, for Handsome Harry had taken her absorption in her unseen neighbours as something more flattering to himself, and now, dropping his hand on to her arm, he suddenly drew her towards him.

With a quick jerk she wriggled free—her violet eyes grew hard as she withdrew her head from the proximity of his—he seemed surprised, and more than a little offended.

'Say, now, what's the trouble, little girl?' he asked in a pained voice. 'You sure don't object to a little friendly kiss—you won't go far in Hollywood if you do.'

Avril lifted her well-marked brows a fraction, she smiled, but it was a chilly smile. 'Indeed—how interesting!' she said gravely. 'Do you know, I adore kissing—but only with good-looking men!'

For a moment Handsome Harry was taken aback by this attack on his world-famous features—he could think of no adequate retort—then he laughed good-naturedly and stood up. 'Say, you're a great kid, Miss Bamborough—I reckon you'll go a long way, but if that's your view I guess we'd better get back to the party.'

She forgave him instantly, he would have been a nice creature, she thought, if it had not been for his incredible vanity. Of course, he had not taken her remark seriously—nothing could penetrate his armour of conceit. They strolled back to the lawns, Handsome quite cheerfully resuming his monologue upon motion pictures as produced, directed and acted by Harry Honeydew.

Avril looked about for Hugo Schultzer, but could not see him—crowds more people had arrived and it seemed a hopeless task to try and find him in that slowly-moving throng.

'Hello, Angie!' Handsome had halted before a small, dark man with olive skin and flashing black eyes. 'What are you doin' in this crush? Is the big boy featurin' in the party?'

'Sure, Mistaire Honeydew, dat guy Mick looka after him, while I tak-a-walk around.'

'Miss Bamborough—meet Mr. Donelli. Miss Bamborough has a rooted objection to kissing any but a handsome man, Angie! I guess you'd better see what you can do to cut me out while I go hit up the drinks!'

With this parting thrust he nodded amiably to Avril and turned away. 'Where did you leave Hinckman, Angie?' he called over his shoulder.

'Over dare—he talka to Lula Valdez.' Angelo pointed the couple out and Handsome Harry walked away.

Avril looked quickly over to where the tall, robust Hinckman stood with the little Mexican star. So that was the great chief of the Trans-Continental Electric Corporation. He was a big man even among this gathering of big men, and she thought he looked it. Angelo drew her away. 'We goa to see der rock garden, yes?—verry pretti there,' and for the second time that afternoon Avril allowed herself to be led into the twisting maze of rock-walled paths, with their sudden vistas of lily pools and miniature cascades.

Angelo found an even more secluded corner. She did not know if he was a star or not, and fearing to offend him by apparent ignorance, enquired what film he was making now.

He waved a beringed hand, and shook his glossy head. 'I no playa da filma—it ees too much work—not enough dolla, unless you coma big star.'

Avril looked at the little man with an amused smile, and asked him what he did do.

'I da boss gunman in Mistaire Hinckman's racket,' he said proudly. 'I—Angelo Donelli—da besta shot in California.'

Avril was mildly horrified, but vastly intrigued. 'Do you really kill people?' she enquired.

He laughed. 'In Chicago I see plenty trouble—that's why I comma here, I wanta da quiet life—I just bodyguard for Mistaire Hinckman—case other guys geta fresh. Mistaire

Hinckman very rich—but da gangs no trouble him while Angelo around!'

After that Angelo told her a number of surprising things about himself. Not only was he the finest shot in California, but he was certainly the most handsome man—the most sought after by the women in Hollywood—from the stars to the cuties in the bread-queue. He was the greatest lover that the world had ever known since his great countryman, that amazing rogue Casanova, had gone the way of all flesh some two hundred years before. With Gallic frankness he told Avril that she surpassed in loveliness all the women he had ever known, and with Latin speed in coming to the essential point suggested that they should leave the party, and adjourn forthwith to enjoy together the oldest pastime in the world.

Avril had had similiar suggestions made to her during her theatrical career by a hundred different types of men, but never before with quite the outspoken abandon of the glossy Angelo. Inwardly she could not help being amused, though outwardly she maintained an expression of chill severity—and really Angelo was becoming a little embarrassing. It looked as though, nothing daunted by her refusal to leave the party, he meant to assault her there and then.

Ronnie Sheringham saved the necessity for strong measures on either side by coming round the corner.

'Hullo!' he said to Angelo. 'The big chief's wanting you—you'd better get back.'

'Mistaire Hinckman,' exclaimed Angelo, standing up. '*Madonna mia*—an' at such a time. Oh 'ell!' He seized Avril's hand and kissed it. 'I seea you again, eh?—we maka da party together—very fine—Angelo maka you so 'appy you do not know,' with which he rushed off to find his charge.

Ronnie's brown face broke into a smile. 'Sorry,' he said, 'I hope I haven't spoilt your fun.'

'On the contrary, your arrival was most opportune,' Avril assured him, 'that funny little Italian was quite, quite mad.'

She was wondering who this young man could be—she had recognised his voice immediately as that of the Englishman she

31

had overheard before, talking so airily about dukes and combines of a hundred million pounds—his face seemed familiar.

'You're Avril Bamborough, aren't you?' Ronnie said. 'I hear you're doing a picture for Ubiquitous.'

'Yes—and I know you, too—only I can't quite place you! I do hope you're not a famous movie star and that I've made an awful gaff!'

He grinned. 'Oh, no—you've seen me at the Embassy—or the Berkeley, in London. I've often seen you there.'

'That must be it,' Avril nodded. 'Tell me—do you know my uncle, John Bamborough? I passed the seat where you were sitting a few moments ago and I thought I heard you mention his name.'

Ronnie went just a shade darker under his tan, he had never met John Bamborough in his life, but he carried off the situation perfectly. 'Oh, John Bamborough! Rather—I don't know him well, of course—but I've met him once or twice down at Hatfield.'

'And did I hear you say you were with his second son at Eton?' Avril was enjoying herself—she knew quite well that he was lying, and wondered why in the world he did not go on the screen. He reminded her of a shorter, more compact edition of Jack Buchanan, and he carried off this difficult situation with such perfect ease.

'Yes—he wasn't in my year, but we were there at the same time.'

'How very queer,' said Avril mildly. 'Uncle John isn't married . . .'

'Really?' Ronnie seemed not the least abashed. 'Perhaps this chap was a nephew, or a different family altogether—it's queer. I felt certain he was John Bamborough's son. Care to stroll back and have an ice?'

As they sauntered across the wide lawns to Clare de la Lune's long, pretentious bungalow, Ronnie pointed out all sorts of interesting people. He seemed as full of information as Uncle Andy, and much more amusing—but Avril could not help wondering how many of his casual statements were actual facts.

They each had a pineapple sundae, and went out into the sunshine again. 'By the bye,' said Ronnie, 'if Hinckman offers you a contract—scrap everything and take it; don't say I told you anything about it, but things are going to happen in Hollywood.'

'What sort of things?' Avril enquired.

'Oh, great changes you know—one or two big men are getting together. I was talking to Cinch of Klein Brothers just now —there's trouble in the wind!' He looked round and laughed suddenly. . . . 'If only these people knew it, and they were a different type!—this might be the lawn of the R.Y.C. at Cowes in July 'fourteen. Ninety per cent of them haven't any idea that things are going to blow up in the next few weeks. Two-thirds of them will be dead, as far as the film world's concerned, this time next year.'

'Dear me—you are an alarming person.'

He ran his hand through his wavy hair. 'Oh, no—but it's just as well to be in on the ground floor—might as well buy British, even if we take the money off the Yanks, mightn't we? I'll have a word with Hinckman about you.'

'That's very nice of you—but I've got a contract with Hugo Schultzer already,' Avril demurred.

Ronnie laughed. 'I wouldn't lose any sleep over that! Hullo —there's Nelson Druce. Hullo, Druce!'

'Hello, Sheringham.' A tall, attractive man paused beside them, he had humorous grey eyes and dark hair brushed smoothly back. Avril imagined him to be about thirty. He spoke with a faint but pleasant American accent. 'What in the world has brought you to Hollywood?'

'Oh, a spot of business and too many writs in London. D'you know Miss Bamborough?—Nelson Druce.'

The American held put his hand, and as Avril took it, she noticed it particularly. It was strong, firm, resilient to the touch, and one of the most beautifully modelled hands that she ever remembered seeing on a man.

'Coming in the Combine?' asked Ronnie casually.

'What do you know about the Combine?' Druce's humorous mouth suddenly hardened into a straight line.

'Oh, quite a bit—you ought to come in—you'll have to in the end.'

'What!—with that swab Hinckman—not on your life. My old man believes in clean business—an' I'll say he's right.'

Ronnie smiled his disarming smile. 'Oh, well—I don't know much about the man, but it's a big idea.'

'Nuts! Trans-Continental Electric haven't got the money to finance it—you'll see, the whole thing'll fizzle out in a fortnight.'

'Maybe—look here, there's a chap over there I want to see, so I'll leave you two—so long!' Ronnie strolled off into the sunshine.

'I know your uncle just sufficient to say I'm acquainted, Miss Bamborough,' said Nelson Druce. 'He's a great man and he's turning out fine pictures now.'

'Oh, Uncle John, yes—he's a dear. I felt an awful beast leaving him, but I was simply dying to see what Hollywood was like. Tell me—I've met so many celebrities today. I hardly know where I am—are you Mr. Druce of Pacific Players?'

He smiled. 'Not exactly—but my old man is, and of course I'm in the business, too. Let's hear what you think of Hollywood now that you've seen it!'

'That's a little difficult, isn't it? after so short a time. Everybody seems very kind, but we should think one or two rather eccentric in England, perhaps!'

'They're not kind, Miss Bamborough, don't you believe it.' Nelson Druce's eyes held hers steadily. 'It's dog eat dog in this rotten town—thank God I'm sailing for Europe in a fortnight's time.'

'For long?'

'I'll be away for a goodish while, and glad to see the back of this darn place—but let's be cheerful! Come and see the rock garden!'

'No, thanks, I've seen it.' said Avril quickly.

Tiny lines wrinkled up round his eyes in sudden merriment. 'Some guy get fresh with you, eh? I'll say they don't lose much time in this town, but I didn't mean a necking party. I'm harmless and engaged—see the fair girl over there?—that's my

34

fiancée—Vitelma Loveday, you may have heard of her.'

Avril had and seen her, too. Starring in the productions that Pacific Players send out all over the world. 'Of course I've seen her on the screen—but she is even more lovely in the flesh. I did have—shall we say—an "experience" in the rock garden with a most unpleasant Italian, who is, I gather, the Captain of Mr. Hinckman's Prætorian Guard!'

'Sure—I know him, rotten little wop. It's a disgrace that Hinckman should keep those gangsters hanging round. It's not really necessary—my old man doesn't, and he's as big as Hinckman any day.'

Avril smiled, she liked this slim, muscular young man. 'That sort of thing doesn't trouble me really—it's unpleasant at the moment, but the Provinces and South Africa taught me how to handle situations like that long ago.'

'Yes,' he nodded. 'I can see by your eyes that you're not the sort of woman to stand for any funny business, but you won't be worried much. The English colony will sure take you up, and then you won't be troubled at all. You'll be as safe among the serious artists as if you had a flat in Kensington. If I may I'd like to introduce you to one or two—they're really nice people, most of them.'

'I should be very pleased if you would—I do feel just a little isolated here, although of course I've got certain introductions.'

'Ach! dere you are—I haf look everywhere for you, Miss Bamborough.' Hugo Schultzer bore down on them.

'Well—I'll certainly look forward to seeing you again.' With a smile Nelson Druce took his leave.

A moment later Avril saw Hinckman coming towards her. She was reminded of a general at an Aldershot Review. On either side, and little behind him moved a small crowd. Ronnie Sheringham was there, and Donelli. She noticed that nobody spoke to the great man unless he addressed them first. The other guests made way before him as if he was Royalty itself.

'How do, Hugo?' He spoke in a sharp voice to the German, and nodded towards Avril without taking off his hat. 'I guess this'll be Miss Bamborough?'

'I 'ave bleasure to bresent to you my new star, Mr. Hinck-man.' Hugo made the formal introduction.

Hinckman twirled his cigar with a quick motion of his lips. 'See here, Schultzer,' he said abruptly, 'I'd like to have Miss Bamborough take the lead in a production I figure to make. "The Forbidden Territory", it's called. Will you take a profit on her contract?'

'No! I haf use for Miss Bamborough in the film I make myself.' The German looked sullen.

'Okay. Now, Miss Bamborough, I'd certainly like to have you in this film of mine—I'll raise your contract price and pay damages—that is if I have to! to Schultzer here. What d'you say?'

Avril looked him straight in the eyes. 'Thank you, Mr. Hinck-man. No—Mr. Schultzer has given me a contract, and no increase of salary would induce me to break it.'

Hinckman shrugged his broad shoulders. 'Okay, Miss Bam-borough—but you're green to Hollywood. Trans-Continental Electric don't hand out star contracts every day. If Hugo should find himself unable to fulfil you'll be on the train back to Europe, or warming up a pew in the agents' office—looking for a job!' He turned away with a quick laugh, and as the little crowd that formed his general staff moved to follow him—Avril heard him say: 'Come on, boys—did you hear that dame? I guess she doesn't know what's coming to her—but it's nix to me.'

3

The Gathering of the Powers

Jos Hinckman took his seat at the end of a long, baize-covered table in a private room of the Excelsior Hotel. Ronnie glanced quickly at his face as he sat down beside him. Hinckman had Red Indian blood in his veins; the big nose, the high cheek

36

bones, and rather narrow eyes with their hard, inscrutable stare, all proclaimed it. His magnificent physique came from a Prussian mother. It was a queer mixture—Red Indian and Prussian. Ronnie thought of cruelty, cunning, and unscrupulous determination—the worst aspects of both races, yet Hinckman was not without a certain rather forceful charm. His joviality, and a veneer of politeness assimilated through his long association with the better types of big business men, served to cloak his real character, but Ronnie Sheringham was a shrewd observer—he felt that removed from his present sphere, or thwarted in some strong desire, Hinckman might easily revert to the ethics of the mining camp in which he had been bred, and take the law into his own hands.

Dismissing Hinckman from his mind for the moment, Ronnie turned his attention to the other nine men who were finding places at the board. They were the key personalities of the giant American film corporations.

No secretaries or stenographers were present. The doors were locked, and Hinckman's men patrolled the corridors. He was anxious that the conference should not be interrupted under any pretext. Each of the magnates had observed certain precautions in the manner of their arrival at the hotel—had entered by a side door, and been shown straight up the service staircase. All were anxious that the public, and more particularly the Press, should remain in ignorance of this meeting, at least until it was over.

Before each place was set a neat pile of white paper—two freshly sharpened pencils, a blotting pad and ash tray. At each end of the table reposed a massive ink-stand, and a quantity of pens with bright new nibs. The blinds were down, and the artificial light threw its pale rays on the baize, struggling—not very successfully—against the strong sunlight which glowed through the shuttered windows. The atmosphere was tense—electric!

'Waal, gentlemen,' Hinckman began, 'you're all here, I see, an' you all know each other, that is with the exception of my young friend, Mr. Sheringham. He was not at our first meeting, and maybe he's not acquainted with you all. That being

37

the case, I'll take the liberty of making him known to you.

'On your right there, Mr. Sheringham, is Uncle Andy Wilson of World Wide Pictures. Next, Mr. Walt Cinch, of Klein Brothers, who I guess you already know. Then Mr. Percy Piplin, who you've seen many a time in his make-up if you haven't seen him in the flesh before; he's the biggest of the big noises in his own concern—Star Artists. Hugo Schultzer's next, of Ubiquitous Films, and at the bottom of the table, Mr. Barton Druce, of Pacific Players. Up the other side, Mr. Rudy Stillman of Stillman's Comedies. Then Handsome Harry Honeydew, whose pictures, I guess, you saw as a kid—he's Reno Films Limited. Next, Mr. Amos McTavish, of Alpha Talkies, and on my other side here, the great little Issey Vandelstein, who's Mozarts.

'Now, gentlemen, Mr. Sheringham is here today because he represents certain very important British interests. Maybe on the other side, the motion picture business in not so powerful as it is in the States, but they're big enough to form a serious opposition, and it is obviously to our advantage to have at least one British corporation toeing the line with us here. I only wish we had one of the Jung group to speak for Germany, but we'll fix that later; anyhow, Mr. Sheringham is here today in the interests of the Britishers.'

A succession of nods, varying in amiability, acknowledged Ronnie's introduction. He smiled genially at each of the others in turn.

Hinckman tapped the ash off his cigar, and went on. 'A fortnight ago I asked you gentlemen to meet me in this room, and I laid before you what to my mind is by far the biggest commercial undertaking of the century. I put it to you, then, that you should consult your boards, and meet me here again—fully empowered by them to discuss this gigantic proposition, and to state their willingness or unwillingness to participate. During the last two weeks I have had the opportunity of going into the possibilities of this thing, even more thoroughly than I did before. And I am today more than ever convinced of the enormous advantages which such a scheme offers to us all. Combination and Amalgamation are the business watchwords

38

of this era. In fifty years' time the world will be full of combines—why wait for our grandchildren to reap the benefits: let's sink our differences—and make big money now! At first sight it may seem that such a mighty conception is impracticable in application, but believe you me—if we get together *it can be done*. At the present moment we are, one and all, in a greater or less degree—up against it financially: put this thing through and it will set the whole industry on its feet in a state of flourishing prosperity such as it has never known before. Now, gentlemen, I'd be glad to hear your views.'

For a full minute there was complete silence—then Mr. Cinch, a small, wizened man with close-set eyes, half-hidden beneath his pince-nez, coughed into his hand, and spoke in a reedy voice.

'Well, people—I've had a talk with one or two of my co-directors in Klein Brothers, and we feel Jos Hinckman is one hundred per cent right. It's a mighty big proposition, I'll allow, but take a think about the profits. A rock-bottom guaranteed market for every film we make!—where'll the Exhibitor be, I'd like to know?—why, in the bread-queue like a lot of other poor bums!—we'll sure hand him a dollar a day and the real rake-off comes to us boys here. I'll hand it to Jos Hinckman for having the big idea—and Walt G. Cinch, who's Klein Brothers, is with him right along the line.'

Mr. Percy Piplin looked quietly round the table, he was also a small man, but very different in appearance to Mr. Cinch. Few of the millions who know his grotesque prototype so well on the screen, would have recognised in his narrow, clever face and greying hair, their beloved Percy.

'I'm afraid, in a way, that I am here under false pretences,' he said with a little smile. 'As you are aware, Star Artists is a corporation which differs in nearly every particular from all others. We produce—direct—*and* star in our own films. In addition to that we have the good fortune to be in the unique position, that the release of one of our films is a great public event. We possess no chains of cinemas or agents in the ordinary sense—we hire other people's houses for the exhibition of our films, very often theatres which are not in the usual

39

way connected with the motion picture business. If every picture house in the world were closed to us tomorrow, we should still take theatres to exhibit our films, and our publicity department would bring them to the notice of the masses. In fact, we are the one example of a group of artists marketing their talents direct to the man in the street. I therefore—and I may say that Mr. and Mrs. Marybanks are at one with me in this matter—can see no possible advantage in entering Mr. Hinckman's Combine. There may be certain advantages in the scheme for other corporations, so I propose to leave you to your deliberations with the best of good wishes, but—gentlemen—the proposition does not interest Star Artists.'

Mr. Percy Piplin then took up a brand-new bowler hat, and, the door having been unlocked for him, shook the dust of the council chamber of his less-fortunate brethren, from off his feet.

'Waal! an' that's that!' said Hinckman with a grin. 'Star Artists are sure in a unique position—I didn't figure for one moment that they'd come in—but praise the Lord, it's the only concern of its kind. Who's next?'

'I'd like to say a word.' Uncle Andy threw out his chest. 'This is how I see it, gentlemen. It's a great proposition that Jos is putting up all right—but is it practical?—that's what I want to know. All of us has got good assets—World Wide has got a whole heap, but all of us has got bad 'uns floating around as well—now, how's that going to pan out in the event of a take-over? I see the bunch of us wrangling like a lot of old washer-women as to whether some flop's contract's worth two cents or ten!—I tell yer another thing—what about the small folks?— we've all got to live, and we're big people—they don't cut no ice—not so's you'd notice it. They don't stop me sendin' my kids' children to Yale or buying another ten-thousand-dollar automobile if my fancy gets that way—let them have their show! If I ever get to heaven I wanta be able to look my Maker in the face! This may be business—but it ain't cricket. I guess you can count me out.'

'Ungle Andy is right, Hinckman.' Hugo Schultzer nodded a ponderous head. 'All der little beoples will be smash, many artist—many gamera mens, many broducers as well. I am big business man, but also I dink for my work-beoples. How, too, would we plend all our schools of broduction?—Ungle Andy has reason. It is not bractical—dis broject—and for Ubiquitous, we brefer that it should not be.'

'You're wrong, Schultzer, at least that's how I see it.' Rudy Stillman took up the argument in a strong nasal twang. His cadaverous face became hard and grim as he leant forward on the table. One lock of his long hair dropped across his high, narrow forehead. 'Methods of production?—nothing—we'd soon shake down to that, and I'm for business—first, last, and all the time. Stillman Comedies pay their way, well, as most things, but it's profits I want to see. It ain't my pigeon to keep a lot of lazy scuts around, not if there's a better way without —and these goddam stars get more grasping every day. If there ain't no competition they get what they're given—an' that's flat. I reckon we people ought to get right down on our knees and thank Jos Hinckman for giving us the lead out of our mess. He's the big boy all right, and Rudy Stillman's with him all the time.'

Hinckman nodded. 'Thanks, Rudy—I wish some of these other boys had your sound horse-sense—but you won't regret it—we're going to see this party through.'

Handsome Harry stood up to speak. In his imagination he faced the camera in his daily life. He posed with one hand resting on the table—the thumb of the other in the armhole of his waistcoat. 'I think you know, gentlemen, that I have been in the moving-picture business as long as most—in fact, I can recall the days when Hollywood Boulevard was . . .'

'Handsome!—Handsome!' Uncle Andy shook his head. 'We folks know more about your history than you do yourself! This is a business party—not a fan lecture! We'll do the reminiscing after, you just give us the low down as you see it on this scheme of Hinckman's.'

Handsome grinned amiably. 'Sure—that's true, I can't tell you boys nothing about Hollywood, but I figure I can tell you a piece about the artist's point of view. I don't happen to have the good fortune to stand in the same position as Piplin and the

Marybanks' crowd—going back a bit there was a time. of course—but that's neither here nor there; anyhow, there's a certain similarity in our positions. . . I produce—direct. and star in my own films. Now. if we form this Combine where does Harry Honeydew hit the shore?—do I get a free hand to make my pictures. or don't I? I owe it to the public who's made me what I am, that they should continue to have that pleasure. to which they all look forward—and see a Honeydew production, starring Harry Honeydew, in their own home town.'

Mr. Cinch tittered. 'Sure it's interestin' to hear about your great public. Handsome—where d'you keep it—in a hat box under yer bed?'

Honeydew turned towards the little man. he was an impressive figure as he stood there. despite his advancing age. Greyhaired. strong-limbed. fine-featured. 'No. *Sir*,' he said without a trace of humour. 'my public is world wide. My fan mail when I made "The Return of Battling Butler" was the biggest ever received by any star in Hollwood.'

'At that date. Handsome—at that date,' said Uncle Andy mildly.

'Well. maybe. but the film I'm making now—it's a great story, I'll tell the world. You boys just wait—and I figure to go on making motion pictures for a few years yet.'

'If you join der Combine. they will choose der films dat dey broduce,' Hugo Schultzer tapped a fat foretinger on the green baize.

'Then if that's how it's goin' to be Reno Films stands out.' Handsome Harry crushed out the stub of his cigarette and sat down.

Hinckman turned to Amos McTavish. a dour. elderly man dressed in sober black. 'Spill the beans. Amos—what's Alpha Talkies got to say?'

Amos McTavish looked round the board with narrowed, half-closed eyes. He spoke with the curious accent of a Scotsman long resident in America. 'It's my considered opeenion, Hinckman. that your scheme has possibeelities. but, as ye know. I'm a man that holds strong views upon oor duty to oor fellow-men. I'll say it certainly is true that the greater majority "know not what they do" an' I'm a strong follower of Mr. Ford in his belief that it's the bounden duty of every great employer of labour to care for the moral welfare of his people. Now Hollywood City has been compared to the iniquitous City of Babylon in ancient times, an' fer close on twenty years I've striven with all the power that the Lord has given me to lift the moral tone of the people I employ; often, perhaps, against their wish, but for their ultimate salvation. The Alpha Talkie Corporation is a shining light in the darkness of this city. Our people get good money, but they know that liquor is not allowed. If they're so much as reported in a speakeasy in this town—they're fired. Non-smokers stand a stronger chance of promotion to a better job. We don't encourage single men after the age of twenty-five, and divorce, or any sort of immorality, means immediate dismissal. Over the stars, of course, I have no the same control, and more's the pity—but it's a great work I'm doin', and I'd certainly be interested to know the attitude of the Combine on this important head. Will they be prepared to follow my example?—to continue the regulations at present enforced by the Alpha Corporation for the moral uplift of the workers, and co-operate in a sincere attempt to clean up this city?'

'There's a lot in what you say, Amos,' Hinckman nodded solemnly, 'an' I reckon we'd undertake to adopt your views. Whatever our private tastes may be we all know the deleterious effects of liquor on the workers from the business point of view, an' neckin' parties in their free time don't make fer better work in the studios either. I'd be proud to associate myself with you in a *genooine* campaign to make Hollywood go clean. I'll go further by pointing out that by forming a combine we'd be able to control the stars as well as the workers. Public scandal in connection with a star would bar them from the Combine sets. That would compel them to give an example of clean living. There's more to it than that even, an' it's a point that I don't know if you gentlemen have sufficiently realised. A combine would be in a position to dictate the subject of its pictures without fear of competition because there'd be no fellers to hand out the hot baby stuff. We'd be able to raise the moral tone of the talking pictures altogether—and thereby influence for good the morality of the entire wurld.'

The Scotsman's eyes were filled with a fanatic gleam. 'That's the finest word I've heard ye speak fer many a day, Jos Hinckman. Amos McTavish is with ye—an' ye have the blessing of the Lord.'

'Vait a minute—vait a minute.' Issey Vandelstein's teeth flashed as he turned on the dour Scot. 'Ain't you forgettin' something, Mister?—you may have all der religion in der world —but you don't 'ave all der shares in Alpha Talkies. No, *Sir* —vat about me?'

'Sure, Mr. Vandelstein, your holding in Alpha is pretty considerable, I know, indeed ye are the biggest indeevidual stockholder, but at ye're own choice ye refused a seat on the board. I speak for meself and my co-directors, and oor holding is certainly equal to ye're own. This scheme of Hinckman's seems to us a fine thing for the Corporation from the strictly business point of view—and after what ye've just heard, it should be a great and splendid force for the moral uplift of the wurld— neverless as oor largest stockholder, and the big noise in Mozarts, I'd be doubly interested to hear ye're point of view.'

Issey Vandelstein shrugged his narrow shoulders. 'Ai don't vant no combines.'

'What are your objections to the scheme, Issey?' Hinckman asked.

'Vell—Mozarts is Mozarts, ain't it?'

The board considered this cryptic utterance in silence for a moment, then Hinckman said, 'That's true, Issey, and Mozarts is certainly a slick concern, but it ain't got nothin' on Trans-Continental Electric for all that. If we see money in this—why not you?'

'Ai don't vant no combines.'

'Maybe, but let's hear what's biting you. I'll say I've never known you to turn down big money before.'

'Ai jus' don't vant no combines,' repeated the little Jew doggedly, and Hinckman was compelled to leave it at that.

Ronnie Sheringham looked round the meeting, he felt that it was time to put in a word. He had attended many similar gatherings in his chequered business career, but never any in which such vast interests hung in the balance. He sat there—brown-faced—blue-eyed and smiling. His hands were buried in his trousers pockets, and he leant a little forward, his coat thrown open, showing a wide expanse of silk shirting, and an old Etonian tie. The fact that he was by many years the youngest man in the room, and the weight of millions that the others represented, awed him not at all. He spoke firmly in his lazy, cultured voice.

'Mr. Hinckman has told you the reason for my presence here, and the interests which I represent are in complete agreement with his plan. It should be a marvellous thing for us all. I think you'll agree, too, that the British end of it is important. Individually, they may not be as big as you, but the question of the quota arises.

'In the event of a Combine being formed here, and the British interests left outside—you'd either have to show their films in America—which might prove popular because they'd make a special line of the cutey films you propose to bar—or and the films of the Combine would be barred out of Britain, and the home market left free for the present producer. If we come in the Combine will work its English studios, the question of the quota will not arise, and we shall be strong enough to wipe our present competitors off the map. As far as that goes it won't matter how much of the English-made stuff you show over here, either, because the profits will go to the Combine just the same. I think from every point of view this scheme will benefit us all.'

Hinckman nodded approval. 'You certainly are a bright young man, Mr. Sheringham—that's just exactly how it'll work. Your people will get a share holding in the Combine, and in a few years' time the Combine'll have the British market in its pocket. Now let's hear what Barton Druce has to say.'

Barton Druce, the great man of Pacific Players, was an elderly grey-haired American. His shrewd eyes belied the easy-going impression created by his kindly face, he spoke with decision in a clear, level voice.

'I've been mighty interested to hear what all you other folks have had to say, and I'm thunderin' glad to learn there's some sound sense left in this community. If Rudy Stillman and Walt Cinch care to go on Hinckman's pay-roll I guess I'm not stoppin' them, but I've been too long in the motion picture business to let any guy or any collection of guys tell me where I get off! I say nothin' against friend Amos' high moral views—some of us has religion, and some of us keeps Pekingese!—but if he figures to see Hinckman featuring in a crusade to wet-nurse movie stars . . . well, I guess he's backed the wrong horse. As for Handsome—it's a pleasure to see that he's at least got enough brains in his good-looking skull to get the fact that his public will have to wait a long, long time before they see his pretty face if a combine buys him up! The British interests don't cut much ice with me. I haven't had the pleasure of meeting Mr. Sheringham before, so what those interests are I don't precisely know, but whatever they may be they can't materially influence the position here in Hollywood. The rest of us—that's Hugo, Issey, and Uncle Andy—are with me. Issey's plain business—Hugo's a careful man—and Uncle Andy wouldn't be the boss of World Wide if he was a fool. They say, and I say, that a combine isn't practical; every man jack of us runs his outfit on different lines—we'd sure fight like hell! Besides, different markets want different pictures; our present individual organisations supply those needs. The elimination of personality in the dead level of a combine output would set the development of the moving picture business back twenty years . . .' He paused, and then went on with sudden intensity: 'And now I come to the most important point of all. *This whole scheme is nothing but a damned ramp*—yes, I mean that! Hinckman, who sits at the end of the table there, is willing to risk the future of the entire industry—to bring dissension amongst us—and suffering to thousands—in this mad attempt to establish a dictatorship! Under the iron heel of a combine thousands of good workers who have grown up with the small concerns would be scrapped and lose their means of livelihood. The industry would suffer irretrievably through lack of healthy competition. Stars—artists—producers—would be faced with ruin, but for the few who were prepared to bow their necks under this

46

tyrannous yoke . . . and this for what? To gratify the avarice and vanity of one unscrupulous man.'

Hinckman's face had gone a deeper shade of red. He had expected opposition from Barton Druce, but never dreamed that he would have to face this devastating personal attack. His hands clenched, his dark eyes blazing between narrow lids, he sat immovable, as though carved from stone, while the flood of oratory poured over his head.

With a sudden movement Barton Druce thrust back his chair and left the table. At the door he turned and spoke again, his voice rising in harsh denunciation.

'I speak for Pacific Players—for my co-directors—my shareholders, and the highest tradition in American business which seeks to protect the people it employs; not only do I refuse to participate in any combine which would bring such misery and ruin in its train, but—should it ever show signs of coming into being—*I will fight it with every means at my command!*'

4

The Spider's Web

The meeting was over, the majority of the potentates had walked quietly down the back stairs of the hotel, hurried to their cars, and then—with every secrecy—been spirited away.

Hinckman, Walt Cinch, Hugo Schultzer, and Ronnie remained. Ronnie and Cinch were talking over the result of the meeting together in a corner—Hinckman had moved round to a seat next to the German's chair.

'Now, Hugo,' he said, twirling his cigar, 'that Bamborough kid—I asked you not to quit with the rest of the bunch so we could have a word about her.'

'I haf told you, Hinckman, I require the young lady for my own broduction.'

'Maybe—maybe—but it's this way, Hugo; I figure to make this picture "The Forbidden Territory". We shan't call it that, of course, but that's the name of the book—incidentally I took the trouble to read the book myself, I was that struck with the synopsis. It's about Russia and those Bolsheviks. A young American gets put behind the bars in Moscow or Vladivostock or some place, and two of his pals go out from London to rescue him. It's a great story—sledge scenes in the snow— aeroplanes—a gun-fight with the Reds in a ruined château, and a dash to the frontier in a high-powered car—marvellous material to work on. It's by a feller named Wheatley—who he is, God knows—but that don't matter. There's plenty of love interest too—a little Princess who got left behind when the Whites cleared out, and a Bolshie actress who's full of pep. It's got the makings of a master film—great spectacle, human interest—and educative value as well.* Now I've got a cutie for the little Princess, but the actress woman must be the real goods—and the moment I set eyes on Miss Bamborough I knew she'd fit right in. I saw what she could do in Titchcock's last, and I've been kicking myself ever since that I didn't sign her up before you got wise—now be a sport an' take a profit on her contract!'

Schultzer shook his head. 'No, Mr. Hinckman—I haf said before, I haf need of Miss Bamborough for my own broduction.'

Hinckman hit the table a resounding blow with his clenched fist. 'You sure make me mad,' he cried angrily. 'Where'll I find another girl who just fits my part? I've been through every star in Hollywood with a toothcomb—there's isn't one that's got just what I want—an' what the hell'll your production be anyhow? A one-horse show compared to this great spectacle of "The Forbidden Territory" I'm going to make. Tell you what I'll do . . . give me the kid an' I'll give you a share in the profits on my picture. Now I can't be fairer than that?'

The German was stubborn. 'Mister Hinckman—your bicture may be a big bicture, but I haf my gondract with Miss Bam-

---

* *The Forbidden Territory*, by Dennis Wheatley. Published by Arrow Books 30p.

borough—and therefore she star in the Ubiquitous broduction.'

'Okay,' said Hinckman wearily, 'but you'll sure get some new ideas before you're much older.' He turned to Ronnie. 'Guess we'll get along.'

The four men went downstairs together. At the door of the hotel they parted—Schultzer and Cinch on their respective businesses, Ronnie and Hinckman in the latter's car to the Garden Palace Hotel, where Lord Gavin and Ronnie were staying.

When they arrived they went straight up to Lord Gavin's sitting-room. He was seated with his tiny childlike body hunched up in a big arm-chair, his small feet dangling. The blinds were drawn, and the black clothes which he invariably wore made him almost imperceptible in the semi-darkness. He turned his big head, and glanced sharply at them as they came in.

'Well, what fortune did you have at your meeting?' he asked in his melodious voice, directly the door closed behind them.

'Oh, not too bad!' Ronnie was already mixing drinks for Hinckman and himself.

'And not so mighty good, either.' Hinckman mopped his large face with a red and white spotted silk handkerchief. 'We've got Cinch and Rudy Stillman for sure, an' that's something. We more or less counted on Cinch from the beginning, but Rudy's a useful man, an' somehow I didn't figure he'd play.'

'With yourself that makes three for certain,' Lord Gavin said quietly. 'Not bad for a beginning—what of the others?'

Ronnie laughed. 'You should have seen Piplin—he just walked out on us!'

'Yep—hi-hatted the whole party,' Hinckman grinned. 'But I told you he would from the word go. Star Artists might own this town from the way they treat folks—still I guess they've a right to please themselves. Uncle Andy wouldn't come in, an' that's a pity. World Wide's a pretty sizeable concern.'

'The G.O.M. talked an awful lot of drivel,' Ronnie supplemented, 'about meeting his God face to face and business not being cricket—who on earth ever said it was, anyhow? I

49

was surprised about Issey Vandelstein though. Ours is just the sort of scheme I should have thought would have appealed to him. What was his grouse, Hinckman? Have you any idea?'

'Lord in heaven knows! I don't. Issey's as cute as they make 'em, I guess he thinks he'll be able to work some kind of graft all on his lonesome. He'll be too clever by half if he's not careful an' burn his yellow fingers—but for the time being he's turned us down flat.'

'Honeydew?' Lord Gavin enquired, 'what had he to say?'

'He's so fond of his own dial, poor mutt, he don't know which way to turn it so's you can focus his profile best—he gave us a lot of yap about his precious public, an' how a combine would be cutting out his films. They would, too—if Jos Hinckman had any say.'

'Amos McTavish was the funniest.' Ronnie grinned reminiscently. 'He wants to turn Hollywood into a seminary for young ladies—Hinckman's going to join the Salvation Army and play the drum!'

'Don't you be so funny, young feller—Amos McTavish is no fool! What if he is bats about religion—it's no bad proposition to get your workpeople on the Halleluja stuff—it keeps 'em off the liquor an' you get better work out of 'em. I'm going to have a little private talk with "smell yer breath Amos" an' I figure he'll come in.'

'What about Issey Vandelstein holding a big block of stock in his company? How's that going to affect us?'

'All depends on Issey—he may have the power to crab the deal or he mayn't. We'll certainly get a copy of the Alpha Corporation's articles of association. That'll give us the lowdown on the share majority necessary to carry through a sale. Amos'll give us the amount of Issey's holding—then we'll be wise.'

'If it is necessary we could consider the advisability of buying Vandelstein out,' suggested Lord Gavin.

Ronnie blew a couple of smoke rings and put his feet up on the opposite chair. 'That would be one way—the old Bosch was pretty strong against us, though.'

'Hugo Schultzer,' Hinckman frowned. 'Yep, he's a stubborn

50

fool, but I guess he doesn't know what's coming to him. I've got a private score against him—that Bamborough kid you put me on to is just the dix for my new super-film—but he won't let up on her contract—wants to hold her for some snide production of his own.'

'Was Barton Druce very antagonistic?' Lord Gavin asked. 'I know you feared he would be.'

'An' how!' Hinckman was emphatic. 'Good as called me a crook to my face, an' said he'd sure fight the Combine all he knew. He'll need some watching if we mean to put this thing through.'

'He was pretty scathing about the others, too, wasn't he?' Ronnie grinned. 'In so many words he told Handsome Harry and "Smell yer breath Amos" that they were a couple of idiots. He wasn't any too polite about me either. He seemed to think the British interests were all eyewash!'

As he spoke, Ronnie pulled up the shade, and the sunlight streaming through the high window caught Lord Gavin's silver hair, making a halo round it as he nodded his head. For a moment Ronnie was reminded of the Black Angel—but Lord Gavin's voice was mild.

'Let us sum up,' he said. 'Cinch and Stillman are definitely with us—Barton Druce, Schultzer, and Andy Wilson definitely against—Vandelstein also, but he presents a separate problem since it seems that he is only antagonistic for some private purpose of his own. We may reasonably suppose that he hopes to make more money by standing out for the time being. By the by—I forgot Piplin, but we have already agreed that the films made by Star Artists are of such an exceptional nature, and so limited in number, that they cannot possibly affect a world combine. We can ignore Piplin and his friends. Amos McTavish seems favourable if we can deal with the interest which Vandelstein holds in his concern. Honeydew is chiefly anxious to ensure his atrocious films should continue to be forced upon an unfortunate public.'

'That's so.' Hinckman put aside the well-chewed butt of his cigar, and took another from Lord Gavin's box.

'It seems then, that Alpha and Honeydew must be our first

consideration—some form of treaty should be possible with the latter.'

'Yep—I guess we'll have to take in Handsome himself someway—but if we get Reno, we get Von Sternheim. He's expensive, but in his own line he's the greatest director in the motion picture business.'

'I know—Von Sternheim is an artist. I have the greatest admiration for his productions. It is he who keeps Reno Films alive. If we can get him it will be worth while saddling ourselves with the dead weight of Honeydew—then, if it is essential, I will purchase Vandelstein's holding in Alpha—that would give us five.'

'Sure—but five ain't seven. We'll never get a stranglehold on little folks or the exhibitors with Pacific, World Wide, Mozarts, Ubiquitous, and Star Artists all out against us.'

'I agree.' Lord Gavin smiled. 'Who are, then, the weakest of the remaining five?'

'Ubiquitous, by a long sight.'

'And after that?'

'World Wide an' Mozarts run about level.'

'If we can secure Honeydew and Alpha, Vandelstein may see the wisdom of joining us before it is too late. In any case he will be frightened, and if we can bring Schultzer down, that should complete his rout.'

'You'll leave Issey an' World Wide out of the picture for the moment then?'

'I think that would be wise. Ronnie, my dear boy, I am expecting a cable from Moscow, would you be so kind as to go down to the hotel office, and see if it has arrived?'

'Rather!' Ronnie got slowly to his feet. 'But I'll phone down —that will be quicker.'

'No, the hotel servants are so careless.' The hard note that Ronnie had already learnt to know, underlay Lord Gavin's quiet voice. 'I should be obliged if you would go down yourself, and if by chance it has not arrived, you might walk as far as the post office to enquire. . . . Thank you so much.'

Ronnie took the hint, and left the two older men together.

'I suppose,' Lord Gavin went on slowly, when they were

alone, 'there is no possibility of the others forming a combine against us?'

Hinckman looked doubtful. 'I don't trust the Jew,' he said, after a moment's thought, 'but I don't figure he'd line up with the others any quicker than he would with us. Barton Druce is the one man I'm scared of—it's just on the cards that they might rally round him.'

'That is rather what I feared myself. I was not sufficiently sanguine to imagine for a moment that we should sweep the board at our first attempt, but we have not done so badly. The one thing we must guard against now is any sort of organised opposition. If they remain as separate entities I am quite confident that we can deal with them at our leisure.'

'That's so—and as I see it our present programme is that we set to work quietly on Handsome and Amos—and go out to smash the German.'

'Exactly. Now tell me, if when we make things uncomfortable for Schultzer he becomes stubborn and refuses to join us—are any of the others likely to come to his assistance?'

'That sure brings us back to Barton Druce—he's the only guy in the bunch strong enough to carr' Schultzer after the trouble that's coming to him from your's t ly.'

'If Druce comes to his rescue, do you consider that any of the others might join up with them?'

'I certainly do. Uncle Andy's thick as thieves with Barton Druce, they'll row in together for sure, an' that'll make us three all—with the other guys hanging in the balance. Gee— what a chance for Issey Vandelstein! He'll go to the highest bidder every time—and what a sum we'd have to pay!' Hinckman sat forward suddenly. 'Now wait a moment—I'm beginning to see things clearer now. That's Issey's game, I'd lay ten grand to a single buck. He'll prod Hugo an' Uncle Andy into forming an opposition group with Barton Druce as leader. That's going to prove mighty awkward!'

Lord Gavin nodded. 'It is the one thing above all others which we must prevent—you say this man Druce was particularly bitter in his opposition?'

'*An' how!*' Hinckman gave a short, hard laugh, then he proceeded to give Gavin Fortescue some of the choicer portions of Barton Druce's scathing denunciation.

'Dear—dear! what vehemence.' Lord Gavin smiled mirthlessly and a sinister light crept into his cold eyes. 'And you say that he is the only individual round whom these other people are likely to gather against us. . . . Well, we had anticipated the possibility of certain serious eventualities arising—it seems that such an eventuality has arisen almost at the beginning, instead of the near the end, of our campaign. It is obvious, my dear Hinckman that this honourable, but stupidly belligerent person must. . . . Now what is that delightful expression which you employ over here? Ah! I remember now, The unfortunate Mr. Druce must be "taken for a ride"!'

5

The 'Z' Projector

Avril Bamborough was reading a novel in the hotel garden. It was a week since the meeting of the powers, although Avril knew nothing of that, and a fortnight since her arrival in Hollywood—but she had not yet started to make Hugo Schultzer's film.

She was anxious to get to work, but when she mentioned that to Hugo he had seemed worried and, for him, ill-tempered. As her salary cheque was sent along at the end of each week, she had no real cause to grumble, and life was quite pleasant lazing in the sunshine. She had discovered that Ronnie Sheringham was staying in the same hotel—the Garden Palace—and she had seen quite a lot of him.

She had met all the other members of the cast who were featuring in Schultzer's production, and a small army of people who had a finger in the pie, every variety of technician and expert. Each one had taken her aside at the first opportunity and explained with the utmost gravity that he or she, as the case might be, was really the one person upon whom the success or failure of the picture depended. The person she would really have liked to have met was the author. She felt that his views on the interpretation of her part might have been of considerable value—but nobody seemed to have heard of him, except the continuity man, who said vaguely that 'He reackoned it 'ud be the same guy he'd met a year or so back in Noo York City, the poor bum hall-roomed in a snide apartment house way out in Brooklyn.'

There were conferences most mornings in the Ubiquitous Studios, where there was much talk but little done. Schultzer and his principal executive—Eberhard Lutsach—were in a constant state of friction, and when one arrived the other walked out. Avril found the unsettled atmosphere trying after the general good feeling she had been used to in the English studios, but it seemed to her that it was not in Ubiquitous alone that a state of unrest existed. There were endless comings and goings between the key men of the other studios, and constant whisperings in corners. She wondered more than once if Hollywood was always in this ferment or if there really was anything significant in that strange conversation which she had overheard at Clair de la Lune's garden party. Ronnie Sheringham went completely vague when she questioned him about it.

Avril had been to a number of parties, and was beginning to find out which invitations it was safe to accept. On two occasions during the first week she had landed herself in the type of entertainment which was very definitely not the kind she was prepared to enjoy. She had left early with her rather large mouth very tightly shut. Angelo Donelli had been present at both. He hovered in the background of her existence all the time, and although she did not wish to hurt the little man's feelings she disliked his blatant attempts at seduction intensely, and she was just a little bit afraid of him. He was an unclean little beast, but possessed of a devilish persistency. Returning the flowers he sent, and refusing all his invitations failed to discourage him in the least.

A shadow fell across Avril's book, and looking up she saw him standing before her.

'Afternoon!' he cried gaily, with a sweep of his soft hat. 'You coma joy-ride with Angelo in his new automobile, eh?'

She shook her head. 'No, thank you—I am expecting Mr. Schultzer at any moment.'

'Ah, no matter—you coma with Angelo—verrie nice—we maka da whoopee—yes?'

'No, really, Mr. Donelli—it's quite impossible this afternoon.'

'You verrie unkind to poor Angelo—what for dis evenin' den?—Angelo throw a party, eh?—plenty people—plenty talk—you coma as star guest, we maka one great time.'

'No, I'm afraid I'm fixed up for this evening, and all next week—after that I shall be working on my picture, so I shan't go out at all.'

The Italian's eyes went dark, he fingered his small moustache with a beringed hand as he scowled at her. 'You high-hatta Angelo, eh!—Allaright!—Angelo not der boy to be high hat in 'urrey! He maka plenty trouble—you see!'

Avril thought he was one of the most unpleasant people that she had ever met. There was something utterly indecent about his hot, lecherous stare—he seemed to strip the very clothes from her body by his hungry glance.

'I have no wish to high-hat anybody,' she said sharply, 'but I've told you before, Mr. Donelli, that you are wasting your time, and the sooner you realise it, the better.'

'Goot day to you, Miss Bamborough—der gar is outside if you are ready.'

Avril turned gratefully to Schultzer as he joined them, then, picking up her gloves and parasol, she gave a brief nod to the scowling Italian, and left him.

As she crossed the lawn she caught sight of Ronnie, lazing in the sunshine on the first floor balcony of the hotel, his hands in his pockets, his feet on the rail. He smiled a greeting to her as she went past with Schultzer and she waved in reply. She had not realised until then that his room must be next door but one to her own.

56

When they were seated in the back of Schultzer's car, the German turned heavily towards her. 'I take you dis afternoon to der house of Barton Druce—you haf nod met him pefore, I dink.'

'No—I met Nelson Druce the first day I was here—but I've never met the father.'

'So!—he is a goot friend to me—I hope to make goot pusiness with him.' After which announcement Mr. Schultzer lapsed into heavy silence.

The big car tore along the dusty road, eating up the miles that lay between Hollywood City and the beautiful residential district of Beverley Hills. At last they turned into a long, straight avenue with wide lawns on either hand, and a well-kept garden gay with flowers. The long, low house rose up to meet them, and the car came to a standstill in front of a pillared porch.

Barton Druce himself came out to welcome them. In his well-cut white flannels and grey jacket, his iron-grey hair brushed smoothly back, he looked a fine example of the best type of American big business man.

'Mr. Druce, I haf bleasure to bresent to you the young lady that I mention—Miss Avril Bamborough.' Schultzer made a little stiff, jerky bow.

'Delighted to make your acquaintance, Miss Bamborough— come right in. Glad to see you, Hugo—how's things?' Barton Druce led the way through three wide, airy rooms, leading one into another, to his study at the back of the house.

'Not goot—not goot at all.' The elderly German looked very tired as he sank into a chair.

Barton Druce nodded. 'Well, I guess you'd better spill the beans; I figure Miss Bamborough is acquainted with the situation more or less?'

'She will haf to know—and Miss Bamborough will unterstand that what we haf to say is gonfidential.'

Avril smiled. 'Of course,' she said, 'or would you rather that I left you? I am dying to walk round Mr. Druce's lovely garden.'

'For der moment—no, later berhaps.' Schultzer turned to

Druce. 'I haf more drouble with Lutsach—dis morning he throw up his gondract—he has gone now to Hinckman.'

'Is that so? That's sure hard on you, Hugo—you can sue for damages, of course—but lord knows when you'll get 'em, and that don't give you back your best man.'

'With him goes also Tzarkowski, my best gamera hand. How I can replace these beoples I do not know.'

'It lets you out of their high salaries, anyhow—I've got a whole bunch myself that I'd be glad to see the back of—if the T.C.E. would take 'em.'

'Jawohl—but in der meantime how do I make my bictures? Last week I lost also Penson, who is der best exbert in Hollywood for motion bicture dress design. Vendy Clauss also makes drouble—she ask a new gondract yesterday—she will haf more money or else she break der bresent one. If she go also, how will I my historic bicture gomblete?'

'Well, I guess we must do what we can to help you out, Hugo, and about Miss Bamborough's picture we'll come to some arrangement—I'm sure not goin' to let that rouster Hinckman have it all his own way.'

As Avril looked out through the open window she saw a tall, fair girl, who was swinging a sun-bonnet in one hand, stroll across the lawn towards them, and she recognised her at once as Nelson Druce's fiancée, Vitelma Loveday.

Barton Druce had seen her, too, and hailed her. 'Come here, kid, and meet Miss Bamborough—take her for a walk around to see the flowers. Miss Bamborough—meet Miss Loveday, my little daughter-to-be!'

The little daughter-to-be held out a carefully manicured hand. 'I'm real glad to be acquainted, Miss Bamborough.' She smiled a lazy, affected smile. 'I guess we'll leave the big boys to talk their business, while I pick your brains on the latest things from Paris in the glad rags line.'

Avril thought Miss Loveday an extraordinarily handsome girl—she had enormous eyes, and perfect features, her figure was straight and slim. Side by side they sauntered round the garden.

'Are you making a film just now?' Avril enquired.

'Me?—not likely!' The fair girl looked surprised. 'I'll be Mrs. Pacific Players Junior, in the fall—why should I worry to make pictures any more?'

'I should have thought that, as a star, you would want to go on for your own satisfaction—I think I should.'

'You don't say! Well, maybe it's all right for those who like it, but it's too near hard work for me, an' anyhow a star's life's limited—what's the good of hanging on? It's sure better to get out while the goin's good.'

Avril paused in front of a herbaceous border which was a riot of gorgeous colour. 'Isn't that divine?' she said.

Vitelma Loveday shrugged her beautiful shoulders. 'I'll say it's swell,' she condescended, 'but you should see the exotics. You can keep the garden flowers—it's exotics for mine!'

Avril found the strain of making conversation to this blasé young woman very fatiguing, but it suddenly occurred to her that the subject of Nelson Druce might make her hostess talk —so she remarked:

'I think I met your fiancé at Clare de la Lune's garden party.'

'What, Nelson!—oh, yes, that's so—he was talking about you the other day; said he'd promised to make you acquainted with some of the English stars, but he's that absent-minded you'd be surprised. I guess he's so wrapped up in his invention he doesn't even realise that I'm around half the time.'

'I didn't know that he was an inventor,' said Avril, with sudden interest.

'Sort of—he's got some new kind of lens he's just crazy about. He says it'll revolutionise the motion picture business— but I guess that's just his talk.'

'It sounds most awfully interesting.'

'Well—I suppose it is in a way.' Vitelma sounded doubtful. 'I don't get half he tells me about it, but I figure it's some gadget that'll throw the folks who're featured into strong relief—so that they'll stand right out of the picture when it's shown. A whole heap of people have been boilin' their heads over that idea for years. The "Z" Projector, Nelson calls it. We'll take a walk round to the Lab; if it 'ud amuse you any— an' get him off the job.'

'Do you think we ought to disturb him?' asked Avril doubtfully. 'I expect he hates being bothered while he is at work.'

'Oh, I wouldn't let that worry you—he sure spends too much time tinkering in there as it is, an' it's his job to be around with me, else folk'll start a rumour that we're not engaged at all.' Miss Loveday gave a little sharp, affected laugh, and it was quite obvious that she thought far too much of her own attractions to imagine anything of the kind. Then she led the way to a big glass-roofed building which had evidently been added to the house at a recent date.

Nelson Druce, in clean white overalls, was busy washing slides in a bath of chemicals when the two girls came in. His brows contracted when he first looked up, then he smiled.

'Hello, Honey! Why, how do, Miss Bamborough.' He wiped his hands on a rag, and came towards them.

'Guess it's time you quit messin',' said Vitelma, with a frown, 'Miss Bamborough'd like to see the exotics—be a good boy and take us round.'

'Why, certainly—I owe Miss Bamborough an apology too for not fixing those introductions I promised—I'll be with you right away.' He began to shut up various cases and cabinets, locking each one carefully.

'It doesn't matter a bit about the introductions,' said Avril, 'and please don't bother to leave your work on my account.' She looked round the big laboratory with its neat rows of glass bottles, and white tiled walls. She would have liked to have asked him about his invention, but he showed no sign of mentioning it, and hurried them out of the building as soon as possible. He smiled pleasantly at Avril and said, 'I can easily come back later—I'm sure it 'ud be a real pleasure to show you round.'

He took them to the hot-houses and surprised Avril by the knowledge he displayed. She knew little of orchids, only the names of the particular kinds which she liked to wear, but she could see at once from the easy way in which Nelson Druce talked about them, that he was genuinely interested in his father's collection.

She liked him even better than she had done at their first

brief meeting, and found herself watching for the fascinating little wrinkles to crinkle up at the corners of his eyes as he smiled.

Vitelma played the part of chorus, and Avril wished that she would keep quiet or go away. She began to wonder what had induced Nelson to get engaged to this vapid girl. Of course, she was beautiful—too beautiful for words, and Avril knew that good looks counted tremendously with men even if there was nothing behind them, but it seemed to her a pity that Druce, who obviously had more intelligence than the average young man, couldn't have found a woman with a little brain as well as beauty.

After the glass-houses, they walked round the garden again. Druce halted before the long border that Avril had admired so much.

'This is the bit I like,' he said. 'The orchids are interesting caus' they're curious and rare—but they're only freak stuff, and I'd scrap the orchids every time if I had to choose between them and *this*.'

Vitelma's beautiful mouth went sulky, and Avril smiled to herself, but thought it best to change the conversation. 'I thought you were going to Europe?' she said to Druce.

'Sure—I'm off day after tomorrow.'

'You're a poor sort of beau—I'll say.' Vitelma's voice was acid. 'From the tone you use I guess Miss Bamborough'll think you're just waiting on the chance to quit Hollywood—an' me.'

'No, Honey—no. You've got me all wrong. It's not you I wanta quit—but my work I want to get on with. I've just *got* to go to Europe for that.' He drew Vitelma's arms through his affectionately, and patted her hand, on which sparkled a large diamond solitaire ring.

'Well—why can't you take me along?—I'm overdue for a trip to Paris, an' I wanta whole heap of new clothes.'

'But I'm not going to Paris, Honey—you know that—I'll be in London most of the time. London and Berlin—working seventeen hours a day in the laboratories—what chance 'ud I have to take you places. Hello, Hugo! How's tricks?'

They had reached the french windows of the study once

61

more. Barton Druce waved them inside and led Avril to a chair.

'Now, Miss Bamborough,' he said, 'Hugo and I have had our little talk—you'll be acquainted with his difficulties from what he said just now, and I'll bet a packet you've heard some of the queer rumours that are going around. The T.C.E. are trying to put over some funny stuff an' leave us all without a livin'. Of course that don't concern you none, but for the fact that it's going to make it darned hard for Hugo to produce you as you deserve to be produced now all his technicians and experts have been taken off him, but I figure you don't want to sit around doin' nothing while he imports others from Europe and gets them trained. That's going to take a longish time—an' you're an expensive young lady to have idle, so I've offered to buy your contract off Hugo and star you in Pacific Players right away. How's that with you?'

Avril smiled in Barton Druce's level eyes. 'I'm very, very sorry to hear about Mr. Schultzer's difficulties,' she said, 'and I refused a rise in salary from Mr. Hinckman when he asked me to break my contract the first day I was in Hollywood— but this is quite different—if Mr. Schultzer is willing, I shall be very pleased to accept your offer.'

'Okay—that's great stuff, and I'm mighty glad to hear that you turned Hinckman down. I take it that I can rely on your good faith, Miss Bamborough, to refuse any similar offer in the future?'

'Once I have signed a contract,' said Avril gravely, 'I should never dream of breaking it.'

'Then we'll get down to the details right away. Pacific contracts differ in some ways from Ubiquitous, but not in essentials—we'll fix the main points now—get the contract drafted tomorrow, and you can sign up the day after.'

He moved over to his big desk with Avril and Schultzer beside him. Vitelma and Nelson were left standing at the other end of the room.

'What in heck possessed you to bring that wench into my Lab?' he asked angrily, nodding in Avril's direction.

Vitelma's eyes opened wide. 'Just listen to the boy friend now!' she appealed to the empty air. 'If that isn't the limit.

62

Why, I thought she was a little friend of yours—you both got worked up enough about the exotics—I'll say—seemed to me you'd made a proper hit.'

'Ah, you don't understand—she's a nice kid all right—I got nothin' against her, but I wish you'd get wise to it for good an' all that the work I'm doin's secret. The "Z" Projector's the most important thing in motion pictures since the talkies hit the screen. I don't want half Hollywood to know what I'm on —there's plenty of people'd take a chance on shooting me up if they knew what I'd got in my Lab and thought they could lay hands on it. You haven't done no harm today, I don't suppose, but for the Lord's sake act sensible another time and don't come butting in with strangers.'

'All right—all right—don't get sore, Honey! People aren't all that interested in your little box of tricks—you're not the only clever boy in Hollywood—there's scores of other fellers got labs, an' they don't make all this fuss.'

Nelson Druce smiled quickly. 'I'm sorry, Honey—don't go and get all het up. I'm just a bit worried, that's all. Now smile a little and be your angelic self—there—that's the way, you sure are the loveliest darling in all the world—and I'm bats about you.'

Barton Druce got up from his desk. 'That's fine, Miss Bamborough. I'll introduce you to Cyril de Rille, my principal producer, tomorrow, then we can go right ahead. By the by, does it happen you're free tomorrow evening?'

'Yes.' Avril nodded. 'I don't think I am doing anything.'

'Then I'd be glad if you'd join us for dinner, we're going after to the Premiere of "This Brave New World", it's not a Pacific production, but Trans-Continental Electric's new super film. Hinckman and I don't love each other none, but we still shoot each other free seats for our new shows—trade custom— an' they tell me it's a great spectacle. Nelson and Vitelma'll be here, and it 'ud be great to have you come along. Okay?—I'll send the car to pick you up at your hotel—where're you staying—Garden Palace, isn't it?'

Avril's 'Yes' was almost drowned in the roar of a high-powered engine. At first it sounded almost like an aeroplane, but as it stopped they realised that it was a huge car with an open exhaust which had pulled up at the front door.

'Now who in the world'll that be?' Barton Druce looked out through the vista of wide rooms to the hall. 'Why, it's Handsome!' he exclaimed. 'Come right in, Handsome. How de do?'

Handsome Harry Honeydew strolled in, a broad smile on his face. 'Waal, folks?' he asked. 'Heard the great news?'

'I'll buy it,' said Barton Druce.

Handsome's smile broadened into a grin. 'I'm going to produce—direct—and star, in three great Super Films—can yer beat it?'

Barton Druce's face became grave. 'You're sure crazy, the way things are at the moment,' he said seriously.

'Not on your life, I'm not. Trans-Continental Electric are financing them—and they're to be made on their lot.'

'Handsome! You don't mean that! You ain't gone in with that bunch, have you?'

'I certainly do. They took over Reno Limited this afternoon, and I'm to make three Super Films.'

Vitelma clapped her hands. 'Oh, boy—now isn't that just great—what a marvellous break!'

The knuckles of Barton Druce's hand showed white as he clutched the back of his chair. 'You stupid fool!' he burst out. 'If you'd held your interest in Reno's you'd still have been making motion pictures in ten years' time. As it is—you may make these three—but after that they'll never let you make another. Haven't you the sense to see? It's Von Sternheim they've bought—not you!'

6

This Brave (?) New World

The following evening Barton Druce sent for Avril as he had promised, and she dined quietly with him, Nelson and Vitelma.

After dinner, as they drove into the great Trans-Continental Electric cinema—the Ocean Palace—Avril became quite excited; she had attended many first nights in London, both of the Theatre and the Screen, but this was her first Hollywood Première.

Outside, the night signs flashed, the streets were thronged. On such occasions the crowds of Hollywood never fail to turn out in force to see the famous stars and the great producers arrive; those magnates upon whom the very life blood of their city depends.

Inside, the foyer was packed with people, and as Avril looked about her she found that now she knew quite a number of faces with certainty, whereas a fortnight before they would have been only vaguely reminiscent through the medium of the screen.

The vast house was a blaze of light when they entered. At the back of the Grand Circle was a tier of private boxes, and Barton Druce, as the head of Pacific Players, had been allotted one of these. Hinckman himself occupied the next box, with him was one of his principal directors, who had made the picture, Handsome Harry Honeydew, and the famous German, Von Sternheim. Walt J. Cinch was in another box further along, and besides him sat the tall, lean figure of Rudy Stillman.

Percy Piplin was not in evidence, nor were the Marybanks. They remained supreme—aloof—the Olympians of Hollywood. In the seats below Avril caught sight of Ronnie Sheringham. Why didn't the man go on the films, she wondered once more; he positively exuded personality. That fine head of his, the broad shoulders, and the slightly eccentric but beautifully cut evening-clothes—the male stars paled beside him.

The door at the back of the box opened and Angelo came in. Avril's brows contracted into a quick frown. In his be-ringed hand the Italian carried a vast bouquet of flowers. His white teeth flashed into a smile as he presented them.

'I finda you again, eh? Angelo always finda you when he want. Please to accep', Madonna, zis little gif'.'

Avril was angry and embarrassed. The man was becoming something more than a nuisance. She had come to dread the stare of his hot, hungry eyes, and there was something beastly and unclean about his loose, moist mouth. She turned quickly away and looked at the auditorium.

'My—but ain't they lovely!' Vitelma exclaimed, 'exotics, too.'

Nelson Druce came to the rescue, in one swift glance he had realised the situation. 'This is a private box,' he said firmly. 'I guess you'd better fade out of here.'

Angelo, for once in his life, was taken aback by so complete a rebuff. 'I leava de flowers,' he said after a moment. 'Den may-be you taka dem home and dream der happy dream 'bout Angelo.' He laid the bouquet upon the floor and left the box.

Vitelma's beautiful face showed sudden malice as she said sweetly to Avril: 'Well, I'll say you haven't wasted much time getting a boy-friend. But you sure do treat 'em rough.'

'You're nuts, Vitelma,' said Nelson Druce quickly. 'That rotten little wop has been pestering Miss Bamborough ever since she set foot in Hollywood. You sure don't think she'd take one of Hinckman's gunmen for a beau?'

'Say, now.' Vitelma was all eyes. 'Is that what he is? Well, p'raps you're right—I'm all for a quiet life myself—but he's a good-looker all right, in that Italian sort of way.'

Nelson Druce laughed. 'I'll be getting jealous in a moment, Honey.'

Vitelma smiled at him archly. 'If you don't make a fuss of me I'll give you lots of cause.'

He laughed again. 'I guess I won't give you any opportunity, not when I've got you to myself, in the fall.'

Avril had ignored the incident to the best of her ability. She was grateful when the house went dark and the programme opened with a slap-stick comedy.

The film was one of the hundreds which are made annually to fill the yawning maw of a greedy but uncritical multitude. It was mildly funny and exceedingly well-photographed—by the time that it was over every seat in the house was occupied, yet before the big film there was still an Alt Risney Songalogue to come.

Even the sophisticated picture-goers of Hollywood were compelled to laugh at the antics of the absurd fish with owl-like eyes, and the dog which used its tail as a marline-spike and its body as a life-buoy—but Avril missed a good deal of the film because Hinckman had joined them in the box.

He leaned against the door, his hands in his pockets, a cigar between his teeth. 'Evening, Druce,' he said amiably.

'Evening, Hinckman. I hear it's a great film you're giving us tonight.'

'Yeah, it's a great film all right. Look here, Druce, old man, about this Combine. Why not cut out high-hatting the rest of us an' come right in?'

'I figured I'd made my views pretty clear at the meeting.'

'Maybe—still, things has happened since then. Handsome's toed the line this afternoon—an' I guess Hugo Schultzer's wishing he'd done the same.'

'Yeah?'

'Yeah.'

'I'm not interested.'

'That so? You'll wish you were 'fore you're through. Why not let us all get together, sink our differences an' become friends—Trans-Continental Electric an' Pacific Players 'ud soon shake down together. If you sign up Uncle Andy'll come in with World Wide—an' Issey Vandelstein with Mozarts—we won't need the rest. There's a packet in this thing for all of us.'

Barton Druce stood up. 'See here, Hinckman, I just hate the thought of bein' rude to you in your own theatre. But what I said the other day goes—every word of it—an' I'll tell you something else. I'm not standing by to see poor old Hugo done dirt, neither—you may've monkeyed with his executives, but his film's going on. Meet Miss Avril Bamborough—she's going to star for me—in Pacific Players.'

Hinckman twitched his cigar from one corner of his mouth to the other. 'You don't say. . . . Waal, I guess you've asked for yours.' Without another word he left the box.

The big film was a marvellous spectacle, every advantage being taken of the scenic possibilities in Aldous Huxley's novel *This Brave New World.* Giant sky-scrapers towered to the clouds, helicopters sailed about in every direction. Upon the dance hall the producer had let himself rip, in a riot of abandoned jazzing. The feelies had been demonstrated by the ingenious device of equipping the audience in the picture with electric wigs—whereby, when the hair of the hero in the film within a film stood up in horror, so also did that of his audience. Clever fakes of the incubating babies in various states of development were shown, and Hollywood had been combed for the most cherubic collection of toddlers that these might duly receive their electric shocks. The remarkable adventures of the lady who was carried off for a love feast in a balloon by a big buck nigger, and her later exploits with her rescuers had, needless to say, been suppressed, also the modern revival of an ancient religious festival when the participants worked themselves into a state of frenzy for the ultimate good of their health. Much had been made of the Native Reservation Scene, but not unnaturally, the Hollywood producer had felt Mexico to be totally inadequate. He preferred Africa, in order that he might more fittingly bring in lions, tigers, elephants, and every other animal that he could lay his hands on.

Much, too, had been made of the Delta minors who moved on all occasions in sinister gangs with downcast heads and shuffling feet, after the manner of the slaves in *Metropolis.* The death-bed scene had been cut out as entirely unsuitable, also that important portion of the book when the young man is scourged by the Mexican Priest. The Alpha plus damsels were the loveliest possible collection of cuties with india-rubber legs. A littler quiverful of soft-tipped arrows had been substituted for the malthusian belts, and these the cuties let fly with delicious abandon at the boy-friends of their choice. Unfortunately a theme song had been introduced for no particular reason, and the whole point of the book lost by the complete elimination of the interview with the Jewish World Controller and its original ending. Instead, the Hollywood editors had substituted a happy understanding with regard to legal union between the more resilient of the rubber-legged cuties and the handsome young savage—the latter being suitably injected with a strong dose of the 'Oh King live for Ever' serum. However, these little alterations were hardly a matter of serious concern since Ronnie Sheringham, Avril Bamborough, and Nelson Druce were probably the only people in the house who had actually read the book, and it is doubtful if more than half a dozen others had ever even heard of Mr. Huxley.

When the film was over Hinckman and the producer, Ring, together with the principal rubber-legged cutie in the flesh and the young savage, looking anything but masochistically inclined, received felicitations in the foyer.

Everybody pushed and shoved to get as near to them as possible and remain in their proximity as long as they were able. The film had definitely got over, but apart from that it was a matter of business policy on the part of each member of the crowd to see to it that the great man of Trans-Continental Electric should register their personal enthusiasm and admiration. From all sides there came a perpetual chorus.

'Oh, Mr. Hinckman, I thought it just grand.'

'Did yer ever see such sweets as all those kids a-playin' with the flowers. I'll certainly say it was a great show, Mr. Hinckman.'

'An' wasn't Babe just "It" with her little bow an arrer. But I reckon that was your idea, Mr. Hinckman.'

'Sure, it's a mighty fine production, Mr. Hinckman. I'll say you've given us the goods this time all right. But then, I guess, you always do.'

'An' them scenes in the jungle with the elephants—I figure you're wise to the public taste all right, Mr. Hinckman. It sure is a hundred-per-cent box-office attraction—an' then some!'

Barton Druce and his son managed to steer Avril and Vitelma through the crush and then step by step, down the broad staircase. Outside in the street a crowd of spectators blocked the sidewalk on each side of the entrance. Little murmurs of excitement went up as the more celebrated stars were ushered to their cars.

As the Druce limousine drew up before the entrance the crowd surged forward. Barton Druce ran neck to neck with Hinckman as the uncrowned King of Hollywood. In addition he had with him Vitelma Loveday, who was a popular favourite, and Avril, the new English star, in whom people were already becoming interested. Most of the commissionaires were some way away, hunting for other cars. The two or three police officers were quite inadequate to deal with the seething multitude. The crowd pressed in on all sides, Avril was nearly swept off her feet, but she clung to Barton Druce, who continued to force his way towards his car. Nelson and Vitelma were just behind, all four completely surrounded, jammed tight against each other in the crush. Avril caught sight of Angelo's olive face, but he was not looking at her, he was on the other side of Barton Druce and his eyes were fixed on the elderly American with a curious expression. Wedged in front of Avril was a tall, red-headed fellow with the long upper lip and blunt nose of the typical Irish peasant, she vaguely remembered having seen him in Hinckman's company on the day of the garden party. His hard blue eyes were also fixed on Druce.

Suddenly there was a deafening report, then another and another. Avril felt Barton Druce's arm twitch. Vitelma screamed, the crowd began to struggle wildly. A fist shot over Avril's shoulder, catching the Irishman with terrific force behind the ear. His head flopped forward as though his neck were broken. Police whistles shrilled, women shrieked, men shouted, people began to run, terrified that there would be further shooting. Nelson Druce had forced his was to Avril's side, his face white and set. He seized the Irishman by the collar just as he was about to slip down onto the pavement through the easing pressure of the crowd. Barton Druce's head hung forward on his chest, his hat had fallen off. The police had begun to use their batons, reinforcements were arriving

70

from every direction. The crowd melted. Avril felt a sudden tug as Barton Druce pitched forward on the pavement. Angelo had disappeared.

After that, to Avril, everything seemed to become a nightmare. The whole thing had been so sudden—so unexpected. A few moments before, this nice elderly American had been talking and laughing with her in the box—now he was stretched out on the pavement, unconscious and bleeding terribly. She saw his son kneeling beside him, shaking him by the arm, and repeating over and over again:

'Dad, say something—for the Lord's sake say something—tell me you're all right.'

She found herself kneeling beside him, and vainly trying to staunch the blood that welled from three blackened holes in the wounded man's shirt-front.

The Irishman, whom Nelson had temporarily knocked out, was being hauled by police into a patrol wagon.

People were carrying the wounded man in through the hall to the privacy of the box-office.

Avril heard Vitelma screaming in a fit of hysteria, and remembered afterwards pulling her together by telling the girl sharply that she was ruining her face.

She saw Barton Druce laid out on the floor, and heard people shouting for a doctor.

Finding a chair in a quiet corner, she sat down—she was feeling sick and giddy—then she fainted.

When she came round, she saw that Hinckman was in the room, a tall and dominating personality—there was a doctor, too, kneeling beside Barton Druce.

As in a dream she heard the doctor say, 'It ain't no good to move him to a clinic. He's just about all in.'

It was then that the full horror of the thing came upon her. That kindly old man with the neatly brushed hair and pleasant smile would never walk round his orchid houses any more, he would never again see the sunlight upon the gay flowers in his garden. . . . He was dead. Murdered. Shot in cold blood by callous, brutal, hired gunmen. Assassinated, she did not doubt,

71

because he had been brave enough to declare against the Combine.

She found herself holding Nelson Druce's hand, it was hot and feverish. He stood there with his face suddenly grown old, glaring at Hinckman across his father's body.

She heard Hinckman mouthing hypocritical condolences. . . . 'Just terrible these gangsters—to think it happened outside my theatre—close it for a week—mark of respect—sincerest sympathy—behalf of the Trans-Continental Electric Corporation.'

She saw Nelson's face, he was staring at Hinckman with hard, bright eyes.

Hinckman was talking again. 'Hear you were figuring to make a trip to Europe—when formalities are over—terrible shock you certainly must have sustained—help to restore you— this appalling tragedy.'

Then she felt Nelson clutch her hand with sudden violence as he spoke, his words coming sharp and rapid like bullets from a gun.

'Am I leaving for Europe, so you can fix a deal on the Pacific Corporation? Am I going to let you pull off your damned Combine? Am I going to let you get away with murder? Am I, hell!'

7

The Rival Factions

On the afternoon following the murder of Barton Druce, Lord Gavin Fortescue held a council of war. His body seemed more puny than ever, and his dark heavy clothes looked curiously out of place on this day of radiant sunshine when everyone else was wearing the lightest garments that were possible. Hinckman towered above him, his long legs spread wide apart, his hands clasped behind his back, the eternal cigar protruding from the corner of his strong mouth. Ronnie lazed in one chair by the window, his smart shoes upon the arm of another; he looked more than ever the perfect film hero in his wide-cut flannels and open shirt. Outside the fierce sun beat down in dazzling brilliance, but in Lord Gavin's private sitting-room it was cool and shady.

'I figure we got 'em on the run,' Hinckman declared.

'I had two little men around this morning both wanting to sell out—but I wouldn't talk. I guess they're going through the hoop an' they know it.'

Lord Gavin smiled. 'The effects of Druce's death are bound to be widespread. Did you see the German?'

'What—Schultzer? Yes, I reckon we got him fixed. Now Eberhard Lusatch has come over to us, Hugo's in a flat spin, an' Wendy Claus signed right on the dotted line last night. She sure knows her stuff—that woman.'

'Do you think Schultzer will play now?' asked Ronnie.

'Sure—he's got to. How else'll he continue to produce? He was figuring on old man Druce to carry him over—this time tomorrow he'll be crying Kamarad—believe you me.'

'T.C.E., Klein Brothers, Stillman, Honeydew, Ubiquitous,' Lord Gavin ticked them off upon small pudgy fingers, 'that is five. What of McTavish?'

'Alpha'll be O.K. I've put Amos wise to the figure we're pre- pared to go to. Issey'll cash in his holding for a cert.'

'Six then—we progress. However, we must bear in mind our liabilities. Schultzer will prove an unwilling partner, and we have saddled ourselves with the necessity of producing these three super films for Honeydew. I shudder to think what they may be like.'

'We shan't start production till the Combine's formed—an' I figure I know enough about the moving picture business to cut out the super—when I want to. What's his redress with the whole board against him? 'Sides, we've got Von Sternheim —he's the cleverest guy in the business, if only you can keep his exes down. Reno Films 'ud have been way under years ago if it hadn't been for him. His box-office draw is darn near as big as a real top-notcher in the star line. I'll say that even Piplin's name on a film don't beat Von Sternheim's that way.'

'That is true—and we have already acquired Eberhard Lusatch from Schultzer—then there is your own man Ring; we shall be exceptionally strong on the production side. The question is, who do we concentrate against next?'

'Waal, there's Vandelstein and Uncle Andy still out against us, both of 'em undamaged so far, and there's the Pacific people, who've lost their big chief.'

'Does Vandelstein show any signs of changing front?'

'No—sir! Issey "don't vant no combines". I sure pressed him all I knew yesterday—but it weren't no good.'

'Why not go for Pacific,' Ronnie put in lazily. 'They're bound to be in a mess now their big noise is out of the game.'

Lord Gavin nodded his silver head. 'Out of the mouths . . .' he murmured. 'After all none of the other people upon the Pacific board appear to me to have more than a very moderate amount of personality or intelligence. It should not be difficult to bring them round to our point of view.'

'There's the young 'un.'

'Nelson Druce. Yes, but even if his father's share-holding comes to him, a considerable time must elapse before he could get control of his company—and he is only a boy; surely you cannot seriously fear his opposition.'

'Sez you!' Hinckman looked thoughtful. 'I guess you should have heard him hand out the rough stuff to me last night. I'll say that kid's got guts, an' he's gone clean crazy 'bout his dad.'

'Yes, yes, an admirable young man. I do not doubt, but hardly a figure whom these older men could be expected to rally round—men like Vandelstein and Uncle Andy would not be prepared to accept the leadership of a boy even if he were sufficiently strong to overawe his own board.'

'That's so! All the same, I'd give a whole heap to know just what that young man's up to at this moment.' Hinckman nodded slowly. 'He's not sitting writin' any *billy-doo* to yours truly. No sir—believe you me!'

Mr. Hinckman's surmise was perfectly correct. Nelson Druce was not employed in writing love letters to him or anyone else; nevertheless he had Hinckman very much in mind.

He was pacing rapidly up and down his father's study. On the

74

open desk many papers lay scattered. They were the confidential reports that each big corporation compiles for its own information, with regard to the doings and position of its rivals. Now and then Nelson stopped to verify a figure in his mind from one of them, then he resumed his restless pacing.

Lord Gavin Fortescue might have been surprised out of his habitual calm had he been present at the board meeting which Nelson Druce had attended that morning.

It would have displeased him intensely to learn of the very considerable respect in which Nelson Druce was held by the older members of the Pacific Players board. It would have displeased him still more to know that, not alone because of his father's enormous stock holding, but largely on account of his own strong personality, Nelson Druce had been elected President of the corporation in his father's place, and that the board had supported a resolution for a firm continuation of its late President's policy, and an open declaration of war upon the promoters of the Combine.

Nelson had expected no less from his colleagues after the murderous attack that had been made upon their President. In America youth is not necessarily regarded as a bar to high positions in big business. Nelson was only thirty, but he had had ten years' experience in the film world, and although he had not done anything spectacular, he had a very good supply of sound common sense, and felt himself quite competent to take his father's place. He was filled with a quiet, cold rage and an unshakable determination to leave nothing undone that might wreck the Combine. With that end in view he had lost no time, but arranged a meeting for this afternoon with Uncle Andy, Issey Vandelstein, Amos McTavish, and Hugo Schultzer. It was to take place at the Druce home to ensure privacy and he was now awaiting the arrival of the other magnates.

Uncle Andy was the first to put in an appearance. He had already telephoned his sympathy in the early morning, but he wrung Nelson's hand again and again. The Great Old Man was so affected by his friend's death that he could hardly speak coherently.

'My boy, my boy,' he kept on saying, 'if this don't beat all.

It sure makes me ashamed to be a citizen of the United States —just to think that such terrible things can happen in this great country of ours. I'm an old man, but I never reckoned I'd live to hear of the shooting of my friend Barton Druce in the dead centre of Hollywood Boulevard. It's a darned disgrace to civilisation.'

Schultzer, too, when he arrived, was almost in tears. In his heavy, sentimental way, the lumbering German had had a very great respect and affection for Barton Druce. Issey Vandelstein, who ever played a lone hand and had had a few dealings with the dead man, confined himself to formal condolences, but as a mark of respect to the host he wore a black tie with his bright green shirt.

McTavish, who completed the party, exhorted Nelson to turn to the Lord in his hour of tribulation, and would have continued in that strain for a considerable time if Nelson had not cut him short by thanking him briefly and suggesting that they get down to business.

When they were all seated Nelson addressed the party. 'It's this way,' he said. 'You're all acquainted with the terrible thing that happened last night, and I'm very grateful for your sympathy, but I'm going to ask you for something more than that. You know just how my old man met his death, and I guess most of you have got your own ideas as to why. It was a frame-up—pure and simple. I gave Mick Downey his myself, an' when the police picked him up he still had the gun in his hand, but only one bullet had been fired from it. Now we all know that Mick Downey's one of Hinckman's bunch, an' he's for the chair all right—I'll see to that; but there were others in the killing too. I spotted that guy Angelo Donelli in the crush an' I reckon he was one of them—anyhow they made their getaway. My point's this, these birds who did the job are only paid gunmen—the man who's behind this whole racket is Hinckman. He knew he couldn't get the old man at his office or in the house here, so he put him on the spot by getting him to the Ocean Theatre. To bring this thing home to Hinckman can't be done. I'm wise to that. He was up in the foyer taking the sugar off the crowd—but do we stand for this sort of thing or don't we, that's what I want to know?'

'I'll be damned if we do!' Uncle Andy hit the desk a resounding blow with his clenched fist.

'Vat yer goin' ter do, Mister Druce?' Issey Vandelstein wanted to know.

'Combine against the Combine,' Nelson announced promptly. 'It'll interest you to know that this morning my board elected me as President of the Pacific Players Corporation. They've given me a free hand to take any steps which I figure to be right an' proper to resist encroachment and organise an active opposition. I want you boys to toe the line and we'll sure smash this swab Hinckman before we're through.'

'Well, I certainly am delighted to hear they put you up, Nelson, an' you can count on World Wide Pictures bein' right alongside you all the time. I guess we're free citizens of the United States of America, an' we don't stand for murder. No, sir—that's flat.'

Nelson Druce took the hand which Uncle Andy extended and shook it warmly. 'Thanks, Uncle Andy,' he said. 'It's great to know I'll have you with me. Now, Vandelstein, what about you?'

'Ai don't vant no combines,' the little Jew shook his head.

'Come on, now,' said Druce persuasively. 'Think again, Issey. What's goin' to happen if Hinckman gets on your tail like he has with Schultzer?'

'Mozarts is Mozarts, aint it?'

'Well, what about it? You're sure as liable to be shot at as the rest of us.'

'Maybe. But Ai jus' don't vant no combines, Mr. Druce.'

'Is that so? Well, I'll say you get me beat—but I guess we'll have to leave it at that for the moment. Let's hear how Mr. McTavish sees this thing?'

'You certainly shall, young man.' The dour, hard-faced Scotsman turned on Nelson suddenly. 'It's my opeenion that ye'll burn your fingers if ye're not careful. The Combine'll be a fine thing for us all—an' a great power for good in this world

77

of darkness. By the opposeetion ye propose ye are thwarting the will of the Lord, an' retribution will be upon ye. Fer meself I'm proud to say that I have entered into certain arrangements this morning which will enable me to take my rightful place in the forefront of this great movement.'

Uncle Andy looked quickly at Issey Vandelstein. 'Have you bin an' let up on your holding, Issey?'

'Sure.' The gold teeth flashed.

'Now what in heck possessed you to do that?'

'Vhy vouldn't Ai? Amos gave me der price Ai vant.'

'You poor boob—ain't you just said you don't want the Combine?'

'Sure—but Alpha is Alpha an' Mozarts is Mozarts, ain't it? Der von's my corporation, der other ain't. Ai don't vant no ill vill from de Alpha people—an' der feller vat takes a profit don't never go broke.'

'In that case I figure we needn't detain Mr. McTavish any longer,' said Nelson coldly, 'an' I'll say it'd be better for the world in general an' his own salvation in particular, if he cut out moralising an' went in with a crowd of decent men instead of a bunch of murderers.'

'Hold on, Nelson.' Uncle Andy laid a restraining hand on his arm. 'That stuff don't cut no ice. Amos'll have to answer for what he's doing one day—an' it may be business but it sure ain't cricket.'

'Young man, I forgive ye them words, because it's the command of the Lord that I should do so, but ye're attitude'll bring ruin upon yerself an' yer friends—an' that I warn you.' With which covert thrust Mr. McTavish, the latest recruit to the Combine, left them.

'Now, Hugo,' Nelson said when they had settled down again. 'It's up to you. After me, I reckon you've been the biggest sufferer so far. I take it you'll come in.'

'I wish that I gould say yes to that, Mr. Truce,' Schultzer replied slowly. 'I haf great respect vor your goot father, also I haf gonfidence in your ability—but I haf many gomplications in my pusiness.'

'Well, as I see it that's all the more reason that you should come in with us. I'm ready to sign up in the Bamborough contract right now if you'll say the word.'

'Ach! it is not alone der gomplication of broduction, it is also I haf gomplication with my go-directors.'

'I certainly had the idea, Hugo, that you were speaking on behalf of Ubiquitous, when we said our piece at Hinckman's meeting,' Uncle Andy put in.

'Jawohl—at that time it was so—put now many members of my poard change dare mind. dis morning I haf meeting with my go-directors. I tink Hinckman has abbroach some of dem, they say let us join der gombine pefore it is too late.'

'That certainly is a difficult situation,' Nelson admitted.

The poor old German was nearly in tears. 'Mr. Truce, I lof your father—he was a goot man. I haf respect for you. Myself, I will retire pefore I do dis ting, but if my go-directors unite against me, Ubiquitous must also of der gombine pecome.'

'Well, it that's how things are, Hugo, I guess we'll have to do without you.' Nelson Druce shook his head. 'I'm sorry though, and I certainly sympathise with the rotten position you find yourself in.' He turned to Uncle Andy with a smile. 'Seems to me—it's you an' I against all-comers.'

'Vi d'yer say dat, Mr. Druce?' Issey Vandelstein grinned suddenly. 'Ai don't vish you no ill vill.'

'Maybe, but you won't come in with us so what's the odds. Now see here—three of us stand a better chance of smashing this ramp than two—why don't you come in?'

'Ai don't vant no combines.'

'Oh, Lordy. What the hell do you want?'

'Ai don't vant nothing and Ai vish you all der luck in der vorld.'

'Well, that's nice of you, Issey.'

' 'Tain't nice, it's business, ain't Ai jus' said Ai don't vant no combines. Vell! Ai'm villing to finance you, Mr. Druce, if you're vanting any help that vay.'

'Is that so? Well, I figure we'll need all the money we can get, if we're going out against Hinckman. Let's hear your proposition.'

The little Jew leaned forward. 'Hinckman's spendin' money

like vater, ain't it? Vat did Reno Films cost 'im? Vat did 'e pay out fer Lusatch an' dat voman Claus?—where did der money come from vat 'e paid fer der Alpha Corporation? 'E can't go on that way. No, sir! An' it's jus' like any other vor—der feller vot's got der shekels vins in der long run.'

Uncle Andy nodded. 'There certainly is a whole heap in what you say, Issey. I figure Hinckman must have sure pawned his weskit by this time.'

'Okay! Now Amos bought my Alphas, ain't it? Ten million dollars vas der price Ai ask. Ten million dollars vas der price Ai get. Vere did der money come from?—not Amos, 'e ain't got a vad like dat, not so he could put 'is 'and on it, anyvay. Der money come from Hinckman. All right, now Ai don't vant der money—so vy vouldn't Ai lend it to Mr. Druce—see?'

For the first time since the tragedy Nelson Druce laughed. 'I'll say you're a great little man, Issey. The idea of fighting Hinckman on his own money suits me fine.'

'Wait a minute, wait a minute.' Uncle Andy put out a large hand. 'If you're game to help us break these swabs—why not come out in the open? Line up along side of us.'

Vandelstein shook his narrow head. 'Dat ain't der same thing at all. Mozarts is Mozarts, ain't it—vell, they stays put. Ai don't vant no combines with Hinckman an' Ai don't vant no combines with you . . . but if Ai'm villing to make a little loan to Mister Druce, that's private—see. Now vill you vant der money or von't you?'

'What security are you asking, Issey?'

'Vell, Mister Druce, Ai figure you got a vad of Pacific stock, ain't it. Ai'm villin' to loan you dem ten million dollars fer ninety days at six per cent, an' Ai'm villing to take Pacifics at par on fifty per cent cover fer security.'

'That's okay, Issey, though I'd certainly like a longer date if you could fix it.'

'Vi vorry about dat? Hinckman vill be up der spout afore then, 'sides, Ai vouldn't like to make it no longer on them terms. Ain't Ai takin' a chance that Pacifics go vonkey as it is.'

'That's true. All right, Issey, we'll call it a deal.'

The little man stood up. 'Vell, you're a vine feller, Mr. Druce, an' Ai vish you all der luck in der vorld.'

When Vandelstein and Schultzer had departed, Uncle Andy and Nelson talked over their plan of campaign. It was decided that they should each call a meeting of their principal executives and place the situation before them, offer new contracts all round to those they wished to retain, at a considerably higher figure, but with very heavy penalties attached. By this means they hoped to bind their lieutenants to them, or in the event of their going over to the Combine, pile up enormous assets for their corporations by way of damages.

'I figure that Issey's getting the best of this deal by a long sight,' Uncle Andy said, as he was leaving.

'Sure,' Nelson grinned. 'He reckons Hinckman's about all in for money, but that it'll pretty near break you an' me to bring him down. Then Master Issey'll be sitting pretty. The only man outside Star Artists in the market, Hinckman bust an' us crippled like hell. I guess that's the reason why he's financed us just to make quite sure we won't go under before the Combine's down and out. Still we meant to fight anyhow, an' this money'll be mighty useful. I figure it'll make just all the difference in pulling us through.'

'Yeah. You'd have been a fool not to take it—an' he didn't ask for what was more than fair. He stands to lose a packet if Pacifics slump. I guess we got no grouse on Issey really.' Uncle Andy climbed into his car and Nelson waved to him as he drove away.

When the car had disappeared from sight Nelson Druce strolled back into the house. He carefully collected and locked away his papers, then he went upstairs to his bedroom.

In the gathering twilight he unlocked a big cabinet containing numerous pigeon holes, most of which were filled with papers and bundles of letters. From one upon the left-hand side he drew a large and ugly-looking automatic, farther in reposed a square box full of cartridges. He weighed the pistol carefully in his hand for a moment as he stood there deep in thought. Gradually his eyes narrowed and his mouth drew down into a set curve full of dangerous determination. Then he took out the box of ammunition, and with those long, nervous fingers that Avril had admired so much, slowly began to load the gun.

8

The Terror in the Night

Avril dined with Ronnie that evening. She had dined with him on two occasions before and enjoyed being in his company. She found his lazy amusing manner delightfully refreshing after the snap and drive of the Americans. They always seemed so frantically anxious to get somewhere, or do something. Even if they were apparently enjoying themselves at a party—they wanted to rush off in their fast cars to some road house or night dive, and when they got there, their first idea seemed to be—to leave it for some other.

She could talk, too, with Ronnie upon all sorts of interesting subjects, whereas everybody else in Hollywood had one theme and one theme only—they chattered endlessly from morning to night as to what they and their acquaintances were doing or about to do in connection with the motion pictures. Avril was getting heartily sick of it. It seemed to her that they were a stupid, brainless lot with the possible exception of a few brilliant intellects, and these locked themselves away in the fastness of their luxury mansions most of the time.

Avril was just a trifle homesick for her own English world, and Ronnie was definitely of it. However much his casualness —to call it by no other name—might lead the unwary to suppose that he had unbounded influence with important people who in actual fact he had hardly met, Avril did find that they really had quite a number of acquaintances in common.

After dinner Ronnie suggested going on to a night place to

dance, but Avril decided that she would rather go back to their hotel and sit in the garden.

The night was fine, and it was cool and pleasant there after the dusty heat of the long day. They sat talking casually as they sipped their iced coffee fortified with brandy from Ronnie's flask. The hotel itself was a blaze of light, but the garden was almost deserted.

'When do you start to do a spot of work?' Ronnie asked lightly.

'In a day or so now, I hope. Barton Druce was to have taken over my contract today, but I expect the Pacific people will when they've had a chance to straighten out his affairs.'

'Nelson Druce is a lucky devil—I bet he comes into a packet.'

'Well, I don't know that one can say that he's altogether lucky. I believe he was very fond of his father, and he must be feeling this terrible thing most frightfully—but of course he'll be a very rich man now.'

'Wonder if he'll run the Pacific show or if he'll sell out.'

'I should think he's almost certain to continue in the business, he seems awfully keen about it. I think he's clever, too, he's carrying out all sort of experiments with new lenses.'

'That must be rather fun.'

'His fiancée told me about it when I was up at the house the day before yesterday—it seems he's got a thing called the "Z" projector. I don't know much about it, but Vitelma Loveday said that he thinks it will revolutionise the whole business?'

'Oh—how?' Ronnie's tone was casual but his blue eyes had quickened with interest.

'I don't quite know, but I gather that it will throw up the actors in relief when the film is shown upon the screen.'

'Um—they've been working on that for years. The Germans perfected one method, but the expense killed it. They had an enormous screen made like the concave side of a saucer tilted up on end, but it had to be made of silver. The ordinary picture palace couldn't possibly have afforded to install it, but it was a marvellous idea. I saw it in Berlin, and when they chopped a chap's head off on the film it looked just as though it was rolling out of the screen right on to the stage.'

'How extraordinary!'

'I wonder of Druce has really solved the secret of showing films in the round, it is bound to come, of course, and if he has there is a fortune in it.'

'Yes, I suppose there is.'

'Rather! Look what Western Electric must be making out of their talkie patents—every theatre in the world has to be fitted with them. I wonder if Druce would care to sell the English rights of this thing.'

Avril smiled. 'What would you do if he would?' she asked curiously. 'Try and sell them to Uncle John?'

'Oh, no. I'd form a company—I don't suppose Bamborough would be willing to give me the price I should want in money down.'

'You must be a very rich young man.'

'No. But I know plenty of people who are. It would be as easy as falling off a log to raise money on a thing like that.'

'Then where would you come in?'

'Oh, shares—and my expenses—man's time, you know.'

'If, as you say, the whole world will have to use this invention I shouldn't think Nelson Druce would be such a fool as to sell the English rights—why should he?—he can't be hard up for money.'

'No, I don't suppose he would—worse luck.' Ronnie whistled thoughtfully, then he said suddenly, 'I say! it's going to make the other companies look a bit silly, isn't it? If Druce decides to fit his new projector in Pacific-owned theatres only.'

'Yes, I should think it will, and I can't say I shall be sorry—your friend Hinckman thoroughly deserves a real good slap in the eye.'

'Oh, I say,' Ronnie protested. 'What's he done, anyway. He's not a bad chap.'

'Indeed, I think you have very curious ideas, Ronnie, I don't know, of course, but I should think it's more than likely that he put those men up to shoot poor Mr. Druce last night, the man they caught was one of his people.'

Ronnie laughed as he tilted back his chair. 'My dear, what

84

utter rot! Hinckman would never have had anything to do with a thing like that. The States are full of gunmen, I expect they shot old Druce up because he refused to pay for protection or something of that sort.'

'I'm not so sure. Anyhow, Hinckman seems to have pretty well smashed up poor old Schultzer.'

'What about it if he has. That's only business. If Schultzer can't keep his directors and technicians he deserves to lose them, and I think you are awfully silly to turn down Hinckman's offer of a contract. This "Forbidden Territory" film is going to be the best thing Trans-Continental Electric have done for years.'

'Perhaps it is—I don't care—I just don't like Mr. Hinckman and I don't approve of his business methods.'

'Well, it's your funeral—but you'd be much wiser to come in. He'll have the whole caboodle under his thumb in a few months' time.'

'If he doesn't go smash first.'

'He won't. And after all, why worry where your screw comes from as long as it's the biggest you can get—I shouldn't care a hoot.'

'No, Ronnie, of course, you wouldn't, and I think you're a darling, but that is just one of the little things in which we don't see eye to eye. And now I'm going to bed.'

Ronnie laughed as he stood up. 'Well, have it your own way, but there's nothing dishonest about it.'

'Nothing dishonest about breaking my contract?'

'No, it's done every day in Hollywood, and your business manager would do it for you if he were over here.'

'Yes, if I let him, but I shouldn't, as it is he drafted my contract before I left London, and that, my dear is that.'

Ronnie saw her as far as the door of her room. He had decided to have an early night himself, and his own room was only just along the corridor.

'Thank you for my nice evening,' said Avril sweetly, 'and lots of happy dreams.'

Ronnie laughed again. 'Thanks. I'll dream I have that contract of yours and I'm scrapping it for a fifty per cent rise with

Hinckman—no, I won't though, that would be too much like hard work. I'll dream that Nelson Druce has made me a present of the "Z" projector. Good night, sleep well.'

Lord Gavin Fortescue was reading when Ronnie entered his private room. He carefully marked his place and put down his book. 'Well, my young friend,' he said placidly, 'how have you been amusing yourself this evening?'

'Oh, I dined Avril Bamborough,' Ronnie replied, as he walked over to mix himself a drink. 'She's intelligent for a woman and I'm sick to death of American cuties. How's Great Headquarters—any news from the Californian Front?'

Lord Gavin stroked his silver hair. 'We progress,' he said slowly. 'You know, of course, that we have taken the Alpha salient, a costly operation, since Vandelstein stuck out for his price, but it straightens our front considerably and gives us five.'

'Yes, we're gaining ground. How about Schultzer?'

'We attack the Schultzer ridge at dawn tomorrow—or to be more strictly accurate, at 10 a.m., Hinckman is to meet the Ubiquitous board. As you know, the position has been well mined, most of their directors are on our side already— Schultzer himself is the main obstacle, but if Hinckman is the strong man I think him we have no need to worry about the result.'

'Um—Hinckman's the big boy all right—and I expect Barton Druce's death has shaken them pretty badly.'

'Yes, a most tragic affair, poor fellow, to be shot in the open street like that. Really, the American Government should do something to put a stop to these crimes of violence. The activities of these gunmen are really too terrible—nobody is safe.' Lord Gavin's voice was mild and sympathetic. He looked like some benovelent prelate as he sat hunched in the big chair.

'It was a ghastly business,' Ronnie agreed. 'I wonder what they had up against him, been trying to soak him and he wouldn't pay, I suppose. Still, one can't help feeling it's a slice of luck for us—it's going to make things much easier. Is there any news from the enemy camp?'

'Intelligence reports that young Nelson Druce has been appointed to his father's old position in the Pacific Company—

86

also that he called a meeting this afternoon.'

'Trying to form a group against us, I suppose?'

'Precisely, but I gather that he did not have much luck. Mc-Tavish was present, and he declared openly for us. The Grand Old Man is joining Druce with World Wide, Schultzer's hands have been successfully tied, and the Jew remains nebulous.'

'Nelson Druce is a clever chap,' Ronnie remarked airily. 'He's just perfected a new projector for showing films in relief.'

Lord Gavin hunched his frail body in the arm-chair, his pale blue eyes filled with quick interest. 'Are you certain of that,' he asked sharply.

Ronnie nodded lazily. 'Yes. I had it from his fiancée.'

'Indeed! This is interesting. It may affect the whole situation profoundly, many people have been working on such inventions for years.'

'I know, it will be as big a thing as when the Talkies first came out. He calls it the "Z" projector.'

'This information is of extreme importance, and my plans are of far too great a magnitude to neglect a possibility of this kind. You have done well, Ronnie.'

'Cough up,' said Ronnie with a laugh.

Lord Gavin took out his note-case and handed over a number of crisp new notes.

Ronnie pocketed them, smiling. 'Well, I think I'll toddle along to my well-earned rest,' he said. 'Good night.'

A few doors along the corridor Avril had just climbed into bed; she took up her book but she did not begin to read at once. She was thinking of Ronnie and their conversation about Nelson Druce.

What a delightful person Nelson was. His comments upon the absurd travesty of Aldous Huxley's book that they had seen the night before, had been most amusing and full of shrewd intelligence. Then afterwards—during that nightmare scene in the box-office—with the old man dying, and the police, and the doctor, and those soulless reporters thrusting their way in, avid for details. She wondered how it was that he had come to be holding her hand, but could not remember, she felt certain that he was quite unconscious that it had been she beside him.

Perhaps he had thought it was Vitelma, but Vitelma had been busy in a corner repairing the ravages that hysterics had made to her face.

It seemed absurd that Nelson Druce should love that beautiful shallow doll. Avril supposed that it was the old story of an intelligent man disliking intelligence in his woman, and just wanting a lovely silky kitten to play with on the heathrug when he returned tired out from business. However, it was not her affair.

She began to wonder if she had been quite wise in mentioning the 'Z' projector to Ronnie, but after all Vitelma had been quite open about it, and there must be dozens of people in Hollywood who were working upon new inventions; what harm could come of it—none that she could see. She dismissed the matter from her mind and began to read one of Mr. A. E. Coppard's delightful short stories. She finished it and read another, then she laid down her book and put out the light.

A gentle glow, the reflection from the lights of the ground-floor rooms on to the garden, showed the tall french windows plainly. It filled the room with a pale, restful twilight which Avril preferred to complete darkness. The thin curtains were sufficient to keep out the morning light, at all events enough to prevent her waking.

For some reason she was restless tonight, and could not get to sleep, She lay for a long time in the semi-darkness, her senses wakeful although her eyes were closed. The sound of faint movements came to her as she lay there, but she thought that they must come from the adjoining room. Then she heard a rustle at her bedside, and in a second sat up, wide awake.

A dark figure stood beside her, the figure of a man, sharply outlined against the faint light of the windows. She snatched at the house telephone on the table by her bed, but with a swift movement he knocked it from her hand. She drew away, opening her mouth to scream, but he was too quick for her. In one spring he had landed on the low bed, forcing her backward, his hand over her mouth.

'Hush,' he said sharply. 'Do not maka da noise. It ees me—Angelo.'

She struggled fiercely but he flung the whole weight of his small lithe body upon her, bearing her down. 'Listen,' he whispered, forcing his face within a few inches of hers. 'I lova you—why you not lova Angelo—Angelo da greata lova. He giva you wonderful time.'

With a terrific wrench she jerked her head free for a second. 'Get out,' she said fiercely. 'I'll scream.' Next minute his hand descended like a clamp upon her mouth again.

In hot, passionate language he began to pour out his love for her. Then a silent, desperate struggle ensued in the darkness. Angelo had no mind to be thwarted in his desire, having got so far. He had not lain in wait behind her trunks in the close, hot darkness of the big clothes closet for nothing. He was a strong, wiry little man and his passions were at fever pitch. He had been brooding over Avril for days past, and the cerebral excitement which with him always accompanied a killing, had not subsided from the night before.

His breath came in hot gasps as he fought and struggled with one hand pressed firmly over Avril's mouth, the other fumbling to tear the bedclothes which separated them, or fending her hand from off his face.

'Ples,' he panted. 'Ples. You lova Angelo, he very nice mans, very gentle too if you be good.'

Avril wriggled and twisted, straining every nerve to free herself and throw him off. Her whole soul revolted at the touch of this brutal little Italian's be-ringed hands upon her flesh. If only she could free her head and call for help. There'd be a scandal, of course, a beastly miserable business—but even that was a thousand times better than submitting to these loathsome caresses. Her night-dress was ripped to her waist, some strands of her hair had caught upon Angelo's gaudy tie-pin and caused her agony every time she moved, but she fought with silent, savage persistence.

'Be sensible,' he hissed. 'I lova you—be sensible, yes; if you not, I usa da chloroform, what you do then, eh?'

The vile little beast. Avril sobbed with rage, and pain, and loathing. He meant to dope her, did he?—she'd heard of such things, read of them in books, or awful cases in the papers.

It had never even entered her mind that such a horror should happen to her. She prayed that Ronnie or a passing waiter in the corridor might hear them struggling, but their movements were almost soundless, except for quick-drawn, gasping breaths, and Angelo's fierce whispers.

She tried to bite into the hand that he held forced against her mouth, but he pressed it down so firmly that she could not get her teeth into it. One of her arms was held crushed, imprisoned under her body, with the other she sought to thrust his face away. He pressed his hot lips again and again upon her throat and eyes. No nightmare that she had ever had had seemed more horrible.

With his free hand he got a small bottle from his pocket, she could feel it as she struck out. With a terrific heave of her body she nearly succeeded in throwing him off, and knocked the bottle from his hand. Unfortunately for her it did not reach the floor, but fell upon the bed. She snatched it up hoping to hurl it way out of his reach, but he caught her hand, and with sudden brutal strength pressed upon her thumb, forcing it back until the pain became excruciating, it was almost at breaking point, she could have screamed with the agony before she finally let go.

He whipped a handkerchief from his pocket and uncorked the bottle with his strong white teeth—then he held them both high out of reach above Avril's head.

'Ef you not careful,' he panted, 'da chloroform, it spill, burna your lovely face, eh? Angelo not wanta hurt you, but he lova you, yes.'

Avril lay frantic beneath his grip, nothing should serve to make her suffer this awful thing. Her strength was almost exhausted, she felt she had been a fool, she should not have fought so desperately, she should have tried cunning before. Suddenly she let all her muscles go limp and lay still.

'Ha—dat is better so,' she could hear the triumph in Angelo's voice. 'You crier an' I spill da chloroform, yes.' He removed his hand from her mouth. She lay there as one dead while Angelo knelt above her.

He tilted the bottle upon the handkerchief. The pungent

smell of the anæsthetic came strongly to her nostrils. She prayed that he might re-cork the bottle, with a gasp of relief she heard it squeak as he pressed it in. Then she gathered all her remaining strength for one supreme effort, and held her breath that her scream might echo through the hotel.

She turned her head slowly towards the window, half-burying it in the pillow that Angelo might have more difficulty in forcing the handkerchief over her mouth. The sickly sweet anæsthetic would render all further resistance impossible. She was half-mad with terror. She opened her mouth to scream with all the power of her lungs.

But even as she did so, she caught her breath in a little gasp. A tall dark figure was standing in the room silhouetted against the pale light of the curtained window. 'Help!' she screamed, 'Help!' and using all her strength in one terrific effort, she succeeded in flinging Angelo from her.

Even as she slipped, terrified and exhausted, to the floor on the far side of the bed, there came a single, shattering report, and a bright flash illuminated the room with sudden violence. With a little choking moan Angelo sank from his knees on to the carpet.

Dazed and bewildered, Avril struggled to her feet, clutching frantically at the shreds of nightdress which hung in ribbons about her; wild-eyed and terrified she looked towards the man.

For a moment he stood there in the half-light, apparently irresolute, peering down at Angelo's still-twitching body. A handkerchief masked the lower part of his face, and a soft hat pulled well down hid his forehead and eyes. He seemed stunned by what he had done, the hand holding the smoking pistol dangled at his side.

As Avril moved round the foot of the bed, he raised it, half-turning towards her. For a moment she was overcome by panic, she feared that he was about to ensure her silence by murdering her too. With a little cry she flung herself upon him, seizing the hand that held the pistol and forcing it with her whole weight, down towards his side.

He pushed her roughly with his other hand and she fell. He tried to wrench the pistol from her grip, dragging her in quick jerks along the floor towards the window, but she clung on desperately, with the unreasoning tenacity of fear. His hand was within a few inches of her face, she could see it clearly in the brighter light between the curtains, as they struggled silently for possession of the pistol, half in the room—half out on the balcony.

A sudden thought flashed into her mind. That hand, so beautifully modelled, with the long sensitive fingers, the carefully tended nails—she knew it, she had seen it before—but where? With a sudden wrench he tore it away, leaving the still warm barrel of the pistol in her grasp. Next moment he had jumped over the railing of the balcony—swarmed down the iron support, and was running, a doubled figure, with head well down, into the shadows of the garden.

Avril lay still in the place to which he had dragged her, shaking and utterly exhausted. She sobbed and panted, overcome with terror and distress. A sudden recognition had flooded into her mind as the man leaped from the balcony. The hand that had saved her from the horror of Angelo—and the hand that had just done murder—was the hand of Nelson Druce.

9

Who killed Angelo Donelli?

How long that grim, breathless struggle with Angelo had lasted Avril did not know. To her it had seemed an eternity, but in actual fact it could not have been more than a few moments, and from the shooting of Angelo to the escape of the murderer over the balcony, had only been a matter of seconds.

She staggered to her feet, still grasping the pistol, and stood for a moment swaying as though about to faint, then she stepped back into the room and clutched at the bed-table for support. She was standing immediately above the body of Angelo. He was quite still now, his legs doubled back, his hands thrown out, his chin tilted in the air, grotesque and un-real, like some horrible dummy figure. She fumbled for the switch of the electric light, but just as her fingers found it she paused—yet another figure stood out in relief against the pale light of the curtains. Someone had come along the balcony.

She suddenly realised that she was almost nude and snatched up her dressing-gown, but the figure did not advance into the room. At first she thought it was a child from what little she could see in the semi-darkness. Then from the attitude she realised that it was a man, small and bent, leaning upon a stick, the head too big and out of all proportion to the slender body. He stood there, seeming fixed and immovable, peering for-ward into the shadows at Avril, and the crumpled body of Angelo Donelli.

Suddenly a quick knocking came upon the door, and Ronnie's voice: 'Avril—are you there—are you all right?'

She shook back her hair and ran to open it. He slipped in at once, closing the door behind him. 'That shot,' he said. 'Was it here? What's happened?'

'It's frightful,' she gasped. 'There was a man—two men—in my room. One of them's been killed I think.'

'Good God! let's have a light.' He found the switches at the door and snapped them on. Avril looked quickly towards the windows, but the small bent figure had vanished noiselessly.

'Why, it's Donelli,' exclaimed Ronnie, as he stepped round the far side of the bed. 'What the devil was he doing here?'

Avril collapsed upon the bed and closed her eyes. 'It was too ghastly,' she sobbed. 'I was asleep, or nearly—he—he sprang on me—ugh!' she shuddered. 'The feel of his hands. I don't think I shall ever feel clean again.'

There were footsteps and excited voices in the corridor, then a loud knocking on the door. Ronnie went over and opened it a few inches. There were a floor-waiter, a chamber-maid, and a number of people from the other rooms, in various stages of attire. 'There's been an accident,' he said briefly. 'Better send for the manager and the house detective.' Then he shut the door again and shot the bolt. 'What happened after that?' he asked Avril.

93

'The brute held his hand over my mouth so that I couldn't cry out. He threatened to chloroform me if—if I wouldn't give way. Then the other man came in—and shot him.'

'How ghastly for you, but how did you get that gun?'

'I was terrified that he meant to shoot me, so I snatched it and hung on. He was afraid that he'd get caught so—so he suddenly let go and bolted.'

The knocking came again. This time it was the hotel manager and the house detective who had arrived from different directions simultaneously. Ronnie let them in and locked the door behind them.

The detective was a tall, lean man, a soft hat was pushed on the back of his head. He looked sharply at Avril, then at the body, and back to Avril again.

'Say, young woman—you been doin' a killing?'

'She didn't shoot him, another chap did,' said Ronnie promptly.

'I wasn't speakin' to you.' The detective's manner was abrupt. 'Come on, sister—answer up.'

'What Mr. Sheringham has said is quite correct.'

'Is that so? Well, I guess this is a matter for the cops. Stay right where you are—both of you.' He took up the telephone and put through a call.

'Touched anything,' he asked briefly, when he had finished speaking.

'No, nothing. It—it only happened a few moments ago.'

'Okay,' he nodded. 'Then I figure we'd best wait for the people from headquarters.'

He strolled over to the window with his hands in his pockets, and looked out onto the balcony, then he turned, pushed a piece of chewing-gum into his mouth, and stood there, his jaws moving slowly, while his sharp eyes ran up and down the room.

The manager said nothing. He was a sleek, dark-haired American with a suggestion of Jew in his make-up. His black eyes were fixed on Avril with a speculative look.

Avril sat huddled on the end of her bed, a small tragic figure, her hair disordered, her beautiful face flushed and strained by the ordeal which she had just been through. Only

94

the exercise of the greatest control and Ronnie's sympathetic presence had enabled her to force a desire to give way to a fit of screaming hysterics.

It was a quarter of an hour before the police arrived. A short, tubby man with thick bushy black eyebrows, dressed in a suit of grey checks, and two others, both plain-clothes men. None of them worried about removing their hats.

'Evenin', Bob. What's the trouble?' asked the fat man.

The house detective nodded. 'Skirt's gone an' killed a guy. That's how I see it, Captain Rudd.'

'That so?' the other turned to Avril. 'Say yer piece, girlie.'

'This man was shot by another who got away,' said Avril firmly.

'You don't say!' his bushy eyebrows went up. 'Let's have yer name.'

'Avril Bamborough.'

'What's yer job?'

'Actress and screen star.'

'You British?'

'Yes.'

'You know this guy?'

'Yes.'

'Since when,'

'A little over a fortnight.'

'He yer boy-friend '

'No.'

'You bring him to yer room?'

'Certainly not.'

'How'd he get in?'

'I don't know—through the window, I suppose, or he may have been hiding in the clothes cupboard when I came up to bed.'

'That so! When d'you come acquainted that he was in the room?'

'When I was in bed, I saw him standing near me.'

'Was yer light on?'

'No.'

'Were yer asleep?'

'No.'

'Queer you never saw him, ain't it? Did yer yell?'

'No.'

'Why?'

'He sprang om me and held his hand over my mouth.'

'That so? Where d'you get that gun?'

'I snatched if from the other man.'

'What other man?'

'The man who came in by the window while we were struggling.'

'D'you know him?'

For a second Avril paused, then: 'No,' she said. 'He had a handkerchief over his face, and it was dark.'

'This guy what's been shot—you say you know 'im? What's his name?'

'Angelo Donelli.'

'Sure—you're right. What's his job?'

'I don't know, but from what he said I gathered he was what you call a gunman.'

'He told you that, eh? Right again, I've known him years. When d'yer see him last?'

'In the crowd outside the Ocean Palace last night—just before Mr. Barton Druce was killed.'

'That so?—when afore that?'

'He came to the box where I was with Mr. Druce.'

'Why?'

Avril hesitated. 'He came to bring me some flowers.'

'Yet he wasn't yer boy-friend?'

'No.'

'When d'you see him afore that?'

'After lunch the day before yesterday, in the hotel garden here.'

'What'd he come see yer for—then?'

'He wanted me to go for a run with him in his car, or dine with him that evening.'

'Yet he wasn't yer boy-friend?'

'No, he was not,' Avril snapped angrily.

'All right, all right. Had he bunched you afore?'

'What—sent me flowers?—yes.'

'How offen?'

'I don't know—several times. I sent them back.'

'Ever mealed wi' him?'

'No—well, yes—but at a party where other people were present.'

'How offen you bin places wi' him?'

'I've never been to a party with him. It only happens that he had been present at two parties when I chanced to be there as well. Just a coincidence, nothing more.'

'He drop in at the hotel—other times?'

'Yes.'

'How often?'

'Oh, I don't know—several times.'

'Where'd yer see him—here, or in the hotel parlour?'

'In the lounge, of course, or in the garden—never here.'

'See him every time he dropped in?'

'Only when I had to—to avoid a scene.'

'Had any letters from him?'

'Yes.'

'Let's see 'em.'

'I tore them up.'

'That so? What time d'you come to bed?'

'About eleven o'clock.'

'Where d'you feed s'evening?'

'The Ambassadors.'

'Who with?'

'Mr. Sheringham.'

'What d'you do after?'

'We sat in the garden for a little while, then I went to bed.'

'Did you lock your door?'

'Yes.'

'Where's the coat you wore s'evening?'

'In the clothes cupboard.'

'You hung it up?'

'Yes.'

'I guess I'll take a look at that cupboard.' He walked across the room and opened the door. It was one of those big closets which are a feature of American luxury hotel bedrooms; in fact, a small room. Avril's frocks and coats were hung in a long line upon a row of hangers, above, on a shelf, were her hats, on the floor about a dozen pairs of shoes . . . Avril was exceedingly proud of her small feet. At one end of the closet, her trunks and boxes were stacked in a pile. 'Show us the coat,' said Captain Rudd.

Avril pointed it out. He placed one hand on the hanger and looked round.

'Guess you couldn't have missed seein' a guy if he was hid in here, there ain't no place for him to hide.'

'Unless he was behind the trunks,' suggested Ronnie.

'Who are you, son?'

'My name's Sheringham.'

'That so! Then I figure you're the guy what dined this dame s'evening?'

'Yes.'

'What d'you do then?'

'Came back here, sat in the garden, and then went to bed.'

'D'you go to bed in them clothes?'

'Well, I mean I was just going to bed.'

'You take a mighty long time—I'll say.'

'Oh, I was talking to a friend of mine in his sitting-room along the passage, and I'd just left him to go to bed when I heard the shot.'

'Then why in heck don't yer say what yer mean. Where's yer room?'

'Next but one.' Ronnie jerked his head casually in the direction of his bedroom.

'What d'yer do when yer heard the shot?'

'I came along here to see what was the matter. I knocked and Miss Bamborough let me in.'

'Was she holding that gun?'

'Yes—I think so.'

'I don't want no thinking—were she or weren't she?'

'Yes, she was.'

Captain Rudd swung suddenly upon Avril. 'How long yer had that gun?'

'I've told you—I wrenched it from the second man's hand.'

'You stick to that yarn, eh?'

'Yes, it is the truth.'

'Yeah, so you say. You bin usin' chloroform?'

'No, but on that handkerchief. Donelli tried to render me unconscious.'

'That so? How many shots were fired?'

'Only one.'

'Where was he standing?'

'He was kneeling on the floor.'

'Thought you said he was a-top of you?'

'I threw him off.'

'Then yer hands were free?'

'Yes, at that moment.'

'An' he was kneelin' in front of yer by the bed.'

'Yes.'

'I figure there'd be about three or four feet between you an' him?'

'I suppose so.'

'Then that 'ud be the distance between you—when you pulled the gun?'

'I didn't have the gun,' Avril protested, 'not till afterwards— the other man shot him.'

'Is that so? An' where would he be standin'?'

'Over by the window.'

'You don't say—now, that's real queer. Angelo was kneeling in front of you—he'd have his back to the window, yet he were shot in the chest. You sure don't figure that you can put it across about this other guy, do you?'

'It's the truth, I tell you.' Avril was very nearly in tears. 'And how do I know which way Donelli was facing—I kicked him off my bed onto the floor. It was dark—I couldn't see— as he was shot in the chest he must have been facing the win- dow when he got to his knees.'

'Yeah—so you say—but yer hands were free?'

'Yes.'

'An' yer face—why didn't yer yell for help?'

'I did.'

'Why didn't no one come?'

'The shot was fired almost at the same second.'

'Where d'you buy that gun?'

'Oh, I tell you—it's not mine. I wrenched it from the other man.'

'Yeah—so you say. How long you bin in the States?'

'About three weeks.'

'An' Hollywood?'

'Just over a fortnight.'

'Then you know Donelli pretty well since you stepped off the train?'

'I met him the first day after I arrived.'

'An' he sent yer flowers, an' love-letters—an' took you places, an' he's been in yer bedroom in the middle of the night —yet yer say he's not your boy-friend.'

'He is not my boy-friend, he did not take me places, and if he was here in the middle of the night, it's through no fault of mine. He came in at the window when I was half asleep, or else was hiding in the clothes cupboard.'

'Yeah—so you say. Now, if he weren't your boy-friend, I'd be mighty interested to know who is?'

'I haven't got a boy-friend,' declared Avril angrily.

'She ain't got a boy-friend,' he repeated with a grin. 'Now ain't that queer. Did you ever hear of a movie star that hadn't got a boy-friend? You're sure like the gangster lady, that hadn't got no gun. Are you married?'

'No.'

'Have yer ever bin married?'

'No.'

'She ain't never been married, and she ain't got no boy-friend. Waal, I always did think you Britishers were slow—but tonight I'm learnin' a whole heap. Hand us over that gun. . . . Hoy! don't point the darn thing at me.' He took it gingerly by the barrel and turned it from side to side, taking care not to disturb the fingerprints on the butt.

'I'll say it's a neat affair,' he commented casually, 'outa date pattern though. Had one like it meself once—sold it off cheap, a few months back, fer twenty-five bucks. They cost about

100

eighty when they're new. I guess this has seen a bit of service, though. What did they soak you for it, sister?'

'It's not mine,' declared Avril again, with rising temper. 'And I should be glad if you would stop your absurd attempts to trap me into admissions which are not true. I've told you what happened and I'm absolutely done up after this terrible affair.'

'You don't say.'

'I do.' She turned to the manager. 'I should be glad if you would have my things moved into another room as quickly as possible. I shall never be able to sleep after this, but I would like to get to bed at once.'

'Wait a minute, wait a minute.' Captain Rudd stepped up to her. 'You sure are in a hurry to see the back of us boys, but I guess you've got the situation all wrong. Let's see yer hands.'

Avril held them out obediently, then before she could realise what he meant to do, the fat detective had snapped a pair of handcuffs on her wrists.

'You're mad!' she cried. 'You can't do this—I didn't do it—you're mad!'

'That so!' He seemed mildly amused at her panic-stricken face. 'Waàl, maybe, but I'm sane enough to know my job, an' it don't take no highbrow detectin' to figure who gave Angelo his. Get your coat, sister. We're beating it to Headquarters right away. I'm arresting you for the murder of Angelo Donelli.'

10

Avril Bamborough faces the Third Degree

Avril was taken at once to Police Headquarters. Captain Rudd had offered to remove her handcuffs if she wished to dress before leaving the hotel, but her refusal to dress herself with five men present had only given rise to some amusement on the part of the detectives. They thought it queer that a movie star

101

should possess any delicacy of feeling. Her request that she should be allowed to use her private bathroom had been absurdly refused. It seemed that Captain Rudd was responsible for his prisoner, and he feared that if she were left alone she might seize the opportunity to commit suicide and thus defeat the ends of justice. He had made up his mind beyond all question that she had shot Angelo Donelli, and nothing would satisfy him but her immediate removal.

Certain necessities that she asked for were crammed into her dressing-case, and the clothes that she wished to take hurriedly packed in one of her portmanteaux, then, just as she was, in her tattered nightdress and a dressing-gown, she was escorted downstairs to a waiting patrol wagon. Captain Rudd, his two henchmen, and the gum-chewing house-detective climbed in beside her, and they were whirled away to the station.

Ronnie had done everything that he could for her, and before she left the hotel, promised that he would get in touch with Schultzer first thing the following morning and cable John Bamborough. In addition he had undertaken to find out the best English lawyer resident in Hollywood, or if necessary in Los Angeles, and secure his services in her defence.

This was but cold comfort for Avril during the draughty ride to Police Headquarters, and still less reassuring when, after a wardress had taken her to a cell and allowed her to dress, she was led out again to a bare bleak room for further examination.

Captain Rudd was a great believer in, and a practised exponent of, the famous third degree methods of the American Police. Avril was placed in a hard chair before an empty deal table. He took his seat opposite to her and his two satellites sat upon his left and right. He then proceeded to ply her with endless questions. And however absurd and irrelevant to the matter in hand those questions appeared to be, Avril soon discovered that they inevitably led back to the old subjects of her exact degree of intimacy with the deceased Angelo or the ownership of the automatic.

Sometimes Rudd endeavoured to trap her into admissions by

a display of false goodwill. 'Come on, girlie,' he would urge her, 'why don' cher come clean. Let's get this thing over. I guess we'd all like to hit the hay.'

Sometimes he flatly contradicted her statements and called her every name under the sun.

When he tired his lieutenants took up the game. The theory of the third degree being, that if you plug away at a prisoner long enough, and wear down their resistance, eventually they will reach such a state of exhaustion or hysteria that they will confess to anything, provided they are left in peace. Owing to the fact that there are innumerable detectives always available for an important case, the prisoner, however strong his mentality, stands no chance of wearing down his questioners. They work in relays, often going out for meals or sleep while others take their place, and then return refreshed to the attack.

In a very large number of cases the theory works, particularly if the person questioned happens to be guilty. Even if they are not, they often make false confessions to escape further torment, as did the unfortunates who suffered the torture of the boot, the water, or the iron virgin in the Tower of London or the Bastille.

In the endless repetition of the same question there is a certain similarity to the Chinese method, whereby through the incessant dropping of water upon the prisoner's head, at the rate of one drop per minute, he is finally driven mad.

It would be unfair to hold the American police responsible for this brutality. Individually they are for the most part brave and capable men, and they cannot be blamed for using every means which the law allows to bring criminals to justice. It is, nevertheless, a terrible ordeal for the prisoner who undergoes it.

By three o'clock in the morning Avril was bordering on a breakdown. Her eyelids were drooping, her face haggard, her head splitting. She felt as though great wedges were being driven into the centre of her skull. The small room was thick with the smoke of cheap cigars and cigarettes.

Captain Rudd sat before her, one hand on his hip, an elbow on his knee. Again and again he went over the same ground, leading up to the same questions in a slightly different way. At last Avril could bear it no longer.

'It's no good,' she said. 'I've told you everything I know. I refuse to answer any more questions.'

Rudd took no notice, he just went on as though he had not heard, but she closed her eyes and would not answer.

He came round to her side of the table and sat upon it, one leg dangling from the edge.

'See here, girlie, that stuff won't get you nowhere—you jus' put us wise on how you gave Angelo his an' we'll call it a day.'

She sat there in silence, pale and weary, her mouth tightly shut, her eyelids drooped, veiling her tired eyes.

He gave her shoulder a gently shove.

Still she refused to answer, so he began to rock her slowly backwards and forwards.

At last she opened her eyes again and pushing back her chair, stood up. She felt that the time had come to make a stand if she were not to break down altogether. She must try to make Rudd cease his maddening questions for tonight at all events, so she gathered her remaining strength.

'Listen to me for one moment, please. I don't wish to interfere with your duty, and I have told you everything I can. I do not know much about American law—but I do not believe that the police are allowed to use force in an endeavour to extract false confessions from their prisoners. You have been using what I think is called the third degree upon me. Now I'm sure you don't want any sort of unpleasantness, and neither do I, but if you persist, I shall complain through my solicitor tomorrow to the British Consul in Los Angeles, and have him take the matter up with the Ambassador in Washington. I don't want to make capital out of the fact, but I am a very well-known actress in England and the papers both there and here will make a terrific fuss out of the story of my illtreatment. That cannot possibly do you any good, and I promise you that you will not get one word more out of me tonight. Now please take me to my cell.'

Captain Rudd regarded her thoughtfully for a moment. He

knew from the quiet, firm way in which she spoke that she meant every word of it. His experience of human nature was very wide and he realised that he was not dealing with any rubber-legged cutie on this occasion. He doubted if he would get any more out of her in any case. 'Better let up for the night,' he thought, there was just a chance, too, that there might be trouble with the big people in Washington, if he went too far. He gave in with a good grace.

'I guess you win, girlie,' he said with a grin. 'Though don't you figure that you've got me scared about those bums in Washington, nor the British Government, neither. They don't cut no ice. Take her away, boys, she's got her story set, she won't alter any now.'

Avril was led back to her cell. She was so exhausted that she hardly had the strength to undress, but when at last she had shed her clothes she was unutterably thankful to creep into the small hard bed. The wardress brought her some bromide, which eased the twitching of her nerves a little, but despite her utter weariness she could not get to sleep.

Over and over in her mind the incidents of that terrible evening succeeded each other in her tired brain. The struggle with Angelo—the brilliant flash of the pistol illuminating the whole room as the shot was fired—the nerve-racking reiteration of those questions by the police. One incident above all came to her again and again. The moment when she had been left holding the automatic and recognised the hand of Nelson Druce.

She wondered what strange impulse had caused her to suppress that information and deny all knowledge of the murderer. Of course there was just a possibility that it might not have been him. She had not seen his face, but the man was of the same height and the same build. Besides, he had a definite motive in killing Angelo; Mick Downey had been caught, he would go to the electric chair, but Angelo had got away, there was not a scrap of evidence against him. No more, in fact, than against herself or any other member of the crowd. Yet he had been there, and he was the chief of Hinckman's gunmen; Nelson might assume with reason that the Italian had a part in his father's assassination. It was a terrible thing, Avril thought, to take the law into one's own hands like that and kill a man. Yet if ever there were a case in which it was justified, surely it was in this. Nelson Druce must have known that it would be impossible to bring the murderer to justice and decided to avenge his father in the age-old way.

Bitterly Avril regretted her frantic action in seizing and clinging to the gun. Druce could not have meant to kill her, nor could he have foreseen that she would struggle with him. He probably did not even know that it was her room to which he had tracked Angelo. If only she had not flung herself upon him, he would have got away and with him would have gone that wretched pistol. There would not have been the least evidence against her, or against him, for that matter.

She wondered if he realised who the woman was with whom he had struggled in the dark—she was inclined to doubt it. Would he have stayed, she wondered, if he had. But it had all happened so quickly—he would not have had time to realise the terrible situation in which he was leaving her and if he had stayed he would certainly have been caught—that would have meant death for him.

What should she do tomorrow—stick to her story or tell about that hand? The more she thought of it, the more certain she felt that she could not have been mistaken. Those long, sensitive fingers could belong to no one but Nelson Druce. Could they bring it home to him if she added that information to her story? He was a clever, intelligent man, surely he would not set out to commit a murder without first arranging an alibi. There was the pistol, of course, that might be traced to him, also there might still be finger-prints upon it, but she doubted that. When she had managed to get possession of the weapon she had reversed it and held it by the butt, her own markings would have destroyed those of anybody who had held it before.

Perhaps when he heard that she had been arrested and accused of this crime, he would come forward and give himself up, or use his freedom to disappear, leaving a confession behind in order to clear her.

She was surprised to find that she felt no revulsion against

Nelson Druce because he had committed murder. To kill that loathsome Italian assassin might be murder in the eyes of the law, but to Avril, having been present the night before, at that brutal killing of an elderly, kindly man, who had no means of defence—it was an execution.

Nelson Druce's lean, pleasant face came again to her mind, his smooth dark hair, and nice grey eyes that had the little wrinkles round them when he smiled. He was, she thought, by far the nicest person she had met in Hollywood. His crisp, direct frankness appealed to her tremendously. It would be a terrible thing if he were arrested and executed for the murder. Suddenly she made up her mind, she would not tell the police about her recognition of his hand unless it became vitally necessary—fresh evidence might be forthcoming in the morning—perhaps that strange figure which had appeared and disappeared so silently from the window might come forward and give evidence; marks might be found of the struggle on the balcony—in any case, for the present she would keep her knowledge to herself.

At last she fell into a restless, fitful sleep; she awoke once to find herself kicking and screaming, with the perspiration pouring from her. She had suffered the agony of Angelo's attack repeated in a dream. She shuddered as she lay in the narrow bed, it seemed that only a moment before she had felt those hot lips pressed to her throat and shoulders.

The wardress was a kindly soul and brought her aspirin in hot milk, after that she dozed off again, and slept until she was awakened in the morning.

She was warned that she would have to appear before a court and made her toilet as best she could. Then she sat waiting for what seemed to be an endless time, but at last Captain Rudd came for her and she was led through a long echoing corridor to the Court-room, which was at the other end of the same building.

Ronnie was there and smiled cheerfully as she came in, beside him was a round-faced elderly man whom he introduced as Mr. Smithson, an English lawyer practising in Los Angeles.

Captain Rudd with his squad was very much in evidence,

also the house detective and the manager from the hotel. The magistrate was an Irish-American with bright, sharp, blue eyes. He studied her curiously as she was led to the dock.

Only formal evidence was given, in which the events of the night before were described. Ronnie, the house detective, the hotel manager, and Captain Rudd, all were called. Mr. Smithson entered a plea of Not Guilty on her behalf, reserving the defence. The magistrate committed her for trial.

Avril expected to be led back to her cell at once, and she was surprised when Smithson applied for bail. She had not known that bail was granted even on a charge of murder, in the United States.

There seemed no difficulty about the matter, either. The magistrate asked the names of the sureties, and Avril, to her amazement, heard Hinckman's name mentioned. She could only assume that Ronnie had used his influence with the great man, having been unable to secure Schultzer. She had noticed that the German was nowhere to be seen.

After a short consultation between Smithson, Ronnie, and the magistrate, bail was settled at ten thousand dollars, and Avril, to her joy, found that she was free to leave the Court.

Ronnie led her out into the vestibule, Smithson joined them a few moments later. He smiled at her.

'This is a rotten business for you, Miss Bamborough. I expect they put you through it last night?'

She sighed. 'They did. It was simply ghastly—you can't imagine how glad I am to be out of their clutches, even it it's only for the time being.'

'You won't have to appear again for a long while yet,' he assured her. 'We shall get bail renewed from time to time, while we gradually build up the case for the defence.'

'I suppose nothing has been heard of the man who did it?' she enquired.

The lawyer seemed surprised. He looked round carefully, and said in a low voice, 'Miss Bamborough, I know that's the story that you put up, and, of course, if you wish to stick to it, well, it's my business to accept your instructions. But before you decide anything definite I'd like you to bear in mind that this man Donelli was a notorious character and we should have an absolutely clear case if you plead self-defence. There's plenty of evidence that you were attacked, and there's not a doubt that we'd get clear away with it.'

'But I didn't shoot him,' Avril protested.

'Well, don't let's talk about it now, this is hardly the place, and I imagine you're pretty done up. I think you'd better rest for today, then we can go into the whole thing thoroughly to-morrow morning. You will have had time to think things over then, but bear in mind what I've said. If you'll excuse me now —I've got another case.'

'Oh, certainly.' Avril was a little bewildered. 'Tomorrow morning, then, at the the Hotel.'

'Yes, round about ten o'clock.' With a quick smile he hurried away.

'Well, that's that,' said Ronnie cheerfully.

'My dear.' Avril smiled a little wanly. 'It's sweet of you to have got hold of Mr. Smithson, and quite marvellous of you to have arranged about my being let out on bail—but I still have a charge of murder hanging over me.'

As they walked down the steps of the Court-house they were surrounded by a throng of reporters and cameramen. Ronnie laughed as he thrust a way through them and said quickly in her ear: 'I shouldn't worry too much about that—this is America, not England—things are different here, everything will be quite all right, it's marvellous what chaps like Hinckman can do, who've got a pull.'

'Hinckman?' she said, and at that moment she caught sight of the Trans-Continental Electric magnate seated in the back of his big car a few yards away.

'Yes, didn't you hear? It was he who went bail for you.' Ronnie flung open the door of Hinckman's car.

The big man leaned forward with a smile as Avril climbed in. She was thoroughly bewildered.

'Mornin', Miss Bamborough.' He moved so that she could sit down beside him. 'I guess it's a pretty tough experience you've been through, but that rotten little wop who was on my staff sure asked for it—and he got it.'

'It was very kind of you, Mr. Hinckman, to have gone bail for me,' she said slowly, as Ronnie settled himself in one of the smaller seats.

He laughed. 'Why, don't say another thing, Miss Bamborough, I'm real glad to have bin of assistance. I sure couldn't go leavin' one of my Stars in the lock-up.'

'I'm afraid I don't quite understand, Mr. Hinckman. I think you know I'm with Ubiquitous. And, Ronnie—what happened to Mr. Schultzer?'

'Hugo,' Hinckman grinned. 'Now see here, Miss Bamborough, Ring wants you to play Valerie Petrovna in "The Forbidden Territory", an' I certainly got to humour him, I feel that way myself, too, have done ever since I saw you, else you'd be making a trip back to Europe, like I said—even if you hadn't got the rats and shot poor Angelo.'

'I'm very, very grateful, Mr. Hinckman, for what you've done, but my contract is with Mr. Schultzer to play under Eberhard Lusatch.'

'Contract?' he laughed. 'You're crazy. You haven't got a contract unless you like to fight me in the courts. Hugo sold Ubiquitous to me this morning for a packet of bird-seed. I guess he was a wise man all the same. He knew Hollywood wouldn't be healthy for him if he hadn't.'

11

The Hand that held the Gun

Directly they arrived at the Hotel, Avril had to face another battery of cameras and a small army of reporters, all fighting to secure copy. She refused to be interviewed, and Ronnie saved her from their importunity by saying that he would give them the story instead. Her belongings had been moved to another room, and she went straight to bed. This time she slept soundly and did not wake until four o'clock in the afternoon.

Having been quite unable to eat breakfast provided at Police Headquarters that morning, and having slept through lunch, she awoke ravenously hungry, so she ordered a large plate of her favourite sandwiches to be sent up to her room, with her tea.

As her sharp white teeth bit into the appetising little squares of bread and smoked tongue, she began to think over her wretched situation. However cheerful the casual Ronnie and the all-powerful Hinckman might be, a charge of murder was no light matter. By the next morning she had to make up her mind what her line of defence was to be. She could accuse Nelson Druce, but it might be very difficult to prove that he had committed the murder. On the other hand, she could accept the line of least resistance which the lawyer offered— make a false confession about having shot Angelo herself and plead self-defence. If she accused Druce and they failed to get evidence against him, her own position might become a very serious one. Besides, she shrank from the thought of being instrumental in bringing about his death, but then it seemed that only by convicting him could she clear herself. The only alternative was to take the murder on her own shoulders, which meant that for the rest of her life she would be known as 'The woman who shot that chap in Hollywood—don't you remember?' and Avril did not relish that at all. In addition it might not be quite so easy to get a clear acquittal on a plea of self-defence as Mr. Smithson seemed to think.

The more Avril thought it over, the more convinced she became that she must see Nelson Druce at the earliest possible moment; she rang down for the car which she had hired during her stay in Hollywood, and began to dress.

Her five hours' sleep had restored her to something like her normal self, although there were still dark lines under her big eyes, but by the time she went downstairs she was looking very charming, and the violet shadows added, if anything, an extra interest to her lovely face.

As the car bore her along the wide roads towards the Beverley Hills reservation, Avril was thinking, not of Nelson Druce, but of Hinckman. She had known, ever since she had over-heard Ronnie's conversation with Cinch on her first day in Hollywood, that strange things were taking place behind the scenes. During the last week she had seen quite enough to realise that all was not well with Ubiquitous. Then three after-noons before, when Schultzer had taken her to Barton Druce, she had suddenly realised the full import of Ronnie's casual statements about this Combine. Barton Druce had been killed before her new contract with him had been signed, and now Schultzer had gone down, powerless against their onslaught.

She realised that had it not been for Hinckman, she would most probably still be in prison. It is not easy to find ten thousand dollars' bail. Of course, she knew that he was serving his own interests; he evidently felt that nobody else would fill this part in 'The Forbidden Territory' as well as herself—and it seemed that Ring, his principal director, wanted her for it too. Avril wondered where she stood legally with regard to her contract, she must cable to her agent in London and find out.

If Trans-Continental Electric had taken over Ubiquitous doubtless they had taken over the Ubiquitous contracts as well. In any case she did not doubt that her agent would advise her to accept a T.C.E. contract. If she had never met Hinckman, she would have been only too pleased to do so a few months ago—but knowing what she did, she was determined not to do so if she could legally withdraw. She wished desperately that she were free to take the train back to New York, then Hey ho! for England and dear old Uncle John.

Yet even if she was not bound legally to Hinckman by her contract, there was this terrible affair of Angelo Donelli. It seemed a ghastly tangle. She could only hope that Nelson Druce would be able to see some way out for her and also for him-self.

To Avril's intense annoyance when she arrived she was greeted by the vacuous Vitelma.

'Now if this isn't just fine, Miss Bamborough. To have you calling on us like an old friend. I'll say it's a terrible time you've been through.'

'Thank you,' said Avril. 'It has been quite terrible, but I'm

112

feeling a little better now, and I particularly wanted to see Mr. Druce.'

'What, Nelson? I guess he's around somewhere. I'll go get him.'

'Thank you so much.' Avril sank into a chair.

Tall, fair Vitelma left the room, and a few moments later returned with Nelson. He seemed calm and collected, his hand was dry and firm as he took Avril's, she looked down quickly at it—yes, that was the hand that had held the gun.

'Sorry to hear about the bad time you've had, Miss Bamborough,' he said. 'I understand Hinckman's bailed you. I thought he would, or, rather, Schultzer.'

'Why?' asked Avril sharply.

'Well, you're one of his people now he's got Ubiquitous. I figure I should have done the same, if we'd bought them up.'

'Why didn't you take them over? I understood that Schultzer had arranged something with your father the day we came up here, at least about my contract in any case.'

'That's so, and as a matter of fact I offered to sign it yesterday—only unfortunately Hugo had changed his mind. Hinckman had been getting at his co-directors, and he no longer had a free hand, so the deal fell through.'

Avril was a little mollified. She had felt that Nelson at least might have carried out his father's wishes regarding her contract before Hinckman took over Ubiquitous. She was glad to find that he had not intentionally let her down. That was a small matter, however, compared to the business she had actually come to see him upon, but she could not mention it with Vitelma present.

The fair girl lay back on a low arm-chair, her slender legs crossed, showing a long expanse of silk stocking; she showed no intention of leaving them together. On the contrary, she said at once:

'I'm just dying to hear about your thrilling experience, Miss Bamborough. Was there three men in your room, or four? People do say such things, you just can't tell what to believe. I'd be tickled to death to hear the real story.'

'I'd rather not discuss it at present, if you don't mind,' said

Avril quietly. 'It's so very recent, and it was all most terribly unpleasant.'

'Oh, well, if that's the way you feel.' Vitelma's mouth went sulky. 'But I guess you'll get all the publicity you want, anyhow. It's not every star's luck to have a shootin' in her room.'

'I'm afraid it's not the sort of publicity that I care about,' Avril replied, a little sharply, 'and to be quite truthful I came here because I was particularly anxious to discuss a private matter with Mr. Druce. Would you think me terribly rude if I asked for a few moments with him alone?'

Vitelma became openly hostile. 'I'd be glad if you'd remember, Miss Bamborough, that Nelson Druce is my fiancé, an' I just can't figure that he has any sort of business that's too private for me to hear.'

'Mr. Druce is the best judge of that,' said Avril coldly.

Nelson Druce gave her a quick look. He said nothing for a moment, then he turned to Vitelma.

'Now, Honey, there's no call to be rude to Miss Bamborough. Maybe she wants my advice as to how she's situated with Hinckman—owing to the Ubiquitous take-over.'

'Well, an' if she does—what then? Ain't I a movie star myself? I'll say there isn't much about motion picture contracts that this child doesn't know.'

'I'm sorry to seem rude,' said Avril, 'and I'm sure that your advice upon my contract would be most valuable, but it is quite another matter that I wish to discuss with Mr. Druce.'

'Is that so? Well, I'd be mighty interested to hear what this so private business is, that you want to talk over with my fiancé. It wouldn't be garden flowers now by any chance, would it?'

Both Nelson and Avril knew exactly to what she referred, but Nelson tried to placate her.

'See here, Vitelma,' he said persuasively, ' 'tisn't everybody who cares about discussing business with a third person present. Be a sport now an' leave us to it.'

'Sez you,' Vitelma burst out. Whenever she was excited her accent became more harsh, and her Americanisms more blatant, yet she looked extraordinarily attractive as she bent

114

forward accusingly towards her fiancé. 'Don't try that stuff
on me, little sweetie bunch. Don't I know you're soft on her.
Didn't you go all gooey when that wop she killed bunched her
in her the box the other night. She figures she's a swell dame
with her English hoo-haw—an' you're just the fool to fall for
it. Well, there's nothin' doin'. See!'

'Oh, Honey—I guess you got me all wrong.' Nelson Druce
shook his head impatiently. 'An' you certainly do a great injustice to Miss Bamborough. People don't go bats about each
other who've only met a couple of times. For the Lord's sake
have a heart.'

Avril felt exceedingly uncomfortable and thought it time to
protest. 'Miss Loveday,' she said seriously, 'I assure you that
your suspicions are quite unfounded. I have been through a
very great deal during the last twenty-four hours, and the very
last thing which I want is another scene. I would not ask to see
Mr. Druce alone, if I were not quite certain that it would be
his own wish as well as mine, and please believe me, it is very
important that I should.'

Nelson Druce looked sharply at her, then with a smile he
took Vitelma's hand gently pulled her to her feet. 'Come
now, Honey—you certainly couldn't pay me a finer compliment than suggesting that Miss Bamborough's interested in me
personally—but you're all wrong. It's just a little business talk
she wants, that's all.'

Vitelma reluctantly allowed herself to be led out of the
room. As Nelson Druce closed the door behind her, he turned
suddenly and leant upon it. His expression had completely
changed. He had become tense, expectant, but he was still quite
calm.

'Now—let's have it.' His brown eyes looked steadily into
Avril's.

Avril did not beat about the bush. 'It was you who shot
Angelo Donelli,' she said quietly.

'Is that so!' His glance never wavered. 'And what makes you
suppose that?'

'I recognised your hand when we were struggling for the
pistol, I saw it distinctly in the light on the balcony.'

'Well, that's not much to go on. I've never known a case of a man being identified by his hand alone before.'

'No.' Avril's voice was even. 'Most men's hands are not worth looking at twice; unfortunately for you as it happens—yours are—but I expect you know that.'

He glanced swiftly down at his right hand, then he gave a sudden laugh. 'They are nice—that's true—but I don't figure having nice hands would be enough to bring a man to the chair.'

'No, perhaps not,' Avril admitted. 'But there are other things.'

'Is that so? And what are they?'

'You believe that Donnelli shot your father.'

'I know he did.' Nelson's eyes went hard.

'How?'

'Does that matter?'

Avril shook her head slowly. 'No, but aren't you rather giving yourself away?—if you knew that for certain, surely it makes the motive even stronger. People will say that you killed Donelli in revenge.'

'What folks say is one thing, what they can prove is another.'

'There is the pistol.'

'Well, what about it?'

'There may be finger-prints.'

'There won't be.'

Avril wondered how he could be so certain about that. 'They may trace the ownership of the pistol,' she suggested.

'They may,' he admitted, but he did not seem at all concerned.

'And then your movements last night. What about those?'

'I can account for every moment of my time.'

'Mr. Druce,' she said slowly, 'if what you say is true it does seem that the police would have the greatest difficulty in bringing this home to you, but I notice one thing, you do not actually deny having done it.'

'Would it set your mind at rest if I did?'

'No, it would not. Since I have see your hand again I am

116

quite certain that it was you with whom I struggled for that pistol.'

'If that's so, why didn't you tell the police?'

'How do you know that I haven't?'

'They would have pulled me out of bed to get a statement, last night, if you had.'

'Yes, I suppose so, anyway you're quite right. I have said nothing about my suspicions for the moment.'

'For the moment?'

'Yes. Now just for the sake of argument let us suppose for the time being that you did do it.'

'Well, what then?'

'Have you considered the terrible position in which the man who did it left me?'

'I have. I've been thinking quite a lot about you today, Miss Bamborough.'

'Not a very chivalrous attitude, is it? To commit murder and fasten it on a woman.'

'Now, wait a minute—that's not quite true. From the report I've heard, you were found with the gun—you say that you struggled with me—the man who did it, and wrenched that gun away from him; if you hadn't, no gun would have been found, and you would never have been accused. It's a bit strong to say that fellow deliberately fixed the killing on you.'

'I know. At the time I was afraid that you—I mean he, was going to shoot me, too. I don't say that he deliberately fixed it on me, but through what took place the police have come to believe that I did it.'

'Sure, you're right there, but let's see what's happened so far. If the fellow had stayed, he'd certainly have been caught —and that would have meant the chair for him, he wasn't to know that by making his getaway the police would fix it on you.'

'No—but he does know now.'

'That's true. Say he heard first thing this morning that they'd picked on you, I figure he'd know enough about American law to guess they'd give you bail. If he'd got any sort of decency.

117

I reckon he'd fix that himself, providing he was in a position to do so.'

'Surely you're not suggesting that it was Hinckman or Ronnie Sheringham.'

'Not on your life. But just supposing it was me. Well, I made arrangements to bail you in any case—if Hinckman hadn't fixed it, I'd have done so myself.'

'But you didn't—Hinckman did.'

'Sure!—but my attorney was in court just the same, with instructions to act if Schultzer failed to do what was necessary. I didn't know that Ubiquitous had finally gone over to Hinckman then. It was the more natural that your own Corporation should bail you—so we let them have first option. The only thing that matters is—you're out.'

'That was very nice of you, but surely it is an admission that it was you last night.'

He smiled. 'Not in the least, Miss Bamborough. It's when you're in a jam you find out who's your real friends. I just did myself the honour of considering myself one of yours—that's all.'

Avril studied the face of this calm young man. It gave her a little thrill of pleasure to know that he had taken steps to protect her, although she was convinced that he had done the shooting. What, she wondered, did he mean to do now? She took out a cigarette and he came forward to light it for her. She looked him straight in the eyes.

'I am only out on bail,' she said slowly, 'and tomorrow I have to prepare my defence. Is this man coming forward to take responsibility for his crime, or am I to be left to defend myself as best I can?'

'I've been wondering quite a piece about that.' He stood looking down upon her—a lean, agile figure. 'It's this way—supposing again that I am the man who gave Angelo the works. If I go and give myself up it involves a whole lot of people beside myself. I think you know more or less what's going on in Hollywood just now—it's the most terrible and sinister thing that's happened in America for years, a deliberate attempt to suborn a gigantic industry in the interests of a

118

small group of unscrupulous men. If they win, it means ruin to thousands, and they're out to win. Nothing's too rotten or too crooked for them. They don't even stop at murdering an innocent man, as you know. Now circumstances have forced me into the position of leader of the opposition, an' it's war to the knife between Hinckman and me. If I surrender to the police maybe I'll get bail, but maybe I won't—Hinckman 'ud pull every wire he knows to keep me behind the bars once I'm put. Anyhow, I'd not be allowed to leave the country, and I figure I'll want to before we're through. This war's got to be fought out in Europe as well as here. . . . So you'll see it's not quite the simple proposition it looks at first sight. I reckon you'll believe me when I say it never entered my head that I'd get you fixed in a jam like this, an' I guess it's up to me to let you out. But if I chuck in my hand it's a hundred to one on the Combine sweeping the board. That means thousands of folks'll lose their jobs an' no place to get others. It means starvation, bankruptcy, suicide for these poor people I'm trying to protect. If that darn Combine once gets going, the misery that it'll cause is just too awful to think about. So there you've got it, Miss Bamborough. If I was the man who did this job I'd be in a pretty difficult situation, wouldn't I?'

'Yes, but if you were, surely you should have thought of all this yesterday.' said Avril quietly.

'Sure—you're dead right. I ought to have realised that I wasn't a free man, however bad I felt, till I'd smashed Hinckman and the Combine. I ought to have waited and traced up Donelli's record back to Chicago—maybe I'd have been able to fix him up for some job in the past, since I couldn't get him legally for the killing here. I can hardly expect you to understand how I felt, but I was just terrible fond of my old man, he was more a big brother than a father to me, an' all day yesterday I was just clean cold with rage. I did my business like a machine, not like a man at all. Then at night I went out to get Angelo. I didn't mean to kill him to start with—that's the truth—I meant to force a confession at the point of my gun. I trailed him to your room, though I hadn't an idea it was your room at the time. I figured he was out on some more dirty work so I thought I'd get him red-handed. After your light went out I waited a bit in the garden, then I got scared he'd quit through the passage an' the front entrance, so I came up to see. I heard what he said about the chloroform and guessed what he was at. Honest, I believe it was that made me go clean crazy and plump for outing him then and there—a swine who'd do that sort of thing on a woman added to all the rest. I didn't dare shoot then 'cause you were all mixed up, an' I couldn't interfere 'cause he'd sure have had a gun—he'd have shot me if I'd tried. I'm no match for a professional gunman, so I had to wait my chance—then when you kicked him off the bed. . . . Well, I guess you know what happened then.'

'You do admit, then, that you did it?'

Nelson Druce smiled grimly. 'I saw Mick Downey in prison yesterday, I offered to settle a sum on his wife and kid if he'd talk, so I could get Angelo legally—but he wouldn't split to the police. He told me, though . . . Donelli fired the other two shots that killed my old man. There's not one scrap of evidence, there aren't even finger-prints, because I greased the gun. But I did it—the brute wasn't fit to live and so I killed him; call it murder if you like, but I say it's justice—and now you know.'

The door was suddenly flung open. Vitelma stood there, pale and trembling. She had overheard every word.

12

'Shanghaied'

Avril and Nelson Druce stared at the girl. Neither of them had foreseen the possibility of her learning the truth about the murder in such a manner. Both were wondering what result this dangerous knowledge might have in the hands of such a woman as Vitelma.

She flung herself on Nelson, gripping the lapels of his coat. 'It isn't true,' she whimpered. 'Don't be a fool Nelson, say it's not true; she did the killing, not you.'

'I'm afraid it is true,' he said quietly. 'Miss Bamborough was not in the least to blame. It was just her bad luck that Donelli chose her room to hide in, though as far as it goes it's just as well perhaps that I turned up when I did.'

Avril nodded. 'Yes, at least I have to thank you for that.'

'But, you a murderer,' gulped Vitelma. 'Oh, Nelson, what'll happen to us if the cops find out?'

'They won't,' he said grimly, 'not till I've smashed the Combine, anyhow.'

'Really,' said Avril, raising her eyebrows, 'I don't remember having said that I am prepared to shield you, or take the responsibility upon myself by pleading self-defence.'

'You don't have to.'

'Indeed. Then what do you propose to do?'

Nelson ignored her question and turned to Vitelma, who had burst into tears. 'See here, Honey—it's no good carrying on like that. Let's face it, I guess you brought this trouble on yourself by listening at that door. I did it, there's no getting away from that, and you can call it murder if you like—I don't, but that's another matter.'

'To kill a guy's murder, ain't it?' Vitelma sniffed.

'Sure—that's so in the eyes of the law, and I'll go to the chair if they get me—but if you feel that way about it, we'd better call it a day. I'll release you from your promise to marry me right now.'

Vitelma ceased crying as suddenly as she had begun. A vision of having to resume work arose before her. How would the producers view her return to the screen? She knew that it is not always easy to come back. She thanked her gods that in the good days she had had the sense to buy that property in Detroit, and after all in New York there would be plenty of rich husbands for the asking. Vitelma Loveday had no fear of being left an old maid. Still, Nelson Druce was a multi-millionaire now his father was dead, and she was fond of him

121

in a way. It would not be easy to find another fiancé with all his advantages.

'I guess I'll have to think about that,' she hedged cautiously.

He laughed a little bitterly. 'Okay, Honey, just as you say, but I should have thought a girl would know if she wanted to stick by her man or not. Anyhow, it's me and Miss Bamborough that have got to do the thinking at the moment. . . . You'd best do yours elsewhere.'

'Oh, Nelson, that's real unkind.'

'No, it's not, but you can't help us any, and this jam's quite bad enough. You'd best go home an' we can talk things over in the morning.' His manner was abrupt, but he now seemed worried and upset.

Vitelma allowed herself to be persuaded, but not without difficulty. Eventually he got her in her car, and returned to Avril, who had been left sitting in the gathering dusk.

'I'm awfully sorry,' she said, when he returned, 'that Miss Loveday should have learnt about this through my coming here, it would have been so much better if you had told her in your own time.'

'It wasn't your fault, but it's a darn nuisance that she's found out all the same. I shouldn't have told her, not unless it became necessary. There are some women that you can tell everything to and some you can't; Vitelma's a darling when she likes, all right, but she just isn't capable of keeping a thing like this to herself—she'll be spilling the whole outfit to her maid in half an hour—you see.' With a rueful smile he flung himself down in a chair.

'In that case, the police will learn about the part you played sooner or later, whether I decide to speak or not.'

He shook his head quickly. 'Nope—what Vitelma says she overheard isn't evidence, and she'd deny it if they put it to her —I can rely on her for that. What you may say is another thing altogether. I figure it would be best if you stay here to dinner, Miss Bamborough, then we can talk this thing out.'

Avril glanced at her wrist watch. 'Yes, it is getting late, isn't it—all right, I will if you wish.'

'Thanks.' He left her to give instructions and returned a few minutes later with a cocktail-shaker and ice.

'I don't know how you feel, but I guess a little drink wouldn't do us any harm,' he said as he began to shoot the contents of various bottles into the shaker.

Avril sat silent, watching his quick, graceful movements, and when he had finished, accepted the glass of golden creaming liquid with its layer of froth that he offered her.

It was a good cocktail. Avril drank little but she was something of a judge. The reaction of the night before was setting in again, and the stimulant revived her. She had another, almost immediately afterwards dinner was announced. Nelson bent towards her quickly.

'We'll cut out business over dinner if you don't mind. We'd sure be interrupted all the time. Let's try and forget our worries for the moment.' Then he did a quaint, old-fashioned thing that surprised Avril, he offered her his arm to take her in.

She responded immediately, wondering if he always did this with Vitelma—somehow she could hardly picture it.

He settled her himself in a place on his right at the big table. It was a pleasant room, if a trifle heavy for a Californian home. Barton Druce had been something of an art connoisseur in addition to being an orchid fancier.

The food was simple, but beautifully cooked. The service perfect. A grave-faced English butler superintended the two coloured men, in neat white jackets, who waited at table. Avril found herself wondering if the late Mr. Druce had ever employed his butler in his productions. The man was a perfect type.

Nelson Druce seemed to pull himself together in an amazing manner once they were at table. He chatted lightly and pleasantly upon a hundred different subjects. His comments were shrewd and amusing. At first Avril found it difficult to throw off the weight of the terrible thing that they were facing, despite her ability as an actress, but gradually she found herself responding. She wondered if the young man's apparent lightheartedness was due to an iron control whereby he had put away from himself completely for the time being all

123

thought of the night before and the future—or if he were thinking about it all the time, but playing a part.

When coffee had been served they were left alone and he began to talk about his trip to Europe. He calmly announced that it would have to be put off for a week or so in order that he might go into his father's affairs, but he thought that he would be able to leave Hollywood in about a fortnight's time.

'You're business over there must be very urgent,' said Avril.

'It is,' he agreed. 'I've been working on a new invention, and it is essential that I go see people in London and Berlin.'

'The "Z" projector.' she suggested.

He frowned for a moment, then smiled quickly. 'That's so, but where did you learn about it?—I'd be interested to know.'

'Vitelma Loveday told me.'

'That so! Yes, I might have guessed. Well, since you know, there is no harm in talking about it. I figure it will revolutionise the motion picture business.'

'Yes—so I understand.'

'What's more, it'll about break the Combine—if nothing else does. That's why I'm going to Europe, it's too big a risk to go making a film with it here in Hollywood. I figure to collect a bunch of artists and technicians on the other side. I'll make the picture in six weeks—an' then we'll show the world.'

She smiled. 'Aren't you taking rather a risk in telling me all this?'

'Not a bit.' He shook his head. 'I've a feeling that you're the sort of person a fellow can tell things to without fear of their going any further.'

Avril felt a little stab of conscience. 'Yes,' she said slowly. 'In the ordinary way that's quite true, but I'm afraid I have been careless enough to mention your invention to someone already.'

'Oh—who?' he asked sharply.

'Ronnie Sheringham. It was at dinner last night. I only spoke about it in quite a casual way when we were discussing motion pictures in general, and of course I had no idea at the time that there was any special secrecy about it. Vitelma Loveday

124

did not seem to attach any more importance to it than to lots of other experiments that are going on.'

'She wouldn't—but it is, and it's unfortunate that you should have mentioned it to Sheringham, he's a nice fellow, but he's too much in with Hinckman for my liking. Still, what's done's done, and it wasn't your fault, Miss Bamborough.'

'No, I should never have said a word if I'd known. I wish Vitelma Loveday had told me at the time, although I don't want you to think that I am trying to put the blame on her. Perhaps she did say something, but I didn't understand her.'

'I'll say she didn't. I know Vitelma too well to believe that story; she simply cannot hold her tongue. I guess you think it's pretty rotten of me, Miss Bamborough, to talk about her like I do—and I wouldn't to anyone else—but as things are it's no good you an' I trying to kid each other, this thing's too important, and we've got to know where we stand. Vitelma's just the loveliest thing in the world and she's got the sweetest nature when you get to know her—I'm crazy about her, but her having tumbled in on this isn't going to make it any easier—that's a fact.'

Avril had a very different opinion of Miss Loveday's nature from what little she had seen of her, but she contented herself with saying:

'I perfectly understand—and I do hope that she sticks to you, I feel sure she will, when she thinks things over.'

He did not reply, and they fell silent. Avril felt that the time had come when something should be settled, so she said quietly, 'I think you had better tell me now, what you intend to do.'

'We'll see,' he replied ambiguously. 'It's almighty hot tonight and there's people about. How about taking the car and running down to Golden Point, my speedboat's lying there. Out on the water with no one around we can talk as much as we like. What d'you say?'

'If you wish,' Avril assented. 'It should be lovely on the water. It's a pity that we shall have to spoil it by discussing this terrible business, but I'm afraid we must. Anyway we shall be safe there from being overheard.'

He nodded. 'Sure—an' Vitelma may be back, it's as well that we should be out of the way in case she takes a fancy to beat us up. I'll get your coat.'

A little later Avril was beside him in his two-seater, speeding down the gradients towards the coast. Her own car had been sent back to the hotel.

At Golden Point the speedboat was in readiness, a smart sailor with the Druce monogram on his cap ran the craft out of the boat-house and alongside the wharf. Nelson Druce took the tiller himself and dismissed the man.

He made Avril comfortable upon the cushions in the stern near him. The engine coughed and then settled into a steady purr. In a great sweep the boat headed for the open water of the bay.

The night was fine and cloudless, a myriad stars twinkled overhead and the lights of Los Angeles made it look like a fairy city spreading for miles along the dark, violet coast.

There were few other craft about, but Nelson Druce did not shut off the engine. When they were some way out, he turned the speedboat down the coast. They skimmed the water at a rapid pace, a foaming cascade of dancing spray tumbling in their wake, the engine throbbing steadily. For the time being Avril was content to sit watching the lights play upon the waters, and the phosphorus brighten every little wavelet as its crest broke and disappeared in the wide waste of the Pacific.

A dark hull loomed up out of the blackness in front of them. It was a ship anchored in the roadstead, a small single-funnelled steamer lying low in the water; about its masts clung innumerable derricks. Nelson circled it once and then shut off his engine.

'A tramp,' said Avril quietly.

'That's so—the good ship *Plymouth Hoe*—homeward bound for Cardiff via Singapore and Colombo. I know her Captain, he's a friend of mine.'

'Really—how queer!'

'Well, he has been since this morning.' Nelson was busy throwing out his bumpers. A figure had appeared on deck, a ladder of rope and wood was cast over the rail. Nelson re-

sumed his place by the engine and brought the speedboat smartly alongside. He made her fast both at the bow and
the stern, with quick, practiced fingers.

'What are you doing?' Avril asked uneasily.

He drew her to her feet and gripped the ladder with the
other hand. 'Little visit to my friend the Captain. Up you go,'
he said firmly.

'But I don't want to,' Avril protested, drawing back.

'Do you walk, or do I carry you?' said Nelson Druce.

Avril was thoroughly alarmed. Had he suddenly gone mad?
she wondered. Perhaps this business had unhinged his mind.

He stood there, tall, and for the moment menacing, beside
her in the darkness. She felt that he could easily overpower
her, and if there was a struggle they might both fall into the
water. Avril could swim, but the bay was supposed to be alive
with sharks. There were men on the ship, surely they would
protect her if he had lost his reason? It seemed best to obey.

The ladder was difficult to climb, it swayed and gave under
her, but the distance was short.

' 'Ang on, Missy,' came a cheerful voice from above, 'we'll
soon 'ave you aboard.'

A red-faced man gripped her by the arms and drew her in
over the side. She landed safely on the deck, panting a little.

Nelson Druce jumped lightly down beside her. 'Evening
Captain,' he cried cheerfully. 'I guess you're waiting to up-
anchor, but I'd just like to have a look around.'

'Evening, sir.' The sailor touched his cap politely. Despite
the warmness of the night he wore a thick woollen muffler
round his neck, the ends tucked into his pea-jacket. 'If you'll
come this way, sir—mind the 'awser.'

Nelson took Avril by the arm and led her after the Captain.
He seemed quite normal again now; she did not know what to
make of this strange visit to his friend the Captain of the
tramp.

They climbed a steep ladder and the Captain led them to a
deck-house on the poop. He flung open the door and switched
on the light. 'There we are,' he said. 'Me own cabin.'

127

Avril looked inside. It was spotlessly clean and much larger than the average cabin on a liner.

'Them's the things you sent aboard this afternoon,' went on the Captain, indicating a great stack of parcels. Avril noticed the handle of a dressing-case protruding from the brown-paper cover of one, and on another the label of a well-known Hollywood book-store. A little apart from the rest reposed one of those long decorative boxes in which florists deliver flowers.

The Captain turned to Avril with a grin. 'You can 'ave yer meals sent up 'ere, Missy, an' you'll be as snug as a bug in a rug. Now if you're ready, sir, I'll be gettin' up on the bridge.'

'What does this mean?' cried Avril, turning a white, angry face to Nelson Druce. 'If this is a joke it's in atrocious taste, and it's gone far enough. If it's not, you're to take me ashore at once.'

The Captain must have heard her outburst, but he took no notice. The solid bulk of his broad figure was disappearing in the darkness.

'It's not a joke, and you're not going ashore,' said Nelson quietly. 'You're going home to England. I'm sorry that I've had to do this, but I'm going to fight this Combine until the roof falls in—that's why I can't take responsibility for what I've done—and I just had to get you out of it some way.'

'I'll protest to the Captain—I'll shout for help to the crew,' she stormed.

'No good,' he said. 'I've bought the Captain an' I guess he can handle his crew. He thinks you're a mild kind of loony and that your name's Miss Benson. I took the trouble to get the proper papers off a snide doctor this morning—in fact I mapped out the whole party. If you hadn't come up to the house I would have phoned you for a meeting, you'd have been here just the same.'

'But you can't do this—you simply can't—ship me off on a tramp steamer—it's impossible.'

'It's not, believe you me, it's what used to be known in the old days as Shanghai-ing—and in this case it's best for both of us.'

'It doesn't clear me of the charge of murder.'

128

'That's true, but it gives me a free hand for a bit to deal with that skunk Hinckman. After that, we'll see.'

With a sudden push, Avril thrust him aside and rushed towards the ladder. She was down it in a second, jumping the last four feet; she slithered upon the deck, but regaining her balance, dashed towards the place at the ship's side beneath which she knew the speed-boat to be.

Nelson Druce came pounding after her. She heard him land with a heavy thud upon the deck. She was in the rigging now and had found the top of the ladder. The boat lay peacefully rocking below. Druce was racing across the deck, suddenly he caught his foot in a coil of rope and tripped, he went down full length with a terrific crash. The Captain bellowed something from the bridge, a light flashed in the fo'c'sle. The crew came running. Avril was over the side, clinging to the ropes, her feet feeling wildly for the wooden slats; they slipped and swayed beneath her. She found the second and third, her head disappeared below the iron bulwark. Suddenly a head appeared above her, a hand gripped her wrist so tightly that she almost screamed with pain. It was Nelson.

'You little fool!' he gasped. 'There's sharks—dozens of 'em —in that water; for the Lord's sake take care.'

She found her feet slipping. Next moment she was dangling in the air, suspended by the wrist he held. He grabbed for her other hand and got it, then with a terrific heave he pulled her up. Other hands clutched at her and she was hauled in over the side.

The crew gave back, and shambled off to the fo'c'sle. They had had their instructions and were getting double pay. It was not their business.

'Might 'ave drowned yerself,' said the Captain. He seemed not so much angry as concerned. 'If you gets any of them fits, Missy, we'll 'ave to lock yer up, for yer own sake. Think she's all right now, gov'ner?'

'Yes,' panted Nelson, who was mopping the blood from an ugly cut upon his hand. 'She sure won't do it again.'

The Captain left them, but Avril was not all right. With a sudden fury she attacked the man before her.

'How dare you—how dare you?' she cried, as she struck at him with her fists.

He seized her arms and held them to her sides. 'Now listen, Avril—Miss Bamborough, I mean—I wouldn't do this if it wasn't necessary. Honest, I hate it—but you'll be all right, the Captain's a decent sort, he'll look after you, and you'll find I've done everything I can to make you comfortable.'

'Let me go,' she screamed. 'Let me go,' and she began to struggle desperately.

'Not unless you promise not to try going over the side again, I won't.'

'Why not?' she sneered with sudden fury. 'If I were dead you'd be out of all your troubles. I wonder you didn't murder me.'

He released his hold so quickly that she nearly fell. He stood stock-still in silence a few feet away from her.

'Well?' she panted.

'Come on,' he said, and his voice had suddenly gone tone-less. 'If that's the way you feel I'll take you ashore right now. I'm just terribly sorry about all this, but I did want to smash that Combine. Don't worry any more—I'll surrender to the police in the morning.'

For the moment Avril remained speechless. There was no doubt that he meant it, and when she realised that, a sudden revulsion of feeling came over her; he looked very boyish standing there and utterly miserable.

'Let me bind up your hand,' she said.

'Thanks.' He held it out and a blood-stained handkerchief.

She took the long, beautifully-shaped hand in her white fingers and commenced to bandage the cut. 'I suppose it is the only way?' she said slowly.

He nodded. 'Yes—I shall plead the old man's death and call Mike Downey—he may talk now Angelo's dead. Perhaps I'll get off with fifteen years.'

'No,' she said softly. 'I mean for me to leave America to-night in the *Plymouth Hoe*.'

PART TWO

HOSTILITIES SPREAD TO EUROPE

13

The Menace comes to London

'And that, darling, is Hollywood!' Avril sipped her second glass of port and looked across at Uncle John. It was two months since she had left Los Angeles in the *Plymouth Hoe*, and she had reached England only that morning.

He sat there, bald and fat and smiling, well fed, well groomed. The white waistcoat that he wore beneath his dinner-jacket, just a trifle tight over the ever-increasing tummy with which he fought a continuous but losing battle. 'My dear!' he said. 'You have had a thin time! But I'm delighted to see you home again.'

She patted his hand affectionately. She was very fond of Uncle John, and he was so splendidly reassuring. She had lost her own father and mother when she was quite young and been brought up by the Bamborough Aunts, Uncle John had acted as her guardian.

Since she had not lived in the same house with him, he had never been called upon to exercise the restraining influence of a parent in small, tiresome matters; but in times of trouble he had always been on hand. When she was at boarding-school it had been his habit to turn up from time to time, stand gargantuan teas to herself and all her friends, tip her lavishly, and roll away, a comfortable, jovial figure in his big car. He never forgot her birthday, and she was one of the very few people whom he trusted with those precious books from his fine collection. His library was his hobby.

When she was eighteen he had taken her for a holiday to Paris, and in addition to the usual sights they had visited a number of curious places of which the aunts would not have approved at all. 'If you are going to act,' he had told her, 'you must know life—the best of it, and the worst of it, from the roots up. If you don't you will never do any good.' And Avril had found that strange tuition into the possible depravity of human nature, a very great asset in some of the rôles which she had played afterwards.

Perhaps the thing that had endeared her to him most, was his thought for her on that dreary South African tour, which she had undertaken two years before. At every town where they played, large or small, the local florist had received instructions to send her a bouquet of flowers on the opening night from 'Uncle John'. Avril loved flowers, and she knew the pains he must have taken in order to arrange that she should receive them.

'You don't think I shall have trouble with the American police?' Avril asked. 'I was terrified this morning when I landed that there would be a policeman waiting for me on the quay.'

He shook his head. 'It's possible, but the amount of shooting that goes on in the States is so appalling that I shouldn't think they'd bother. If they do we can get in touch with this young fellow Druce—but that Italian seems to have needed killing pretty badly and they've got your bail, so I don't think you need worry.'

She laughed. 'Isn't it too delicious . . . Hinckman's ten thousand dollars? I was awfully tickled when I realised that.'

'Tell me more about your journey.'

'It was rather fun, really. The most marvellous rest for the first part of the way. The old Captain was a perfect dear, I enjoyed it ever so much better than the liner I took on from Singapore. I was sorry afterwards that I changed ships, but at the time I was a bit fed up with nobody to talk to—and, of course, it would have taken so much longer if I'd come the whole way in the *Plymouth Hoe*.'

'I should have thought the food was pretty shockin' on the tramp.' Food was an important matter with Uncle John.

'Some of it was rather queer, but Nelson Druce had been quite wonderful. I really give him full marks. Of course, the clothes he bought me didn't fit, one couldn't expect that; I looked a perfect guy, but he must have spent about a hundred pounds on special food for me—hams and tongues and fruit, and every sort of tinned things you can think of. I gave two-thirds of it away to the Captain, but there was still lots over when we arrived at Singapore.'

'What do you mean to do now?—another play—or are you coming back to me?'

'I'd like to do another film with you, Uncle John, if you'll have me. I picked up all sorts of tips at Hollywood, although I never really got going. The conferences with Lusatch were quite interesting. Will you take me back?'

He laughed. 'Why, of course I will, I would never have let you go if I hadn't thought that the experience would be good for you. Things have been moving in the film world, though.'

'Have they? I haven't seen a soul, and there's nothing in the papers—at least not in those little rags they issue on the ship.'

'There wouldn't be—there's hardly a murmur in the daily Press itself as yet, but there's a lot going on behind the scenes.'

'Is there? I'm terribly anxious to hear all about it.'

Uncle John finished his port and snicked the end off a Punch cigar. 'Let's move into the other room,' he said, 'then I'll tell you.'

They settled themselves in his comfortable library. In most houses of a similar kind it would have been the drawing-room, but it was the only room in the house which was large enough to contain John Bamborough's fine collection of books. He was a bachelor and never entertained on a large scale, so he used it as his library and living room. The big windows opened onto the balcony in front of the house, and across the road a gentle breeze ruffled the leaves of the trees in Regent's Park.

John Bamborough brushed some imaginary ash from his white shirt front; his round, good-humoured face wore a puzzled frown. 'To tell you the truth, I don't know what to make of it,' he confessed at last. 'What you've been telling me about this amazing idea of a combine sheds a little light in the darkness, if it's true.'

Avril nodded slowly. 'Yes, it's true,' she said, 'I'm quite certain of that.'

'Well, most of the big people in America seem to be behaving in an extraordinary manner. Any number of films that should have been completed last month seem to have been stopped half-way, and there are all sorts of quaint rumours about. Reno Films have stopped production altogether, so they say, and I heard a story that Harry Honeydew is to start work on a great new super-film for Trans-Continental Electric.'

'Yes, that is true,' said Avril.

'Oh, you know that, do you? Well, all I can say is, God bless 'em, so much the better for our British Talkies if they start trying to put that sort of trash over. Then there's Ubiquitous, the people you went out to. As you know, their agent markets a certain amount of our stuff in America, but I can't get a line out of the feller, I haven't been able to for weeks, he simply ignores my cables, damn him.'

'I'm not surprised at that. As I told you, Eberhard Lusatch left them and lost their best technicians as well; poor old Hugo Schultzer wasn't strong enough to hold Ubiquitous up in the end, and they went over to the Combine, too. Have you heard anything about Mozarts?'

'What?—that Jew feller Vandelstein. Yes, any amount, but I don't know what to believe. One day there's a rumour that he's gone in with the Trans-Continental Electric crowd, the next, that he's joined young Druce. One thing I do know is that he's producing at tremendous speed, the market is simply flooded with Mozart stuff. He's gone in for the type of thing that Renos and Ubiquitous used to produce in addition to his own, at least that's the report, and he's sent over some quite unusual stuff during the last few weeks.'

'What about Trans-Continental Electric themselves—what are they doing?'

'Oh, they're at it night and day, from what I hear. Bigger and Better Pictures is their slogan. In addition to the Honeydew tripe. Von Sternheim, Ring and Lusatch are all working on big pictures for them, and they're turning out any amount of small films. Do you really think that there is anything in this Combine business, Avril? I can hardly believe it, it seems such a gigantic undertaking.'

'Uncle, darling, I haven't a doubt about it. Hollywood was in a ferment by the time I left. Just think of it, I was there holding his arm when they shot that poor Mr. Barton Druce, and I'm certain it was because he was determined to wreck the Combine.'

'It will be a terrible thing for us, you know, if it's true; that is, unless the Government help us further with the quota, and from what I know of them, they'll let us all go smash first and then have a Royal Commission to talk about helping us afterwards.'

'Perhaps they'll offer to take you in,' Avril remarked, curious to see what effect the suggestion would have on her uncle.

'Perhaps they will,' he replied shortly, 'but I don't fancy having American masters.' For a moment he puffed thoughtfully at his cigar, then he went on: 'It's the magnitude of the thing which so astounds me. Do you realise the power these people will have?'

Avril nodded. 'I didn't until Nelson Druce explained it to me, but I do now. For the film trade it will be simply terrible, thousands of people thrown out of work, bankruptcies and suicides galore, and the power of the Press won't be anything compared to the power of the Film Dictators. They will be able to colour the thoughts of the masses in every country, and in the most subtle way of all—through their principal amusement. By continuous propaganda they would even be able to make the people of one country hate the people of another to the extent of going to war, or turn the whole world Bolshevik, if they wanted to.'

For a little time they sat in silence, thinking of this tremendous upheaval which was taking place in their world unknown to the man in the street. Big business gone mad, and letting loose the forces of crime in a supreme endeavour to corner a vast market, using the weight of millions to crush and ruin scores of individual businesses. Then John Bamborough spoke again.

'What was the name of that young fellow that you met out there, the Englishman, I mean?'

'Do you mean Ronnie Sheringham?'

'Yes, that's it—Sheringham. I was wondering where I'd heard that name before when you mentioned it at dinner. He was down at Hatfield last week.'

'Ronnie. How very queer! What did he want?'

'I don't know that he wanted anything exactly. I didn't see him for more than a few moments myself—he came down with the usual sort of introduction and said he'd be interested to see over the studio, so I passed him on to somebody and he was taken round. That reminds me though, he did say something about having some proposition to put up—and asked me what day this week would be convenient to see me about it?'

'What did you say?' Avril leaned forward quickly.

'Well, to tell you the truth I didn't think much of it at the time, he seemed such a boy. I told him that I could give him half an hour tomorrow morning or Thursday, I forget which, but it's down in my diary. I'd forgotten all about it till now.'

'I should love to know just what Master Ronnie is after. He didn't say anything about the "Z" Projector, did he?'

'No, he didn't say anything about that. What is it, anyway?'

'Well, it is supposed to be strictly confidential, but I know Nelson Druce wouldn't mind my telling you. It is a new invention that he's been working on. A lens which will show films in relief. Have you heard anything about it?'

'Have I not, my dear. I haven't heard it called the "Z" projector before, but I know quite a lot about the thing you mean. The idea's not new, of course, but if young Druce has really perfected an invention that will do the trick it will be a tremendous thing.'

'Well, tell me what you've heard about it.'

John Bamborough looked thoughtful. 'It's supposed to be a secret, of course, but you know how these things leak out, Druce has taken the old Blue Hall Studio at Frensham—it's a tiny place but I suppose it suits his purpose. They say that he's producing a film there with this "Z" Projector thing.'

Avril felt a sudden glow of excitement run through her. 'He is in England then?' she said quickly.

'I don't think he is at present, I believe he is over in Berlin, but I don't know for certain. He has been here, of course, and he will be back again quite shortly.'

'Do you know what he is doing in Germany?'

'No, but there is a rumour that he and the Jung people are negotiating. I imagine after what you tell me that he is trying to secure them in order to keep Hinckman out.'

'How thrilling!' Avril's dark eyes shone. 'I do hope he pulls it off. I should simply hate to see Hinckman get the best of him. Has he approached you?'

'Not exactly, but I had a letter from him before he left for Berlin, saying that he had some important business that he would like to talk over with me—and suggesting a meeting for some time next week. I just wrote back saying that I'd be pleased to see him, but I have heard no more. That's what makes me fairly certain that he will come back, though—that and his new studio. I expect it is about this Combine that he wants to see me.'

Avril leaned forward; she clasped her hands together and rested her elbows on her knees as she looked at her uncle.

'Uncle John,' she hesitated. 'Will you tell me what you intend to do if he asks you to join him?'

'My dear, it's impossible to say until I know more about it, I'm quite content on my own. I don't want to go in with any-body—but I consider that this Combine is a definite menace to all of us. If it is some scheme for mutual defence that young Druce has to suggest, I shall certainly consider it.'

Avril gave a little sigh of relief. 'That's splendid, Uncle John, I do hope you will help him.'

His eyebrows went up and a smile twitched the corners of his lips. 'I have only met Nelson Druce once, and that was when he was over some years ago. I don't remember him very clearly—may I assume that he is a very attractive young man?'

Avril felt the colour rising to her face and her laugh was just

137

a trifle forced. 'Oh, he's quite nice, intelligent, you know, and not bad looking.'

John Bamborough nodded. 'I see, is that all? For the moment I thought that—er—well!'

'Oh, don't be absurd—you're quite, quite wrong, darling. He's engaged to Vitelma Loveday, anyhow.'

'Dear me—what a pity.'

'Uncle John, I think you're a perfect beast! But seriously— I do want you to help him all you can.'

'Well,' John Bamborough's answer was cut short by the shrilling of the telephone at his side. He picked it up. 'Hello! . . . Yes . . . Yes, this is John Bamborough speaking.'

He listened for a moment and then put his hand over the receiver. 'It's young Sheringham,' he said quickly.

'Ronnie.' Avril hesitated. 'What does he want?' she asked. And then upon a sudden impulse: 'Better say that I'm not here, if he mentions me.'

John Bamborough nodded and spoke into the mouthpiece again. 'Yes, what is it? The Carlton, yes. I see. . . . Oh, indeed. Yes, by all means. Eleven o'clock. All right, I will be there Good night.' He hung up the receiver slowly.

'Well, what did he want?' Avril enquired curiously.

Uncle John looked thoughtful. 'It was about his appointment. It is for tomorrow, and he wants me to meet him at the Carlton instead of down at Hatfield.'

'I see, and you're going?'

'Yes, why not?'

'Then what are you looking so thoughtful about?'

John Bamborough threw away the butt of his cigar and stood up. 'I'm afraid, my dear, that we are in for a worrying time. . . . He says that Hinckman will be with him.'

14

How Hinckman dealt with Bamborough

Two days later Avril was busy putting the finishing touches to her flat in South Audley Street; she had had a thousand things to see to on her return, and the place had not been lived in for more than three months, while she had been journeying round the world. She was engaged in putting away the books that Nelson Druce had so thoughtfully sent on board the *Plymouth Hoe*.

As she fitted the volumes into her bookshelves, she was thinking about their donor. She had thought about him a very great deal during these last few days; in fact, more than she had thought about him for a month. It was Uncle John who had started the trouble by his half-humorous suggestion that she had a little more than a strictly business interest in the young man.

Uncle John was an exceedingly shrewd person, and Avril wondered what she could possibly have said to give him that impression. It wasn't true, she had told herself at the time. Avril was not one of those women who regard other women's men as fair game. At Hollywood she had certainly never considered Nelson in any other light than as a pleasant acquaintance. On the boat of course it had been different, during the first part of the struggle she had been so furiously angry that she felt she hated him, but afterwards—when he gave way—she had to admit to herself that some current of understanding had passed between them then, that could never leave them quite the same again.

After her first day out from Los Angeles, she had firmly put any such idea out of her mind. The whole Hollywood party had proved a terrible fiasco as far as she was concerned, and she hoped that she might never again meet any of the people that she had known there. She knew quite well that she would meet many of them some time in the future, but she persuaded herself that it was not likely to be for some considerable time. She had managed, not without some little difficulty, to class Druce among the rest. The fact that she was eating the sweets and wearing the clothes that he had chosen for her, did not make it any easier, but the very fact that something that had happened to her on the last tempestuous night, had made her more determined than ever to get him out of her mind—and she had succeeded.

Now Uncle John had upset the whole apple-cart again and compelled her to think, but even so she refused to admit that she was in love with him—to do so would be an absurd weakness, and Avril was not weak. He had not given the least sign of any interest in her except that which circumstances had forced him to show, and anyhow there was Vitelma.

'Damn the woman—how I hate her!' said Avril aloud. Then she realised what she had said, she laughed suddenly and sat down in a chair.

She pulled a little face at herself in the Italian mirror which stood upon a small table at her side and heaved a sigh. 'Well, at all events,' she consoled her reflection, 'now we do know where we are—still we must try and play the game,' and then she deliberately turned her thoughts to business.

Uncle John had kept his appointment with Hinckman and Ronnie; Avril had heard the details from her uncle that same day over luncheon.

Hinckman had come to the point at once. It seemed that the Combine had definitely made up their minds that Uncle John's company was the strongest in the British film industry, and frankly declared their intention of operating through it. The only question was, did John Bamborough come in himself to handle the British end, or did they buy him out.

He had politely indicated that he had no intention of coming in, and he had no intention of selling out.

After that declaration Hinckman had become unpleasant. He had laid his cards on the table and told John Bamborough plainly that time was an important factor in the Combine's programme. They had definitely secured control of six out of the ten big American producing companies, and expected

140

Mozarts to come in any day. Three small companies had already crashed, principally through nervous excitement, the others would follow for a very different reason directly the Combine got going. Star Artists would remain independent—they did not count—but World Wide and Pacific Players would gradually be squeezed out of business. In the meantime they wanted an English house at once, through which to market his productions; then when Mozarts came in their long and arduous campaign would be completed, and they could float the Combine. He promised to wipe out Uncle John's competitors in six months.

John Bamborough in his kindly, affable way had told Hinckman something of his views upon the evils of combines in general, and got up to go.

Then, the Trans-Continental Electric magnate had handed him a detailed draft for the purchase of his business and a twenty-four hour ultimatum, to decide whether he would accept it, or if the whole force of the Combine was to be directed against him. 'And,' said Hinckman, 'I guess you know where Ubiquitous got off.'

Uncle John replied that he knew that and several other things besides. Then with British bluntness he had torn the draft agreement up and flung the pieces on the floor.

Avril pondered the situation. What would Hinckman do now? she wondered. He must certainly be getting very worried to try and force a deal in such a manner. The Star buying seemed to be proving too much of a drain upon his resources, and yet he was prepared to pay Uncle John a tremendous sum for the Hatfield studios. She knew, too, that Hinckman had not let the matter drop where Uncle John had left it. He had forwarded another copy of the purchase agreement by special messenger, together with a brief note saying that his offer of twenty-four hours in which Uncle John could make up his mind was now reduced to twenty-three.

The time limit was already up—it had been since mid-day—and Avril was anxious to hear if there were any further developments. However, she would not be able to see her uncle until his return from Hatfield, and she did not wish to worry him by telephoning. It was still early in the afternoon, so she decided to go for a walk in Bond Street, where she had several things to do—it was not likely that Uncle John would be back at Regent's Park until about seven o'clock.

It was just at the end of what is left of the London Season, and Bond Street was crowded in the brief rush that precedes the general exodus to the moors of Scotland and the French coast resorts. In twenty minutes Avril saw almost as many people that she knew. Even in her shoe shop and the little place just round the corner where she procured her exquisite lingerie, she met people eager to talk to her after her long absence.

As she turned into Bond Street again she ran right into Ronnie Sheringham.

'Hello!' he exclaimed, 'back from the dead, my dear?—what fun.' He was dressed with his usual careless good taste, his soft hat at a jaunty angle on his attractive head; his blue eyes showed nothing but friendliness and delight.

'How are the writs?' Avril asked, smiling.

'Wilting a bit—I returned from America in funds. Nothing like throwing the dog a bone when you've got it, is there?'

'Ronnie, you're impossible.'

'I like that!' he protested. 'What about you—skipping your bail? Ten thousand dollars, too! You've no idea of the trouble I had with Hinckman—he was livid.'

'I would rather not talk about that,' said Avril hurriedly.

'Right oh! Come and have a cocktail. I'm dying for a drink and it's just about time. What about the Seven Hundred?'

'I'd love to—shopping is tiring work.'

'Come along, then. When did you get back?' He led her into the less-crowded Albermarle Street.

'The day before yesterday.'

'How in the world did you manage it? They fairly tumbled over themselves when they found you'd cleared out. You won't be able to get back to America in a hurry.'

'I don't suppose so, and I haven't got the least desire to, either. As to how I got away—that is a little secret, my dear Ronnie, which I do not propose to share.'

'Oh, just as you like.'

142

'Do you—er—think there will be trouble over here? I haven't heard anything, but I'm a little bit frightened about the American police.'

'Lord, no. I shouldn't worry about that, they are far too busy. Besides, you know, that lawyer chap, Smithson, dug up a man who had seen the chap that you said did it, running off through the garden. That doesn't let you out entirely, but it substantiates the statement that you made sufficiently for them to drop the case, I think, and after all they collected ten grand on the deal.'

Avril gave a little sigh of relief. 'My dear,' she said, 'I am glad I met you. You've no idea what a weight that is off my mind.'

As she spoke they entered the narrow passage that led downstairs to the Club. They found a vacant table in one of the little alcoves at the far end, under the street, and Ronnie ordered drinks.

After a moment he said casually: 'Seen anything of Nelson Druce?'

She shook her head. 'No,' she said, quite truthfully.

'Really?' He seemed quite surprised, then after a moment he shrugged his shoulders. 'But of course you wouldn't have, you've only been back two days. He is in Germany now—getting busy with the "Z" Projector, or whatever he calls it.'

'Is he?' Avril's large eyes opened wide in seeming ignorance.

'Yes, didn't you know? I should have thought John Bamborough would have told you—you've seen him, of course?'

'Oh, yes.'

'He's been getting pretty thick with Nelson Druce.'

'Why do you suppose that?'

'Well, I daresay you've heard, Hinckman made Bamborough an offer yesterday, and he simply wouldn't look at it. He never would have behaved like that if he hadn't been got at first by Nelson Druce.'

'I don't know about that. Uncle John is hardly the sort of person to stand being dictated to, by Hinckman or anybody else. He probably refused entirely on his own account.'

143

'Do you really think so?—Hinckman doesn't, I know.'

'Well, you say yourself that Nelson Druce is in Germany.'

'Yes but Hinckman has an idea that Bamborough came to some arrangement with him before he left.'

Avril finished her cocktail and carefully set down the glass. 'No,' she said, 'I don't think he did.'

'Well, in that case what about it?' Ronnie leant forward eagerly. 'It's not too late; can't you persuade your uncle to come in?'

'No, my dear, it's nothing to do with me, and I can tell you quite frankly, Ronnie, that if it was, I should advise him to stand out.'

'But why?'

'Oh, there are a thousand reasons, and we've been over them all before.'

Ronnie ran his fingers through his curly hair; he looked quickly first one way, then the other, and spoke rapidly, in a low voice.

'Look here, I don't know everything that Hinckman does by a long chalk—and as a matter of fact, I'm very glad that I don't —but I do know one thing—he is out to smash absolutely any organised opposition—of that I'm certain, and he thinks your uncle has joined up with Druce. For goodness' sake tell him to be careful—Bamborough I mean. What Hinckman will do I haven't an idea; but just think of any dirty trick you like and I wouldn't put it past him.'

Avril studied Ronnie's face carefully, he was very much in earnest, although he sat there stuffing salted almonds into his mouth one after the other just like a handsome spoilt child. 'Thank you,' she said. 'It's nice of you to warn me—but why in the world do you work for such a man if you really believe that about him?'

He laughed. 'I don't work for Hinckman, as a matter of fact, but it's part of my job to keep in with him, and after all I've got to find the money for my drinks. You get me a nice job at a thousand a year and expenses—man's time you know—and I'll chuck Hinckman's crowd tomorrow.'

'A thousand a year is quite a lot of money. Ronnie, in England anyhow, and one has to do something to earn it.'

'Well, five hundred if you like. I'm not greedy, really.'

'But would you stay in it—settle down to work, I mean?'

'Ah! there you are.' He laughed again and finished his drink. 'Somehow one always means to, but one never does; besides, my talents really lie in this direction. I like the excitement of big business, and although i says it as shouldn't, I am quite useful as a negotiator. I've got a flair for bringing people together. Some day I'll tumble into a fortune. I should have made one over this in the last few weeks if I had had the capital—I may yet, as far as it goes. These people will find me pretty difficult to get rid of unless I get my fair whack of the spoils.'

Avril smiled. 'Well, my dear, I only hope that you don't come a cropper. I must get along—thanks for the drinks.'

He escorted her upstairs to the entrance of the Club and saw her into a taxi, then stood on the pavement waving and smiling as the taxi bowled away.

Avril sat back, thinking over the situation once more. It was a pity that Hinckman should already have anticipated what she hoped might come about upon Nelson Druce's return from Germany. She found herself thinking how extraordinarily fortunate it was that they were in England and not America, that surely should help to cramp Hinckman's style.

She had hoped to find her uncle when she arrived at his house in Regent's Park, but the parlourmaid informed her that he had not yet returned. She decided to wait and was shown up at once to the pleasant library.

His man Mills was there. He had just finished telephoning and she saw at once that something was wrong—as he put down the receiver his face was scared and white.

'What is it, Mills?' she asked at once. 'Is anything the matter?' She caught her breath with a sudden, awful fear.

'It's Mr. Bamborough, Miss—they've just telephoned from Hatfield.' Mills was an old and faithful servant; suddenly without warning he burst into unmanly tears.

Avril ran to him and shook him by the shoulder. 'What is it?' she cried. 'What is it? Tell me.'

'The poor Master's dead, Miss,' he gasped between his sobs. 'Knocked down and killed, as he left the Studios this afternoon, by a racing car. And—and the swine . . . Oh, Miss, they never even stopped.'

15

The Midnight Visitor

That evening Avril was so overcome with grief and shock that she went to bed and refused to see anyone. She thought of those flowers which used to brighten the small bedrooms of the cheap hotels in the South African townships. She could remember clearly her bitter disappointment when the company had made a sudden change of plans and passed over one town in its itinerary, so that Uncle John's bouquet had failed to reach her on that Monday night.

And now he was dead. Avril wept bitter tears, her heart filled with grief and rage. Grief, for the pleasant, kindly man who had always been so good to her. Rage, because she felt certain that this was no ordinary motoring fatality.

She had telephoned to Hatfield for particulars directly she heard the news at Regent's Park. It seemed that there had been some misunderstanding about her uncle's car. His chauffeur, Radcliffe, had received a message that he had business in the village and would meet him at the cross-roads. Radcliffe, suspecting nothing, had driven the car out of the Studio car-park. A quarter of an hour afterwards John Bamborough left his office. He found his car gone but was told that it was waiting down the road. It was only a few hundred yards so he decided to walk; he had not covered more than half the distance when a big racing car hurtled down the hill past the Studio gates. It dashed on to the pathway and hit him with terrific force. He had been picked up twenty yards from the spot, a crumpled figure in the hedge. The car dashed on; Radcliffe, from where he was waiting, saw it swerve dangerously to the left and tear away along the London Road. No one could describe the driver, since he and his companions were wearing leather helmets and big goggles. The police had been informed immediately, but they had been unable to trace the car beyond the outskirts of London; there, it had completely disappeared.

Avril had not a doubt in her mind. That could never have been a simple accident through reckless driving. It was plain murder. Every bit as much as the shooting of Barton Druce upon Hollywood's main Boulevard, and for the same reason, because her uncle had dared to resist the Combine. It seemed that the men behind it were utterly ruthless, and determined, whatever the cost in human life or suffering, to bring their gigantic scheme to fruition.

Avril went straight home from Regent's Park and gave way completely to her passionate grief.

The following morning Mr. Ledger, of Ledger, Style, and Ledger, telephoned to her. He was the old family solicitor and she had known him ever since she was a child. He wished to know if she could come down and see him, and she agreed to call at twelve o'clock.

When she arrived at the dusty office, with its piles of aged deed-boxes, and rows of musty ledgers, the old man seemed genuinely upset. 'A terrible affair—quite terrible,' he kept repeating, as he led her to a chair. He took his seat on the opposite side of the desk, and his spectacles propped well forward on his narrow nose, began to make known the wishes of the deceased.

Avril had always thought that John Bamborough would leave her a certain amount of money in his will, nevertheless she was surprised at its contents. She had imagined that the bulk of his fortune would go to her cousins—his nephews—but this was not the case. He had left them a handsome legacy, there was also a large number of pensions to old actors of his acquaintance and bequests to his friends, but his fine library and the major part of his estate fell to her. There was a special clause in the will which read:

'It is my wish that the contents of my library and all my shares in the Hatfield Company together with its associated businesses should go intact to my dear niece, Avril St. John Beachcroft Bamborough.

'I leave them to my niece in the full knowledge that she will reap the same pleasure that I have done from my books, and that she is fully capable of carrying on the business.

'I have taken great pride in building up the Hatfield Company, and have always endeavoured to maintain a spirit of fair-minded progress in so doing. I am confident that my niece can be relied upon to continue it in the same tradition because she is a great artist and a fine woman.'

Avril was terribly touched. She knew that Uncle John had been very fond of her, but had had no idea that he held such a high opinion of her character and capabilities. Yet she could not help feeling that this splendid legacy was casting an enormous burden on her shoulders at the present time. The will had been made about six months previously, just after she had made her second picture under Titchcock. At that date her uncle could have had no forewarning that his business might very soon be entering upon a struggle for its existence, and that he himself within a few months, was to fall victim to a world-wide film war.

Avril was only half-listening to Mr. Ledger's platitudes, after he had read the extract from the will. She found that she was standing up and that he had taken her hand in his own dry palm.

'This is indeed a terrible affair,' he was saying, 'but at least it gives me the privilege of congratulating you, my dear young lady, upon becoming the—er—head of one of the largest concerns in this—er—comparatively new industry.'

'Thank you,' said Avril vaguely. 'Thank you.'

'Really, I must go to the pictures more often,' he added in a brighter tone. 'My daughter took me to see Piplin once—most amusing I found it—most amusing.'

'Yes,' said Avril dully, 'I expect so.'

He smiled blandly and led her to the door. 'Good-bye, Miss Bamborough—good-bye—anything that we can do, you know. And I hope you will have a great success—just show these American people a thing or two, eh? Yes, yes, we must look to your generation for that. Good-bye, my dear young lady. Good-bye.'

Avril walked slowly down the stone stairs and into the sunshine of Gray's Inn. 'Show these American people a thing or two,' she was thinking. If only the parchment-like Mr. Ledger could know what was going on behind the scenes at the present moment, how his faded eyes would pop out of his head. But then, of course, had she attempted to tell him the truth he would never have believed it. He would probably have had her certified as insane.

When she got back to the flat she telephoned to Hatfield and spoke to the General Manager, Mr. Mole. She found that he had already been in communication with Mr. Ledger and was aware of the position. He informed her that he had called an emergency meeting of the board for the following morning and hoped that she would be able to attend. She said that she would certainly come down, and after ascertaining from him that the police were still unable to trace the car that had killed her uncle, rang off.

That evening she dined quietly with the Bamborough Aunts. They were two dear old ladies whose life was now devoted to charity matinees and judging the Shakespearian recitals held in girls' schools. They discussed the contents of their brother's will, talked over their memories of his childhood and his early triumphs upon the stage. They also recalled, with something of the panic which they had felt at the time, the terrible family scenes which had occurred when the rebel John had declared his intention of abandoning the great tradition to go into this new-fangled film business.

Avril sat through it all wishing desperately that she could unburden herself and tell the truth about the grim history that lay behind her uncle's death. But it was out of the question for her to say anything to these two elderly ladies—they would only have been shocked and horrified, and were quite incapable of helping or comforting her in any way.

When she got home, she thought of her various men friends, and she had quite a number. One young barrister in particular came to her mind. She would be quite safe in making a confidant of him—should she ring him up? On second thoughts she decided not to. She would wait until she had seen her uncle's co-directors at Hatfield on the following morning.

She drove down to Hatfield in her two-seater, and when she arrived she found that the board had assembled in force. There were seven directors and all were present. She knew most of them already—all, in fact, except two.

Old Colonel Frampton Parker, whom she had met on numerous occasions, took the chair. Avril sat on his right and the General Manager, Mr. Mole, occupied the bottom of the table.

The Colonel opened the meeting with a hesitating, but suitable speech, which he had evidently prepared beforehand. Expression was given to the Company's very deep sorrow at the loss of their Chairman, and the sincerest sympathy offered to his family, with special reference to Avril. At the suggestion of the Colonel, the whole board stood in deep silence with bowed heads for a period of two minutes as a gesture of respect for the deceased, and when this very trying ordeal was over, the business of the meeting proceeded.

The question of electing a new chairman was next upon the agenda. Colonel Frampton Parker spoke again at considerable length—he did not say so in so many words, but between his hums and haws it was quite obvious that he considered himself to be the only suitable person for the office.

A Mr. White, who had at one period of his career humped a camera up and down Brighton front, taking snapshots of engaged couples at sixpence a time, rather bluntly opposed the suggestion. Tact was not among the valuable qualities which had removed Mr. White from the propinquity of the bank-holiday crowds to a seat on the board at Hatfield. He put the matter as kindly as his somewhat limited phraseology would allow, but he pointed out that other qualifications were needed, besides the possession of a certain amount of money, and having fought in the South African War, to cope successfully with the problems which beset a film company.

Avril put a stop to the argument, which seemed likely to ensue, by a prompt declaration that since she was now by far the largest individual shareholder she intended to take the chair herself; a statement which she backed by standing up and plainly indicating that she expected the Colonel to vacate his place.

It was pointed out to her that at the present time she was not even a director, and had only been asked to attend the meeting as a matter of courtesy since she was her uncle's heir.

Mr. Mole, however, said that there was nothing in the articles of the company to prevent them electing her to the board then and there, but her election would have to be confirmed by the shareholders at the next annual general meeting; that being understood, he would certainly have great pleasure in proposing her.

Mr. White seconded her, a show of hands was taken, and she was elected without opposition. Mr. Mole then further suggested, that since it was evident from what little had already been said, that conflicting views were held as to the future chairmanship of the company, Avril should be asked to fill that position in a purely temporary capacity until some permanent decision would be reached.

In a manner that plainly indicated the inward struggle between annoyance and good breeding, Colonel Frampton Parker surrendered his seat. Then Avril sprung her bombshell. 'You are probably not aware,' she said, 'that my uncle was brutally murdered!'

At first they were inclined to suppose that she referred to the criminally reckless driving of the racing car, and the callous manner in which the driver had refused to stop, but she very soon made her true meaning abundantly clear. The members of the board began to regret their sudden decision to appoint a temporary chairman, and assumed that her brain had become unhinged through the shock.

She did not allow them to labour under that delusion for

long. As briefly and as clearly as she could, she outlined the series of events which had taken place since the first day of her arrival in Hollywood three months before.

The board began to look grave, they had all read of her arrest in the papers, and those who took an active part in the business knew sufficient of the recent happenings in America to realise that her story was no wild fabrication. In fact, it enlightened them as to the meaning of many curious events which they had been puzzling over for the past month.

Colonel Frampton Parker, with due deference and politeness to Avril, stroked his fine moustache and pooh-poohed the whole thing. Gradually his remarks tailed away into rambling monosyllables as he realised that he was not receiving the least support from his colleagues. In fact, a deathly silence had fallen on the board and the other members were obviously not listening to him.

'This is a very serious thing, gentlemen,' said Mr. Mole. 'You realise, of course, that if what Miss Bamborough says is true, we do not stand a chance against this big American syndicate, unless we get the Government behind us, and induce them to alter the quota in our favour.'

Mr. White laughed. 'Fine hope you've got of doing that. They're a sight too busy helping Germans and Austrians and all sorts out of their mess to bother about us. It seemes to me they put chaps like us who're trying to bolster up the country last all the time. They never give us a thought until it comes to asking for more Income Tax.'

'There is only one thing for us to do,' said Avril quietly. 'An opposition has already been organised under the leadership of Mr. Nelson Druce, the President of Pacific Players—we must join that opposition.'

A long and wearisome discussion followed, but in the end Avril got her way. A sub-committee of three was appointed consisting of herself, Mr. Mole, and Mr. White, with full powers to take any steps that might be necessary to ensure co-operation with Nelson Druce. To Avril's immense relief the Colonel was shouldered out of being a member of the com-

mittee on the plea that he lived in Sussex, and was not therefore readily available in an emergency.

The length of the meeting had necessitated an interval for
lunch, and business was not finally concluded until well into
the afternoon. Avril drove back to town tired but satisfied. Mr.
Mole had proved himself a loyal adherent throughout, and as
General Manager with a seat upon the board, he was by far
the most important person in the company now that her uncle
was dead. She felt that with his backing she would be able to
handle the others in due course.

When she got home she found a pile of letters awaiting her,
she opened half a dozen, they were all in the same strain,
condolences upon her uncle's death. She pushed the heap
aside, they must be answered some time, but not now, she was
too tired, and she decided to go straight to bed—she would
have a tray brought to her room with a light dinner.

After a bath she felt better, and once she was tucked in bed
more like her normal self. She thought that after all she would
tackle her correspondence now, and had the pile brought in.
The majority could be acknowledged by a formal card, but
many were from relatives and personal friends, which merited
a written answer. After her dinner she settled down to the job,
for she felt that in the next few days she might have much to do
and it was as well to get them off her hands. By half-past ten
she had finished this profitless and melancholy task, she felt
too tired to read, and pushing her bed table away, turned out
the light.

She was dozing, just on the point of falling off to sleep when
a sudden noise disturbed her. She sat up quickly, wide awake at
once. Someone had thrown up a window close at hand. Her
curtains were drawn, she could not see the windows of her bedroom, but she was certain that the sound had not come from
there. It must be the window in her bathroom, she had left
the door ajar. With sudden panic she remembered that the
fire escape ended just below the bathroom window.

'Hinckman!' the thought flashed into her mind. He had
killed Barton Druce, he had killed her uncle. Could he have
heard already that she had taken her uncle's place? Had he

153

made up his mind to kill her, too? Those men in the racing car, his hired murderers, had he sent them to ensure her silence, and make certain that she took no further part in thwarting his plans for the purchase of the Hatfield Studios?

She bent down quickly. In the cupboard of the table beside her bed she kept a property automatic, a useless thing, but good enough to scare the average burglar. It was loaded with blanks. She fumbled for it quickly and her hand closed on the butt. Even as she withdrew it from the cupboard another noise came distinctly from the bathroom—the scraping of a chair. Nobody could have reached the room from any portion of the flat, the only entrance was from her bedroom, and it had been empty when she had brushed her teeth half an hour before.

Avril stepped quickly out of bed, she thought for a moment of calling for help, but her maids would be of little use, the firing of the pistol would raise the alarm at any moment that she wished.

She did not pause to put on her dressing-gown or slippers, but stole softly across the room on her bare feet. If the intruders were Hinckman's grim ambassadors they would make for her bed, believing her asleep. Her heart was thumping in her chest, but her brain was clear and working rapidly. She flattened herself against the wall behind the bathroom door; as they crept into her room she meant to slip out behind them, into the bathroom, slam the door, shoot the bolt, then she could shriek for help from the open window, or if necessary get away down the fire escape.

She paused expectant behind the door, holding her breath while little shudders ran down her frame. A faint ray of light flickered for a moment, evidently the occupant of the bathroom had switched on a torch.

The light went out, the door swung open, Avril could feel the faint waft of air upon her burning cheeks. A figure entered and paused upon the threshold a dark blur in the blackness of the room. The bathroom door shut with a little click, the intruder had closed it carefully behind him.

On went the torch, Avril could see him now, it was a tall man in dark clothes; he switched the small beam of light here and there, it paused for a moment as it rested on her tumbled bed. His back was towards her, she could not see his face, even his head was in the shadow. Avril was terrified—by closing the door he had cut off her retreat—the blood pulsed madly through her veins. In that dark figure peering towards her bed she saw a murderer, one of Hinckman's hirelings who had come by night to silence for ever her suspicions about her uncle's death. She tried to scream, but the muscles of her throat seemed paralysed. Then, steadying her trembling limbs with a supreme effort, she extended the pistol, pointed it at the centre of the man's back just between the shoulder blades, and gasped. 'Hands up! Hands up, or I shoot.'

The man flung his arms above his head and turned with a quick movement towards her. The torch went out, the room was plunged in darkness, but in that brief second as he turned Avril had seen his face. With a little cry she swayed towards him, and he caught her as she fainted.

16

'The Truth Will Out'

When Avril came to, she found herself back in bed once more, the sheets tucked carefully round her. For the moment she did not realise what had happened, then as she saw the figure sitting on the bed, her terrifying experience came back to her.

The lights were on and the intruder was holding a glass of water to her lips. He heaved a sigh of relief as she opened her eyes and set the water down upon the table at the bedside.

It was Nelson Druce, looking more attractive than ever in evening dress. 'Good gracious,' she managed to stammer. 'What a fright you gave me.'

He smiled. 'We're quits if it comes to that, I sure thought

155

you were going to shoot me, but I just can't say how sorry I am that I scared you up this way.'

She closed her eyes for a moment and then opened them again. 'It's all right, I'm better now, but why—why in the world should you come to see me through the bathroom window—why not the front door?'

He looked suddenly grave. 'Sorry—it must seem queer, I know, but I guess I'm being watched. Maybe you are, too, for that matter.'

Avril sat up and pushed back her hair. 'Well, surely that's all the more reason; think of the scandal if somebody saw you come in that way.'

'You don't understand, I threw my fellow off, went in one door of the Dorchester and walked out of the other, but I figured they might have planted another guy on the front door of your block, so I decided for the fire escape and the back way.'

'Well, anyhow my reputation will be simply mud if you are found in my bedroom at this hour of night.'

'I'm sorry, Avril,' she noted that her Christian name came quite unconsciously to his lips, 'but I simply had to see you—it's just terribly important.'

'In that case you'd better go into the sitting-room while I put on some clothes. I expect I'm looking a perfect fright.'

He stood up and the little wrinkles came round his eyes as he smiled down at her. 'No,' he said slowly, 'you're not. In fact, I don't think I ever realised before that you were quite so lovely.'

Avril felt herself go hot all over, she pulled the sheets a little higher and looked away quickly. 'It's the second door on the right down the corridor—you'll find drinks there if you want one,' she said, a little breathlessly.

'Thanks—I can do with a drink.' He smiled again and left her.

She pulled on a few clothes, and then found herself studying her face carefully in the mirror. 'Yes, you are lovely,' she told herself, and there wasn't a doubt about it. Her violet eyes were enormous tonight, and her flushed cheeks added to her beauty. That must be the result of the fright she had received. What a fool she had been to faint—and yet—well, anyhow it was no good thinking about that. She quickly combed back her hair, slipped her small feet into her mules, and went down the passage to the sitting-room.

He had mixed a brandy and soda all ready for her when she came in. 'Take that,' he said, 'it'll steady you up.'

'Thank you.' She sank into a low arm-chair. 'Now tell me—why this midnight visit?'

'Had to see you some way, and I'm getting scared of ordinary procedure. They darn near got me on the Channel boat last night.'

'They—you mean Hinckman, I suppose—you've heard what happened to Uncle John?'

'Yes, it's just terrible. I reckon you know how much I feel for you in that. I only met him once, but he struck me as a real fine fellow.'

'He was,' said Avril briefly.

'Well, he's gone, poor chap—same way as my old man, both of 'em innocent, decent men, murdered in cold blood; but we can't prove it—not a hope. What do you mean to do—that's what I want to know?'

'Anything and everything that I can,' said Avril firmly, 'to help you smash this Combine, and if possible bring Hinckman to justice.'

He stood up and held out his hand. 'Avril—it's just great to hear you say that. Ever since that night on the steamer, you know, when I shipped you off, I've bin thinking a lot about you—it hit me then how most other girls would have behaved, an' it's kept on hitting me ever since. There isn't one in a million would have gone off in that lousy tramp the way you did, just to give a fellow you hardly knew a free hand. I knew from then on that I could count on you.'

'Let's not talk about that night,' she said quickly. 'What is it you wish me to do?'

'I want to know just how much weight you pull at Hatfield. I was meeting John Bamborough next week but that's all gone down the drain now, an' I see from the papers there's

157

a rumour you've been left an interest in the business. Is that true?'

'Yes, Uncle John left me all his shares, and I think I can promise to hold Hatfield for you.' Avril smiled with pardonable pride. 'I was elected to the board and made temporary chairman this afternoon.'

'Now that's just great. It's the best news I've heard in this heap of a while—you just can't know what a weight that is off my mind. I figured your uncle might help, but I couldn't be certain. If that's a fact I reckon we've cooked Hinckman's goose in Europe.'

'How splendid! You've had good luck in Germany then?'

'Yes. It took a bit of time an' the hell of a lot of money, but I've got Jung fixed.'

'I'm so glad, Nelson.' The name slipped out, he looked at her quickly, then he laughed.

'It's nice to have you call me that—an' we'd be crazy to go Mr. and Miss-ing each other when we're together in a thing like this—wouldn't we?'

'I suppose we should. Tell me how you managed with the Germans.'

'I couldn't have pulled it off if it hadn't been for Issey Vandelstein. A couple of months ago he lent me ten million bucks, I thought it would come in handy 'fore we were through—and I'm needing every dime of my own money to keep Pacific Players going. I put most of Issey's money into the Jung concern on certain definite conditions, they were needing money pretty bad.'

'When do you have to pay Vandelstein back?'

'A month hence. At least it's nearer three weeks now, but that won't cause me sleepless nights. I've completed a film with the "Z" Projector, made it at a little place down in the Surrey country—directly it's shown I'll be able to raise all the money I need on that.'

'How marvellous, and you're really certain that it will be a success?'

'Sure. You must come down and see it. The film's all in bits at present, you know how they always are, but it's great

158

stuff, an' we can easy run it through in the trial room. I'd just love you to see it.'

'Of course I'll come, I shall be simply thrilled. What a state Hinckman will be in when you show it publicly.'

'Yes, I figure it'll about put paid to the Combine. Hinckman's up against it now, or he'd never be trying to force things the way he is. His wage bill with all these stars and producers that he bought on forward contract must be just gigantic, and he can't have a cent coming in except from his general revenue.'

'How are things going in America?'

He frowned. 'Not so good. I'm worried about things back home. You heard about the fire?'

'No. I've heard hardly anything, I've only been back three days.'

'It was pretty bad. Three studios burnt right out on the Pacific lot, and miles of film ruined—we'll get the insurance in time, but it sets us back on the production side, and that's important just now. If we make these films again, they'll be out of date by the time they're done.'

'Was it—was it an accident?'

'Not on your life—incendiarism pure and simple.'

'Couldn't you trace it back?'

Nelson laughed grimly. 'We did. Three wops and a German were pinched for it, but that don't help any, they were my own scene hands.'

'But why should they do it?'

'They're all Communists, and they 'fessed up when they were pinched, said it was a demonstration against the capitalist system, I was sweating my labour—but that's a lie—I'll bet my life it was Hinckman. Plenty of these guys'll face a long stretch behind the bars if they're certain of a fat wad when they come out.'

'It's terrible—how can we fight against that sort of thing?'

'I guess we got to or else we'll all go under. You've heard Unifilms crashed today?'

'No! They are biggish people, aren't they?'

'Yes, a pretty sizeable concern. That's the fourth in this last month. I'll say the bread queue in Hollywood can't be nice to see these days—and it'll be a thousand times worse unless we can keep our end up. You'll have heard Rex Dearing shot himself?'

'No, I've heard nothing—what an awful thing.'

'Poor Devil. I figure he was pretty well up against it before the Combine came along, like a heap of these smaller producing concerns. He asked Hinckman to take him in, but he was too small fry. Hinckman just laughed in his face—Dearing told me that himself—that was a day or two after you cleared out. He just went home and blew his brains out.'

Avril looked at Nelson Druce, his face was very lined and tired. She wondered if he could possibly pull through in the face of this ruthless opposition. If the American front caved in she knew that it would only be a matter of time before the European companies were forced out of business. Once Hinckman had captured Hollywood, he would begin cutting right and left. His overheads would be reduced to such an enormous extent that he would be in a position to undercut the remaining opposition until they were driven out of the market one by one. 'What about Uncle Andy,' she asked, 'how is he?'

'The Grand Old Man's just great, he's doing all he knows to keep our end up on the other side, and he's roped in half a dozen of the smaller people—but the trouble is, while we're helping them they're not much use to us—they're a drag if anything, and Uncle Andy's got a whole packet of trouble of his own just now. They haven't forgotten him.'

'Why, what have they done to the dear old man?'

'Fixed a strike on his office staff.'

'Can't he get other employees to carry on, especially if there are so many people out of work already?'

'That's the trouble, he daren't take 'em. How'd he know with a fresh staff that Hinckman wasn't planting people in his pay. They'd get the low-down on World Wide methods and every weakness in the business. The results might be just awful. He's carrying on as best he can with borrowed staff from

160

his bank in New York; they're trustworthy, but they don't know the first thing about the business.'

'Nelson,' Avril spoke slowly, she looked him straight in the eyes, 'don't think I want to back out for one moment, but do you really think we stand a chance of pulling through?'

He was silent for a moment, it was very still in the cool sitting-room of the flat, with only the occasional hum of a belated taxi in the street below breaking the silence of the night. He shrugged his shoulders as he said at last:

'It's a toss up. Hinckman's winning all along the line in the States. He's got six out of the big ten already, Mozarts may go over any day—and let's face it, Uncle Andy and I are getting pretty rattled, a few more fires or strikes, and we'll be out of business for a year—if that happens I doubt we'd ever be able to get back. We're holding our own in Europe, more than our own, now you're with us—but Europe can't fight the States, not for any length of time. On the other hand, time is a factor to be considered, Hinckman can't go spending the way he is for ever, not even if he's got the Equitable Trust behind him. I figure he'll be done by the end of the month unless he can float his Combine and get away with it.'

'What is there to prevent him?'

'The "Z" Projector, nothing else, the rights of that are mine. We'll fix for the premier of the film I've made about a week from now. Make a flotation immediately, then I'll be able to redeem my Pacific stock from Issey; we'll equip the Pacific Studios with the new cameras right away, and let in Uncle Andy, the Jung people, and yourself on reasonable terms for the same equipment. The four of us will be the only people in the world making motion pictures with the new technique, the stock of every other Corporation will go sailing down to zero, and if Hinckman tries to float a Combine, he won't stand a chance in a million.'

Avril's eyes brightened. 'Oh, if only you could do that! But say anything goes wrong?'

'If it does—we're bust. Issey Vandelstein cleans up on my Pacifics, then he'll go over to Hinckman, that's a certainty. But it won't.' Nelson Druce's mouth closed with a snap.

'Can you come down to Hatfield tomorrow? I should like you to meet Mr. Mole, and Mr. White. The three of us have been appointed as a comittee to enter into any arrangement with you that we consider sound.'

'You've done that already, eh? That's fine. Would the afternoon suit you? I'm fixed for the morning.'

'Yes. I can run you down after lunch.'

'Okay. Can you dine in the evening?—we might go down to Frensham after, it'll be all quiet then and I could show you bits of the new film with the "Z" Projector working.'

'I'd love to do that.' Avril stood up. 'And now I think I had better turn you out. Would you prefer to leave by the window or the door?'

Nelson laughed. 'I figure I'd best go by the door. If there was a guy keeping watch on you he'll sure think you're parked for the night by this time, and have quit. I'd hate to be pinched by a cop coming down your fire-ladder.'

'Yes, I should think the front door is safe enough and the porter won't know from which flat you've come.' Avril led the way out into the passage.

Nelson laid a hand on her arm. 'About tomorrow—you won't go out on your own, will you?'

'Why?' she asked quickly.

'Well, I'm scared for you. Hinckman's out to get us, remember, and his information's pretty good. He'll know by now that you've taken over at Hatfield. Best wait in till I call for you after lunch.'

'All right, if you think that, I will.' Avril waved him back and opened the front door a few inches, then she shut it again quickly. 'That's done it!' she exclaimed.

'What's amiss?' he asked in surprise.

'The night porter,' she whispered, 'he was standing right outside, he must have seen me in this get-up, and I'm sure he heard your voice.'

'Say, I'm awfully sorry about that.'

Avril laughed ruefully. She wished that she had taken the trouble to put up her hair, but it was too late to think of that now. 'That brute will believe the worst,' she said, 'and it will be all over the flats tomorrow—it isn't even as if you were going to marry the girl.'

Next second she regretted her words. She had only spoken in jest, but Nelson Druce's eyes suddenly filled with a strange light. Almost before she could realise what he was about to do, he had caught her in his arms. He pressed his lips firmly on hers, she struggled, her hands upon his chest pushing him away. His grip tightened, all at once she relaxed, and swaying backwards, flung one arm about his neck. They clung together for a full minute, and in that minute Avril knew that she had been wanting Nelson Druce to kiss her like that for the past two months.

17

The Defeat of Nelson Druce

Next morning Avril slept late. Unless she gave special instructions she was never called, and her maid waited until she rang to bring her tray and draw her blinds.

When she woke, she lay for a long time thinking before she rang her bell. All the events of the night before came back to her with vivid clearness. . . . Her fright, the long business discussion and then that wild moment of abandoned passion when Nelson Druce had seemed to draw her very soul to her lips.

Afterwards he had thrust her from him almost roughly. Without a word he had turned away, his face dark and set, leaving her breathless against the wall of the passage. He had marched down the corridor, through her bedroom to the bathroom, and so by the fire escape reached the street.

She loved him—of course she loved him. Avril had not a single doubt about that, and he loved her, she was certain. There had been no half-measures about that kiss—but what

163

could come of it? Surely he would have stayed—have said something, if he were free. Avril decided that Vitelma must still be very much in evidence, even if she were in America.

This personal element complicated things terribly. If it were not for business she would have written him a note saying that she would prefer not to see him again unless he were free; as it was she could hardly do that. They had a thousand things to settle that were of vital importance if they were to take measures together against the Combine.

In a few hours now he would be back again, calling for her in order that they might go down to Hatfield; she must put through a call at once to Mr. White and Mr. Mole, to arrange the meeting. She had no doubt whatever that Nelson Druce would come. She wondered what his attitude would be. Would he behave like the declared lover, or seek bashfully to explain away his conduct as midnight madness?

She did her telephoning and got up. Another pile of correspondence was waiting for her, she did her best to cope with it and then lunched in her flat, mindful of her promise not to stir out alone. At half-past two Nelson Druce arrived.

He was neither bashful nor assertive. He gave her one queer look as he was shown into the sitting-room, and then plunged into business right away. It was obvious that he had no intention of referring to his outburst of the night before, and Avril felt that he was wise, with the meeting in front of them it would have been a most ill-chosen time.

They left immediately in her two-seater, and found Mr. White and Mr. Mole both ready to receive them in the board room at Hatfield.

Mr. Mole said little, but it was evident that he had a shrewd grasp of the situation. Mr. White said a lot; he showed plainly from the very beginning that he had no intention of allowing the company with which he was connected to be run by any American—Combine or anti-Combine.

Avril had never seen Nelson Druce at a business meeting before and she was interested to watch the manner in which he handled the situation.

164

To her, he was polite, brief, almost chilling. He knew that he had her with him already, and in some subtle way he managed to convey to the others that although she was responsible for his introduction, he assumed as a matter of course that she would defer entirely to their decision, whatever that might be. With Mr. Mole he played the young man anxious for help and guidance in a difficult situation. Mr. White he humoured, listening patiently to his extraneous utterances upon the greatness of the British Empire, and encouraging him to further attempts at oratory, but he always managed to bring the discussion back to the points at issue by a few quiet words here and there.

When the other two had exhausted their ammunition he spoke for about ten minutes, quoting their own arguments and pointing out what a terrible menace the Combine would be to the happiness and prosperity of everybody engaged in the Film Industry.

It was a brilliant piece of diplomacy, and Avril gave him full marks. He had not persuaded the others against their will, or asked them to agree to anything which could normally prove injurious to their company, but he had worked them up, from a state of lukewarm doubt, to a pitch of genuine enthusiasm in the rightness of his cause.

Technical details were gone into at some length, and Nelson Druce left the meeting, completely assured of the wholehearted support of the heads of the Hatfield Studios.

On the way back to London he talked of the afternoon's meeting, going over the various points again in what Avril felt to be unnecessary detail. She had realised them herself quite clearly at the time, but she guessed that he was only talking in order to avoid an embarrassing silence.

They did not change but dined together in a small restaurant off Jermyn Street. At dinner Nelson tried to keep the conversation light and amusing, but his efforts were a failure. A restraint had fallen upon them and they found themselves each seeking to avoid the other's glance. Avril was heartily glad when the meal was over.

165

She had parked her car in St. James's Square, and directly they had finished dinner, they set off for Frensham.

London was hot and stuffy, but once they were free of the traffic they reaped the benefit of the lovely July evening. Nelson had ceased endeavouring to force conversation and they spun along through the scented twilight in silence.

Darkness had fallen by the time they reached Guildford, and they turned off the highway into the narrow winding lanes. There was little traffic, but Avril drove slowly. In any case she would not have hurried, since she loved the smell of the pines and gorse that came to them on the still night air, but she had a special reason for delay on this occasion. She felt instinctively that once they reached their journey's end, Nelson Druce would speak about the night before, and she was just a little bit afraid of herself—she wanted to put the moment off as long as possible.

The turnings between the dark hedgerows were intricate and by a quiet word from time to time Nelson kept her upon the right road. They passed two long stretches of open moorland and a small pine wood at the end of which he told her to pull up.

She obeyed, looking to right and left for signs of buildings, but she could see none. He answered her unspoken thought.

'The Studio's just around the corner, down the lane, a couple of hundred yards or so; this sandy track's mighty poor going for the car, I guess we'll leave it on the grass here, there's nobody about.'

Avril edged the car onto a triangular slope at the entrance of the lane and they both got out. On the one side lay the pine wood, on the other the open heath. Low above the dark patches of the gorse the moon was rising. They walked a little way in silence, then he stopped abruptly by a fallen tree-trunk.

'I guess this'll do.'

'What?' said Avril, but she knew quite well what was coming.

'I want to talk to you,' he said, ' 'bout last night. Let's sit down.'

166

She made herself as comfortable as possible upon the fallen tree, while he stood by her, obviously restless and ill-at-ease. 'I expect you've been thinking that I'm every sort of cad—taking advantage of you the way I did?'

'No,' she said tonelessly. 'I don't think you're a cad.'

'Well, I am. Let's face it—there's Vitelma, back home.'

'Are you still engaged to her?'

'Yep.'

'I thought as much.'

'Did you? I'll say you didn't behave like it—last night.' He paused suddenly, then went on: 'Say, I never ought to have said a thing like that. It was real mean of me, try and forget it, will you?'

'Why should I? It's quite true, and I'm not a child, Nelson. You kissed me and I kissed you back, surely the time is past when a woman has to pretend that she had no feelings about that sort of thing, our instincts are the same as a man's.'

He looked at her quickly. 'Sure—we all know that, but it isn't everyone will admit it. You're a woman in a million, Avril.'

'No, I'm not. I'm just human, that's all.'

Nelson prodded the pine-needles with the toe of his shoe, then he looked up again. 'I'd been wanting to do what I did last night for two solid months. You mayn't believe it, but even my business has been done two-thirds mechanically.'

He spoke with such intensity that even Avril was taken a little aback. 'You—you care about me as much as that?' she said slowly.

'Yes.' He turned on her almost fiercely. 'I'm clean crazy about you. I've been in love before, but it's never got me this way—and it's not because you're lovely, or smart, or amusing, or sympathetic; I don't know what it is, but I just love you and I guess I'll go on loving you—so there it is.'

'I know,' she said simply.

'What do you mean?'

'Well, I've been thinking things over these last few days. Uncle John said something two nights before he died, then

167

since last night I've been thinking more than ever. I know now that I feel that way about you, too.'

He did not attempt to kiss her but sat down beside her and took her hand very gently in his own. 'D'you mean that? But of course you do—you wouldn't say it, if it weren't true.'

'No, I wouldn't, Nelson, but what are we to do?'

'You mean about Vitelma?'

'Yes, you've got to think of her.'

'She doesn't care two hoots for me really.'

'How do you know that?'

'Look at the way she's gone on since we became engaged. Has she tried to help me with my work? Has she had any thought for me when I've come home played out evenings? . . . Not on your life. All she's wanted is for me to take her places.'

'You must have loved her or you would never have become engaged.'

'That's true, I was carried off my feet. I guess I'm to blame.'

'It's a thing that's liable to happen to anybody—perhaps this is the same.'

'It isn't, and you know it. With her I figure I was just taken by her looks, and proud as any peacock to have her around. I'd be proud of you, not just because you are beautiful and famous—but in a thousand ways that other folks wouldn't see.'

'I'm miserable all the same, Nelson, about that girl. I've always rather prided myself on the fact that I'd never taken another woman's man.'

'Please—don't say that, it's not true, either, you haven't done a single thing to get me going, I've just gone stark crazy about you on my own. Last night didn't count, if you'd smacked my face, as I'd deserved, it wouldn't have made any difference, I'd be loving you just as much today—so get that nonsense about having taken me off Vitelma out of your sweet head right away.'

'What do you intend to do?'

'Write Vitelma by the next air mail, that's the only thing to do as I see it—ask her to release me.'

168

'Do you think she will?'

His mouth turned down into a humorous little smile, Avril just caught it in the half-light. 'Can't say,' he answered slowly. 'Vitelma's fed-up with being a Star. I reckon she figured to be Mrs. Pacific Players—mind you, I'd just hate you to think I'm slinging mud at her. I'm not, but I've learnt a lot about her in the last few months. It's when you're in trouble that you find out who's worth their salt and who's not.'

'I hardly know her, and anyway, I've no right to judge, but if what you say is true, I should think it's very unlikely that she'll give you your freedom.'

'I'm afraid that way myself.' His grip on her hand suddenly tightened. 'I'm a rotten skunk, Avril, to have landed you in for this. I ought never to have said a word until I'd got clear, much less have done what I did last night.'

She laughed a little sadly, as she returned the pressure of his hand. 'You're nothing of the kind, my dear—and you haven't landed me in for anything, I've landed myself.'

'My, how good I'd feel to hear you say that,' he exclaimed suddenly, 'if it weren't for her.'

Avril shook her head. 'But there is a her, and you may be doing her a great injustice. It isn't every woman who can show her affections, and perhaps you've been so worried with business these last few months that you've got on her nerves. If as you say, too, you have been thinking about me all the time, that's hardly giving her a fair chance, is it? Perhaps she loves you far more than you think.'

Nelson Druce groaned. 'Oh, hell! I hate to hurt her, anyhow, but it wouldn't be fair to her, let alone anybody else, to go on as things are.'

'Then you mean to break with her in any case?'

'That's about the size of it. I can't go on as I am, can I?'

'Listen, Nelson.' Avril spoke very softly. 'I've told you I love you, my dear, and I do, but I can't take you that way, I'd never be happy about it if I did. I don't blame you a little bit for what you've done—everybody's liable to make a mistake of that kind, but you did it yourself, nobody forced you. If you feel that you can't go on with Vitelma, that's your

169

affair, it's between you and your conscience, but I will not marry you, not unless she releases you of her own free will, or does something to justify your breaking your engagement.'

He smiled at her in the darkness. 'You say you love me, and then you say that—didn't I say you were a woman in a million? It's hard on me, but it's just as hard on you and it's principle all right—perhaps that's the reason why I love you so —'cause you've got that as well as bein' lovely and sweet.'

For a little time they sat silent, the tension between them gradually relaxing, then Avril asked him for a cigarette. He handed her his case, and felt in his pockets for his matches, but he could not find them.

'There's a lighter in the car,' she suggested, 'let's walk back to it, then we really must go to the Studio.'

They stood up, and as they turned, Avril caught his arm with a little cry. 'Look!' she exclaimed, as she pointed through the trees. 'Look—there's a forest fire.'

'It's not,' he gasped. 'That's the Studio—come on—run.'

Side by side they raced along the sandy track, before they had covered a hundred yards they came full upon it. The Studio only consisted of one big corrugated-iron and wood structure surrounded by a number of small sheds.

The flames were leaping from the main building, and the group of hutments showed clearly in the bright light.

Avril and Nelson halted breathlessly some yards from the burning building; for the moment they could get no nearer, the heat and smoke drove them back. The crackling of the flames almost drowned her voice as she cried:

'The watchman—don't you keep a watchman?'

'Two,' he shouted back. 'I guess this is more of Hinckman's work and they've been knocked on the head. Quick—round this way.'

He led her round to the side of the building away from the columns of flame and sparks that were spurting from its end. They came to a door, he tried it but it was locked. He stepped back, gave a short run, and brought his foot against the lock with all his force. It gave with a snap, the door swung open, dense acrid smoke billowed out towards them.

'Nelson, you can't go in—I won't let you,' she cried, clutching his arm.

'Got to,' he said briefly. 'They may still be in there—go round to the far end—there's a window there, that's the room they use.' As he spoke he was tying a handkerchief over his mouth and nose. With his head well down he dashed through the door.

Inside there was a lurid glare, yet he could not see the flames, the fire had been started at one end, and the whole place was full of smoke. It cleared a little as he fought his way forward, the heat was stifling, he tripped over some lighting wires and fell into a piece of canvas scenery, but he picked himself up and stumbled on. At last he found the door of the small office, he pushed it open and gasped with relief as he breathed in the fresh cool air. He closed it quickly behind him. Only the moonlight lit the room. Through the window he could see Avril standing outside. Inside, a small table was spread for supper—cold meat, cheese, a quart bottle of beer, the latter half empty. The two watchmen were sitting at it apparently fast asleep, one with his head tilted forward resting on his arms, the other leaning back, chin in air snoring loudly.

Nelson ran to the window and flung it open. He seized the nearest man and dragged him to it, thrusting his head out into the open air. The fellow showed no signs of waking. Avril seized his shoulders, they pulled and pushed until he tumbled out upon the ground. Then Nelson took hold of the other round the body and threw him on the window-sill, his slack limbs swung grotesquely. Avril gripped a dangling arm and tugged with all her strength. His coat had caught upon a fastening, suddenly it ripped and he tumbled out in a heap upon the body of the other man.

'Come on,' cried Avril, holding the window wide. 'Quickly, quickly,' but Nelson was adjusting his handkerchief about his face.

'The cameras,' Avril heard him give a muffled shout. 'I must save the cameras,' then she saw him fling open the office door and plunge back into the inferno.

For the moment she did not know whether to remain where

171

she was, or to run round to the door—she decided on the latter.

'Oh, if he's killed—if he's killed,' she kept murmuring to herself, as she clenched and unclenched her hands in terrible anxiety.

Next moment he was beside her, thrusting a great heavy cinematograph camera into her arms; she almost fell under its weight, but recovered her balance and staggered away with it, to a place out of reach of the flames.

Nelson had dashed back into the building once more. Avril was driven from the door by the choking, acrid fumes, she coughed and spluttered as they caught her in the throat. The whole place was a raging furnace now, from the crackling and the reddish glare she knew that the films had caught and the celluloid rolls were flaring up like tinder. Two of the nearest huts had caught, their matchboard sides roared and crackled.

Avril stood there on the edge of the black, billowing smoke, sparks falling all about her; she was frantic with terror that Nelson would never come out of that hell alive. Bitterly now she regretted her high-minded principles that had seemed so sound and right only half an hour before. If only he would come safely back she would marry him anyhow, she loved him, what did it matter if he were engaged a dozen times, or married even—he was hers—she wanted him desperately, madly, with every fibre of her being.

At last he came staggering blindly through the smoke, dragging the other camera, its tripod dangling behind. She ran to him, flinging her arms about him with a little sob, and supporting him to safety out of the range of that terrible heat.

They collapsed together on a little bank, sobbing and gasping, the camera fallen in a ditch. His hands were burnt and blistered, the smell of his singed clothing came strongly to her nostrils, his face was blackened and covered with soot; as he drew the back of his hand across his eyes, the smears showed strongly upon his chalk-white face.

'Those men,' he said hoarsely, jerking himself to his feet. 'They'll sure be roast where they are.'

They stumbled round the corner to the far end of the shed

again. The clothes of the man who was on top were already smouldering. Nelson and Avril pulled them into safety.

'They're not dead?' she asked.

He shook his head. 'No, drugged, the fools! It was in their beer, I reckon.'

They stood there silently. There was nothing to be done, the whole group of buildings was sailing skyward in a cascade of flame and sparks. The local fire-brigade were miles away, nothing but twisted iron and charred wood could remain by the time they arrived upon the scene, even if there were a telephone available to give the alarm immediately.

Avril slipped her arm through his, she knew that nothing she could say would console him at that moment. As she looked up into his face, she saw that tears were coursing silently down his cheeks.

'Darling,' she murmured. 'Darling.'

He withdrew his arm and placed it round her shoulder, drawing her to him. 'We're finished, sweet,' he said hoarsely. 'Every darn foot of film's gone up in smoke. I'll never be able to pay back Issey now.'

18

Police Protection

Lord Gavin Fortescue walked slowly up and down, his small hands clasped behind his back, his heavy head tilted forward on his chest. Although it was July, a fire was burning in the grate of his private sitting-room. His stick was leaning against the side of his arm-chair. Upon the table stood a stack of pass-books.

He was staying at Claridges. Lord Gavin had no home; from year's end to year's end, the restless spirit in his frail body compelled him to wander the face of the earth. At all the best hotels in Europe he was a well-known figure, and a welcome guest. His requirements were small but his payment lavish. He had never been known to question an account provided he was well served, but if he suffered the slightest inconvenience, the management knew that he would never visit their hotel again.

In front of the stack of pass-books on the table lay an eightfold sheet of paper. It was spread open to its full extent and hung over at each end. Upon it were literally hundreds of typed figures, it was the balance sheet which Lord Gavin caused to be prepared each week showing the financial situation of the Combine. The figures were approximate, of course, and it would have taken a qualified accountant a month's hard work to digest their true significance. They were compiled from dozens of other reports and schedules received from the allied American Corporations, Lord Gavin's bankers, and his brokers, in London, Paris, Berlin, and New York.

A small, bald-headed man was at work upon the sheet annotating certain figures in clear, minute writing. From time to time he made a comment in a thin, falsetto voice. His hands were large, the knuckles big and bony, so that at first sight it seemed that they were crippled from acute rheumatism. But that was not the case, such are the signs in the hand which show a born calculator, and this man was a highly gifted accountant. It was he who put the finishing touches to all Lord Gavin's business statements after they had been compiled and checked by his numerous assistants.

'I don't like our margins,' he remarked after a long pause.

'My dear Todd, neither do I,' Lord Gavin answered with some asperity. 'Yet we have completed with less on previous occasions.'

'Yes,' the little man answered slowly, 'but are we near completion?'

'I trust so. I have been forcing the pace a little recently for that very reason.'

'Quite, quite.' Mr. Todd wondered exactly what 'forcing the pace' implied on this occasion. Mr. Todd often wondered about Lord Gavin's doings when he was listening, with half an ear, to his large wife, as she discoursed endlessly upon the human frailty of their neighbours at Tooting. He had some very shrewd suspicions regarding these vast transactions, but he did not seek to verify them. That was not his business, besides, if by chance one fine day anything did go wrong—he had his professional reputation to think of, it was far better that he should know nothing. It sufficed for Mr. Todd that Lord Gavin Fortescue was a very fine client, and incidentally, his brother was a Duke. Even Mr. Todd felt a little reflected glory added to his own monotonous existence by that association.

The door of the sitting-room opened abruptly and Hinckman strode in. Lord Gavin looked up quickly, he made a sign to Todd. 'You may go now—the same time tomorrow.'

Mr. Todd folded his papers and put them in his attaché case. 'Tomorrow, yes—shall we say the end of the month, then?'

Lord Gavin knew quite well to what he referred. He nodded. 'I think so—before, perhaps.'

'Well, I'd like to see this thing cleared up—I think it should be fairly soon. Good day, Lord Gavin.' Mr. Todd closed the door quietly behind him.

Lord Gavin fixed his pale blue eyes on Hinckman's ruddy face. He waited for him to speak.

'It's all okay,' said Hinckman. 'The fire gutted the whole place.'

'So I gathered from what little was in the papers this morning. Did you get the cameras?'

'No, what 'ud we want with the cameras?' Hinckman looked surprised.

'You are certain that they were destroyed as well as the film?'

'Sure.'

'Good . . . all the same, if you had secured them, we might have possessed ourselves of certain information regarding this new projector.'

'That's so—but what'ud be the use—they're patents, we couldn't infringe 'em.'

'No, but we could have placed orders for a number to be manufactured, they would have been ready then for immediate use, and when Pacific smashes we shall secure the patents for a song.'

'I certainly wish I'd thought of that—but I guess it's too late now.'

'No matter. Have you heard from Vandelstein?'

'Yep, he wants till the end of the month to go further into things—says he's gone sick an' can't touch business at the present time 'cause he's in a sanatorium. But I doubt that's true—he as good as says he'll come in, though.'

Lord Gavin nodded. 'He sees that we are getting the upper hand, but it is a pity that he will not decide earlier, time is becoming an important factor.'

'That's so, we can't go on weighing out like this, an' I figure it'ud be fatal to start cutting salaries before the Combine's floated. You'll have heard that the girl's been appointed chairman at Hatfield. She was down there yesterday with young Druce.'

'I see. Well, that does not worry me to any marked extent. We can deal with her.'

'Yep. I'll fix her all right, an' I've a notion that'll get young Druce rattled too.'

'Naturally, if he fears Hatfield is about to slip through his fingers.'

'I don't mean it that way. I've got a hunch he's gone sweet on the girl.'

'Indeed—what leads you to suppose that?'

'Hall porter on her block. Swears Druce was in her apartment night before last, he caught him talking to her in the hallway with her hair all down. Then yesterday, she took him to Hatfield in her own automobile. After, when they got back, they mealed together.'

'That is interesting,' said Lord Gavin thoughtfully. 'Did he go to her flat again last night?'

'Don't know, she parked her auto in St. James's Square while they fed, after, they picked it up again. That fool Lupas lost 'em in the Piccadilly traffic. He figured they'd turn right, into one of those streets running down to Curzon Street, on the way to her flat, but they weren't there when he made it.'

There was a quick knock and Ronnie came in. 'Hullo, chaps!' He flung his soft hat on a chair. 'Heard the news?'

'I'll buy it,' growled Hinckman.

'There was a Studio burnt out near Frensham last night, quite a small place, but they say Nelson Druce was connected with it.'

'You don't say! I figure you bin reading the news-sheets bright and early.'

Ronnie grinned. 'Yes, I spotted it when I was having breakfast, thought you'd be interested. By the by,' he added casually, 'Frensham's down in Surrey—isn't that the place where you've taken a cottage?'

'Yep, nearby—mine's at Cutmill. Why?' Hinckman's face hardened.

'Oh, nothing—though why you want to live out at a place like that while you're in England—God knows.'

' 'Cause I like the air, and 'cause I like quiet—'sides, it's mighty handy sometimes to have a place where every news tout can't drive me batty.'

'Yes, I suppose you do get pestered a good bit by reporters. I wonder what Druce wanted with a little place like that in England when he has those enormous Studios in the States?'

Hinckman did not trouble to answer. He stood up and walked towards the door, addressing Lord Gavin casually over his shoulder. 'My party's fixed for this afternoon. I'll give you a wire if there's trouble, but I figure it'll be the last nail in their coffin. See-yer-later.'

Lord Gavin nodded. 'I shall be interested to hear.'

As the door closed on Hinckman's broad back he turned to Ronnie. 'Nelson Druce?' he said slowly. 'When we were in Hollywood, what did you learn about him—personally, I mean?'

'Not much—just the rather clever young American, reads books, and dabbles in science a bit. I told you about his "Z" Projector at the time, if you remember. He's engaged to Vitelma Loveday, the film star.'

'Do you happen to know Miss Loveday?'

'Oh, rather!—well, that is, I've met her once or twice,' Ronnie hastened to qualify his statement.

'I see—and what is she like?'

'Superior chewing-gum blonde—too, too lovely, of course, but quite dumb.'

Lord Gavin took a small black book from his despatch box. 'Loveday!' he murmured. 'Ah, here we have her record.' He studied the report carefully for a few minutes and then put the book back.

'A vain woman,' he said cryptically, 'is a danger to her acquaintances. I think we must persuade Miss Loveday to honour us with a visit to these shores.'

Some ten minutes later Ronnie took down a carefully coded cablegram for despatch to some person in Hollywood of whom he had never heard.

Less than a quarter of a mile away, Nelson Druce had just joined Avril, in a quiet corner of the lounge at the Dorchester.

'How are the burns?' she asked at once.

He looked down at his bandaged hands. 'Pretty painful, but I guess they might be worse.' His eyes were red-rimmed and bloodshot, but otherwise his face had not suffered at all.

'I've been thinking,' said Avril. 'I've had an idea.'

'Well, we certainly can do with it,' he smiled at her. 'I was turning things over in my mind this morning, and I figure we're pretty well all in.'

'Not yet. Listen, why can't we make that film again?'

'Make it again? What good'll that do us? It took me close on six weeks before, we'd never be able to finish it and exhibit before the month's up—so what's the use?'

'Why not?' Avril leant forward eagerly. 'Let's make it at Hatfield—you saved your cameras, and we've got everything you will need in the way of plant.'

He smiled doubtfully. 'Well, it's a great idea, but it's a question of time. There's two hundred hours' work in that film. I'm afraid it just can't be done.'

'It can—working fourteen hours a day you could make it in a fortnight.'

'That's so—but do you see Myrtle Savage working fourteen hours a day, and remember, the star features in two-thirds of the shots in this production.'

'No,' said Avril, 'I don't, but with Myrtle Savage it's not a question of life or death, with us it is. I will take her part—live down at Hatfield, sleep on the set, if you like, but we'll get it done between us.'

His look suddenly changed from doubt to excitement and delight. 'D'you mean that, Avril? My! But it's a whale of an idea—an' just marvellous of you to think of it. It'll be hell's own grind, but if you're game to do it—I guess it can be done.'

'Splendid,' she cried. 'I knew you'd agree. There's only one thing that's been worrying me—the script, was that burnt, too, last night?'

'No, we're all right there, I've got a copy of the scenario right here in the hotel.'

'Can I have it this afternoon?'

'Sure, we won't waste a single moment. I'll have the same cast down at Hatfield by nine o'clock tomorrow, all except Miss Savage. That'll help a whole heap, they know their parts backward—it'll be easy money for them running through those shots again. I guess you're right, we'll make it in a fortnight. Avril, you've brought me new life.'

'I think you had better move down there, too,' she suggested. 'There's plenty of spare offices, we can fix them up as bed-rooms and the principal people who are to be featured had better stay there as well. Then we can work any hours we like.'

'That's the idea. It'll be a good thing for another reason. I'm scared of you living in that flat all on your own. You'll certainly be safer at Hatfield.'

'Quite safe, I hope. I've been to Scotland Yard this morning, Nelson, I didn't say anything about the fire at Frensham —no particulars, I mean—I thought I'd better leave that to you, there is bound to be an enquiry about your drugged watchmen. I told them that I intended to live down at Hatfield for a time, and then about Barton Druce being shot when I was in America. I told them, too, I wasn't satisfied that Uncle

John's death was altogether an accident, and about the fires in the Pacific Studios in America.'

'What had they got to say?'

'Well, they were just a little difficult, it was an awfully nice inspector man I saw, and he had a very lively mind; once I'd started he wanted to know all sorts of things, but I managed to fob him off fairly well. To tell the whole truth makes an almost unbelieveable story, and we haven't got a shred of evidence against Hinckman. I tried as far as possible to make him believe that these things were the work of Communists and that I was frightened of trouble at Hatfield. I know he thought that there was more in it than that; anyhow he was sufficiently impressed to promise that one of his best men from the special branch should be sent down and half a dozen ordinary detectives.'

'I'm glad you did that. Hinckman's getting pretty desperate, those two poor devils of watchmen would have been roast alive if we hadn't chanced along last night. We've just got to keep our eyes clean skinned from now on. You can be sure Hinckman'll make more trouble for us the moment he hears we're at work again.'

Avril and Nelson lunched together in the Spanish Grill and during the meal he gave her a brief but clear outline of the film that they proposed to make together. Afterwards he dwelt at some length upon the technique of her more important scenes, then he fetched the scenario, and Avril took it back to her flat with her at once, in order that she might dig into it right away.

She had barely settled herself in her sitting-room with the manuscript before her when her parlourmaid came in.

'There's a gentleman to see you, miss.'

Avril looked up, she was expecting no one. 'Did he give his name?'

'Yes, miss, it's a Mr. Hinckman, he said you'd know his name.'

Avril knew his name indeed. Should she refuse to see him? Better not. Obviously he would not be fool enough to attempt any violence against her personally in the middle of the afternoon. He left that sort of thing to his hired gunmen. This was probably some new move in the game. Perhaps he was about to make the same proposal to her as he had to her uncle—it would be best to hear his intentions right away. 'Show him in,' she said quietly.

He entered the room, massive and smiling, he showed no trace of the ill-will which she expected him to bear her for having skipped her bail at Hollywood.

'Well, Miss Bamborough, it's great to see you after all this time.' He flung his hat on the floor and sank into an arm-chair.

'Really,' she said non-committally. 'May I ask you the purpose of this visit?'

'Sure. I'm here to offer congratulations—'tisn't every day a star becomes a big noise on the production side.'

A dangerous gleam came into Avril's eyes. She owed that to her uncle's death, and this man with the high cheekbones and hard eyes was, she was sure, responsible for his murder. 'I do not think I care to talk about that,' she said firmly.

'Well, maybe—let's say a word about the last time we met. I figure you recollect that.'

'Yes.' Avril nodded. 'It was when you took me from the police-court to my hotel in your car.' Never would she forget that awful day and the terrible night that had preceded it.

'That's so. Now see here, Miss Bamborough, I don't want you to think I'm sore about that bail business—I'm not, ten thousand bucks ain't a lily pod to me, and I'll hand it to you for making your getaway the way you did. That certainly was smart business.'

'That's very nice of you, Mr. Hinckman, then may I ask what you do want?'

'Just a little business arrangement, that's all.'

'I see—I thought as much.'

'Then you're a smart woman.' He drew a bulky paper from his pocket and waved it gently in front of him. 'All you have got to do is to sign this little agreement. We're going to cry quits about any differences we may have had in the past, and I guess you won't have to worry your pretty head about business in the future, either—you'll be a rich woman for life.'

'Can you give me any reason why I should sign any document that you choose to produce?' Avril enquired.

He twirled the cigar in the corner of his mouth. 'Because you're a sensible kid—that's why—an' I guess you know where you get off.'

'I'm glad you think that, and as it happens you're quite right.'

Hinckman nodded, misunderstanding her meaning. He spread the paper out on the table at her side. 'This is just a little deal between you an' me, you're turning over your shares in the Hatfield Company to me for a period of six months, and I'm undertaking to issue the equivalent to you in the Combine stock as and when the Combine's floated. If that's not before six months is up—I get an option to continue the agreement for a certain period. If the Combine don't get going your shares are returned to you all complete—but I guess you needn't worry about that part. The Combine'll get going all right—I'll see to that.'

'Dear me, how kind of you to—what is it called?—let me in on the ground floor, Mr. Hinckman.'

He suddenly realised that she was laughing at him. 'Don't be a plumb fool,' he said angrily. 'You sign right here or it'll be the worse for you.'

She stood up quickly. 'And if I refuse?'

'You won't—but if you do there's just one heap of trouble coming your way.'

'Are you threatening me as you did my uncle?'

'No—I guess I don't have to.'

She was standing within a foot of him, her eyes blazing into his. 'I refuse,' she cried. 'I refuse absolutely.'

'Think again,' he snapped. 'If I once say the word, you'll regret it—an' how! Now take this as a warning. If I do what I've a mind to do there ain't no drawing back—and you'll be for it. Be sensible an' I'll save yer skin.'

'Threats,' cried Avril. 'Just as I thought. Now listen, Mr. Hinckman, I'll give you a warning in return. I've been to Scotland Yard today and I'm under police protection. It's you who'll be for it, if you try any more gang murders.'

'Yeah? You don't say!' he sneered, then suddenly he laughed. 'Police protection, eh? well, if that don't beat everything! Now do you sign—or don't you?'

'No.'

'Okay.' He stepped to the door and flung it open. *'I'll give you police protection. . . . Come right in, Rudd!'*

Avril felt a sudden tremor of fear run through her at that well-remembered name. Her maid had said nothing of another caller, but Hinckman must have left him in the passage. Yes, it was Captain Rudd—the little fat American detective who had plied her with questions so remorselessly in Hollywood.

He stepped right up to her at once, producing a sheet of paper from his pocket.

'Afternoon, girlie. I got a warrant here for your extradition to America—on the charge of murdering Angelo Donelli.'

19

A Life Sentence

Captain Rudd took Avril to Scotland Yard in a taxi, where various papers regarding her arrest were signed, and she was duly handed over to the British Police for safe custody. There the American detective left her. Avril was heartily glad to see the back of him, his presence called up too vividly her memories of Hollywood Police Headquarters and the third degree.

Half an hour later she was removed from Scotland Yard to Holloway in a prison van.

At the time of her arrest she had been too stunned by Hinckman's bombshell to realise the full significance of her position, but on the way to Holloway she began to see clearly all that she had to face.

There could be no question now of citing Nelson as the man who had shot Donelli. If she did, it was quite possible that they would convict him. Directly his name was mentioned in the case the motive would stand out with terrible clearness, and there was this new evidence which Smithson had unearthed about the man running off into the hotel garden—that would support her original story to the police. If Nelson was convicted he would get fifteen years at least. Avril gave a little shiver as she thought of that. It was quite clear that she must take the blame upon herself and plead self-defence.

The thought of what that would mean appalled her. All the horrible publicity which the gutter Press would give to such a case. The sordid details of that loathsome little Italian's brutal attack, with full-page photographs of herself for the lewd-minded to gloat over. But worse—it meant the journey back to Hollywood as a prisoner. She could imagine the gaping crowds upon the station platforms and the boat. Her features were so well known that she would be recognised everywhere, and then, most horrible of all, the weeks or months perhaps, in an American prison before the trial came on. Nevertheless she did not consider for one moment any other course. She loved Nelson, loved him desperately, she knew that now beyond all shadow of doubt. Those awful moments when she had feared to lose him for ever, in the fire the night before, had shown that to her plainly. She was prepared to go through anything to save him.

When she arrived at Holloway she asked that Mr. Ledger should be informed of her arrest, and that she would like him to come to her at once. After some little delay she learned that he had left his office early that afternoon, but his partner had taken the message and Mr. Ledger would come to the prison first thing the following morning. Then she sent word to Nelson at the Dorchester, that he might know at once of Hinckman's latest and most devastating operation.

As she sat in her cell she realised why Hinckman had tried so hard to persuade her to agree to his wishes before he sprang his mine. Hinckman could set the law in motion, but even he could not stop it functioning, once he had called it in.

He had not secured Hatfield as he had hoped, but, by this drastic action following upon the fire, he had completely quelled any opposition to the Combine.

It would be impossible now for her to make Nelson's picture, and she doubted if he would be able to get any other competent actress at the eleventh hour, who would be willing to work at such high pressure. It meant fourteen hours a day with emotions keyed up the whole time, day after day without rest or intermission for fourteen days. Nothing but a tremendous determination, engendered by a vital personal interest, could provide the endurance to carry it through.

Nelson might decide to make a shorter film, but that would not serve his purpose. It would be enough to show the possibilities of his invention to the trade—but he was at war with the biggest people in the trade, so they were useless. He needed a film that he could exhibit to a wealthy audience, in order to arouse their interest and float a public company upon their money.

It seemed now that the last hope was gone of marketing the projector in time to pay Vandelstein his ten million, and save Nelson's Pacific shares. He would find his own Company and Mozarts in the hands of the Combine, with Hinckman at its head, overwhelmingly triumphant.

Avril tried to comfort herself with the thought of Nelson's love for her, yet that seemed a ghastly tangle, too. There was Vitelma to be settled with. The blonde Venus might be selfish and shallow perhaps, but Nelson had undoubtedly been extremely fond of her two months before. Try as she would Avril could not rid herself of the thought that she had come between them, and she hated it. If Nelson had been thinking about her during these past two months, what chance could he have given to Vitelma. It did seem terribly unfair to the girl, if she really loved him.

She began to wonder what Nelson would be feeling after he got the news of her arrest. Poor darling, he had been living under an appalling strain ever since his father's death, she hoped that this would not prove the last straw and crack him up completely.

Her miserable conjectures regarding their respective woes were interrupted by the wardress, a pleasant, buxom woman, bringing her dinner. The food was simple, but of a much higher standard than Avril had expected in a prison, and with a little kindly coaxing from the sympathetic wardress, she managed to make quite a respectable meal. Directly afterwards she went straight to bed.

She lay awake for a long time turning the situation over and over in her mind until her brain was weary with it, but she dropped off at last, and not having undergone the terrible ordeal to which she had been submitted under the same circumstances in Hollywood, she slept soundly. When she awoke in the morning she found her brain clear and her body refreshed.

But a new shock awaited her, and one for which she should have been prepared, although for some reason it was a factor which she had failed to take into consideration.

Immediately after breakfast she was led to the Governor's room. He greeted her kindly and asked her to sit down, then he smiled at her across his desk.

'Well, Miss Bamborough, I hope that you haven't found your short stay at Holloway too unpleasant. We have to observe the regulations, of course, but we do everything that we can to make prisoners on remand as comfortable as possible.'

'Yes, yes, I'm sure,' said Avril uncertainly. 'Everybody's been most kind to me.'

He bowed gallantly. 'I'm very glad to hear you say that, and I'm sure it's not often we receive such a charming guest, but all the same I don't doubt you'll be very pleased to hear that I have received instructions to release you.'

Avril's first feeling was one of relief, but it soon gave place to astonishment. What could have happened? Had Hinckman only wanted to frighten her? Was something technically wrong with the warrant for her extradition? Then suddenly a fearful thought came into her mind. Surely it was impossible— he wouldn't be such a fool. She leaned forward quickly.

'Why,' she said, 'why, of course I'm pleased you are letting me go, but why is it? What has happened since yesterday?'

186

'Well, it's really not my province to discuss these things.' He leaned back in his chair and tapped his finger tips gently together. 'But of course I know the reason for your arrest—some shooting affair in America, wasn't it? I remember reading about it in the papers at the time.'

'Yes,' said Avril impatiently, 'yes, that's right.'

'You broke your bail, I believe, to return to England, and of course the American Courts have the right of extradition, but that will not apply now. It seems that a young man gave himself up last night, made a clean breast of things, Druce, I think his name was.'

Avril groaned. Oh, the sweet, stupid fool, what madness had possessed him.

She pulled herself together as well as she could, and thanked the Governor. He placed a paper before her which he requested her to sign, then, having ordered her coat and hat to be brought to his room, he showed her out himself. A policeman secured her a taxi.

Avril drove straight to her lawyer, hoping that he would call at his office before going to see her at Holloway as had been arranged. It was early yet, only a quarter past nine, if she were lucky she would catch him. She had every faith in elderly Mr. Ledger's capacity for handling the ordinary legal business of the family, but little confidence in his ability to advise her in her present trouble—nevertheless, she felt he should be able at least to find out for her what was likely to happen to Nelson and if it would be possible for her to see him.

As the taxi threaded a way through the traffic towards the Gray's Inn, Avril sat forward on the edge of the seat. She was really worried now, and infinitely more unhappy than she had been the night before. Then, she had felt that there might be many miserable weeks in front of her, but eventually she would be freed, now it was a case of Nelson's life. If he had confessed, how could he defend himself?—at best he could only ask for the mercy of the court and plead his father's assassination as extenuating circumstances. A complete acquittal was out of the question. He had said himself that it would mean fifteen years in prison at least.

She beat her clenched fist angrily upon her knee. Why? Why? Why had the dear beloved fool given himself up? He might have known that she would willingly have gone through the miseries of a trial to save him. What were a few weeks, compared to fifteen years? She thought of the ghastly life that awaited him in one of the overcrowded American prisons, among the gangsters and hardened criminals, the scum of the world, all the worst elements of America's mixed population. How could a man like Nelson Druce, an intellectual—carefully nurtured—used to every comfort that money could buy, stand that? He would go mad, or if he survived, come out a hopeless, broken wreck, prematurely aged and filled with bitterness against the world—the thought was too terrible to contemplate.

For a moment Avril considered returning to Holloway and asking to see the Governor again, telling him that she had shot Donelli in self defence, and that Nelson had made a false confession with the object of taking the blame upon himself because he was her lover. But even as she thought of it she realised that it was no use, they would never believe her. The evidence that Smithson had secured about the man running off into the garden would tell against that story now—and Nelson's own confession had damned him utterly. He had not been suspected before, but now he had associated himself with the crime, the motive stood out so clearly.

All thought of the Combine had passed from Avril's mind, but when, for one brief instant, she did think if it, she damned it roundly. This wretched Combine had got them into all their troubles from the very beginning. Hinckman had won—hands down. Well, let him have his Combine—she didn't care —he could have Hatfield too for that matter if he wanted, the whole miserable business was a mere bagatelle, if only she could see a glimmer of hope for Nelson himself.

'Well! Well!—my dear young lady,' said Mr. Ledger, and a very great deal besides in much the same strain, when Avril caught him at his office. With infinite patience and marvellous restraint, she managed to acquaint him with the situation. It was no easy task, since some of the facts seemed almost beyond his comprehension, but at last she succeeded in making clear her wishes.

He delved into a number of weighty calf-bound volumes that had obviously not been opened for years, and eventually brought the younger Mr. Style to his assistance; the whole affair then had to be explained again.

Mr. Style was a bright young man with very moderate good looks. He was a prominent member of the Beckenham Tennis Club, also of the local dramatic society, and evidently fancied himself as such, but despite his obvious eagerness to impress Avril with his very ordinary personality, he proved of considerable assistance.

He was anxious to help and capable without being clever. There were some further delays while he did some telephoning, then he informed her that Nelson Druce had been removed to Brixton Prison. It was unlikely that he would be transported to America during the present week, and that his London representative and lawyer were with him now. Further, that it would be impossible for her to see him that day, but application should be made in the right quarter and he hoped she would be able to do so the following morning. He then offered himself as an escort.

Avril thanked him as nicely as she was able in her highly nervous state, but declined his offer. She thought that a warder would probably be present when she saw Nelson, and she could not bear the thought of having this self-satisfied little man with her.

She returned to her flat in South Audley Street, still frantic with anxiety for Nelson, but at least comforted with the thought that she would be able to see him.

How she got through that day she never afterwards remembered. She went to bed and got up again. She had slept well during the night, but she felt that even if she had had no sleep for a fortnight she would not have been able to sleep now. Every petty worry in the world seemed to assail her. Three of her more intimate friends, whom she had not seen since Uncle

John's death, thought it time to call and express their sympathy in person. An electrician busied himself in her flat the whole afternoon, following her from room to room with smiling apologies, and an irrepressible desire to discuss the weather and the cricket at Lord's. Colonel Frampton Parker turned up and she simply had to see him, she dared not offend him openly. Reporters and photographers beseiged the place owing to the report of her arrest which had appeared in the previous evening's papers, and then to crown it all, she received an insulting telegram from Hinckman, who showed a callous humour with which she had not credited him. It read: 'Great stuff, kid, congratulations on release, accept Combine's sincerest thanks, Hinckman.' Of course, he knew, and she knew too, that she was only a pawn in the game compared to Nelson Druce—his surrender meant their complete and overwhelming victory.

By the evening Avril was in such a state of nervous tension that she decided to ring up her doctor. He was a youngish man with a pleasant manner and plenty of practical good sense. She knew him well enough to tell him something of her miserable situation, and after twenty minutes' quiet talk he had steadied her considerably. He sent her to bed with a promise that he would call himself at her chemist's on his way home, and have a dose made up for her which would ensure her sleeping, then he left her.

She did not feel equal to dinner, but her maid brought her a tray in bed with some cold soup and raspberries. While she was toying with the fruit a Mr. Drefus rang up. He said that he was a partner in Drefus and Drefus, the solicitors, and that he was acting for Nelson Druce. He had been in communication with young Mr. Style regarding her visit to Brixton Prison, and at Nelson Druce's request he would call for her if it was agreeable at two-thirty the following afternoon. She had told Mr. Style that the morning would be impossible for her, since Uncle John's funeral was to take place at eleven o'clock.

The knowledge that she would at least be certain now of seeing Nelson next day, comforted her considerably, so she took one-half of the doctor's sleeping-draught—and since he was one of those capable practitioners who do not hesitate to use drugs freely when they are really necessary—she was soon asleep.

In the morning she had the ordeal of the funeral to go through and was utterly miserable and depressed by the time Mr. Drefus called for her after lunch in his large car. She found him to be a very different type of man to the elderly Mr. Ledger, or the young and self-satisfied Mr. Style. He was a shrewd-looking Jew, very polished, and in a quiet way very certain of himself.

On the way to Brixton, he impressed her very favourably. It was obvious that he was used to handling really important matters and had a wide knowledge of legal affairs. He told her at once that the case was a difficult and unusual one, but he felt that the very fact of its unusual features might be turned to good account. In the first place he had already taken steps to delay Nelson's extradition to America. International law, he told her, was a very curious thing. Under certain circumstances, the country in which the suspected person was arrested could detain that person. If, for example, he were subpœnaed as a witness to another murder in that country. There had been no murder which they could utilise for this purpose, but there had been attempted murder and arson, in the affair of the burnt Studio at Frensham, the watchmen had been left to burn alive.

'But,' said Avril, 'although we are convinced ourselves that Hinckman was responsible, we can't prove it, we haven't got the slightest evidence.'

'I agree,' replied Mr. Drefus. 'But this is a matter of legal tactics, we shall bring a case just the same. There is the question of the drugged beer, we hope to trace the persons from whom the watchmen procured that. Other things may come to light, but even if we lose, as I expect we shall, it enables us to detain Druce in England as an important witness. In the meantime we shall set to work in the States. Mick Downey has not been executed yet. The defence in his case are creating the usual delays. If we can get at him, we might induce him to speak, or give us a letter to the effect that Donelli was concerned with him in the murder of Druce's father. That would

191

strengthen our hand considerably. As I see it, our best line is to bring Hinckman and the machinations of the Combine into the limelight as much as possible. I hope to stir public opinion in America into such a state of indignation that sympathy for Druce will enable me to get him off with the minimum sentence. If we bring a case against Hinckman for attempted murder here in England, that should go a great way to bring public opprobrium upon him.'

Avril was greatly cheered. Mr. Drefus was evidently no hide-bound lawyer of the old school. He possessed brains and intelligence. She felt that Nelson could not have a better man to act for him.

At Brixton Prison, after the usual formalities had been gone through, Mr. Drefus and Avril were led into a small room with a waist-high partition at one side, above which was a wire grille; beyond was a space about six feet wide in which a warder sat with folded arms upon a wooden chair. Beyond the warder was a second partition and wire grille. After they had waited for a few minutes, Nelson was led in upon the far side of the further partition, so that conversation had to take place through the two screens of wire and across the intervening six feet of space.

He looked tired and worn, Avril thought, but that she knew was partly the accumulated strain of the last two months. He smiled when he saw her. 'Nice of you to come,' he said.

'I would have come yesterday if I could.' She felt how totally inadequate these remarks were on either side to express their real feelings.

'Drefus'll have told you,' he went on, 'what he figures to do.'

She nodded. 'Yes. I do hope that he will be able to stop them taking you out of England. Are they—are they being decent to you?'

'Yes, thanks, they've made me as comfortable as can be expected. Did you have a bad time?'

'No, they were quite kind, and I was only kept at Holloway for one night.'

'Well, I'm real glad about that.'

'Oh, Nelson,' she burst out, 'I'm not. I wish to God I were there still. Why did you do it?'

He smiled. 'I guess there weren't no other way. That was plain from the start. Have you got busy on the film yet?'

'The film?—my dear, I haven't given it a thought, I've been too wretched. Besides, what's the use—now?'

'You're not going to let them get away with it, are you, just 'cause they've got me down?'

For the moment she wanted to burst into tears. What a man he was! A charge of murder hanging over him, a long sentence of imprisonment at the very least, yet he still wanted to carry on the war. She controlled her impulse and tried to smile. 'Do you think I can do it on my own? I was counting on you for the production—but I'll do just what you wish.'

'That's fine, I knew you would. We'll beat 'em yet. An' you can make it. Why not?—you've got Titchcock, an' he's a great guy. Get him to scrap the film he's making at the present time, you've worked under him before and you couldn't have a better man. Pull if off for me, Avril. I want you to.'

'All right—I will. I'll go straight down and see him at Hatfield when I leave here.'

'That's great of you—and I guess I know just what you're feeling, but work'll take your mind off things. Drefus has got the names of the others in the cast. He'll put you wise to them.'

'I'll try and make a start tomorrow then, but time is slipping away so terribly, we've only got eighteen days. I shall never be able to do it in a fortnight if I come up and down to see you every day.'

He shook his head. 'I don't want you to, and you know well enough it's not because I wouldn't look forward to your visits. I'll feel you're safe at Hatfield, with those Yard men looking after you. I'd be scared stiff if I thought you were coming up and down to London. Hinckman 'ud sure try and wreck your car or some swine trick once they learn you're busy on that film—an' these sort of interviews with us both in a cage'll sure only serve to make us more miserable anyway.'

'Yes, that's true,' Avril admitted. 'I won't come again, then, until I've finished making your film.'

'That'll be best, I'll have a quiet mind then about your safety. I guess it was a good thing that you went to Scotland Yard day before yesterday. The fact that you told your story before Drefus set the ball rolling about the fire'll help me a whole heap.'

'Will they let me have the cameras? They are still in your room at the Dorchester, aren't they?'

'Yes, Drefus has got a letter I signed yesterday about that, they are to deliver them to his order. There's another thing—about the "Z" Projector.'

'Yes—what is it?'

'Well, I've been thinking about that a lot. Just supposin' anything goes wrong, that'll fall in to my estate as things are, an' I don't want that. I want you to have it.'

'Oh, Nelson—my dear—don't let's think about such awful things.'

He smiled ruefully. 'I guess we got to, besides, if you can get out the film, exhibit it, I mean, in time, I can't tackle the business of floating the projector on the market from behind the bars here—but you can. Drefus'll help you. Then you can pay off Issey Vandelstein for me, an' we'll have that rotten Combine beaten yet.'

'I see. Well, if you wish me to hold it in trust for you, I will.'

'No, I'm making it over to you absolutely. If the film breaks down, and Vandelstein closes up on me, you'll still have that as the big card. It'll save Hatfield for you, because the Combine won't be able to compete. They can cut their prices to blazes, but your films will be a special thing, standing alone, you'll be in a similar position to Star Artists, and if need be you can take theatres to exhibit, run your own publicity end too. You won't be able to break them, but it'll be stalemate, and after a time they'll leave you to play on your own.'

Avril felt the tears starting to her eyes again, but she checked them with an effort, and said softly: 'Oh, Nelson, you have been marvellous to think out all this in prison. You shouldn't have worried to think of me.'

'What else should I think of?' he said abruptly. 'Let's get

busy or they'll be turning you out. Have you got the papers there, Drefus?'

The lawyer produced a deed from his bag. It was a short agreement in which all rights, patents, and plans—for the manufacture, use, or sale of the 'Z' Projector were made over to Avril Bamborough. He read it through, it was then taken round to Nelson's side of the barrier, where it was duly signed and witnessed.

The warder, who had remained seated throughout the interview, and apparently deaf and dumb, now rose to his feet.

'I'm afraid your time's up, miss.'

Nelson smiled a farewell. 'So long, my dear, don't worry too much about me. And good luck with the film.'

Avril was really crying now, she could not keep her tears back any longer and they rolled silently down her cheeks as she pressed her face to the wire.

'Nelson,' she whispered, 'you know what I said the other night—I mean about Vitelma?'

'Sure—I remember.'

'Well, whatever she says—I'll do just as you wish—and—and—I'll wait for you till you come out.'

He shook his head slowly, but the worn look seemed to drop from his face. 'Vitelma'll set me free anyhow now,' he said. 'You can bet on that, but I guess I wouldn't ask you to wait, I'll be an old man before I'm through with this. You'll just remain my most precious memory.'

Mr. Drefus led her weeping from the cell. In his car he tried to comfort her as he ran her back to London. After a little she stopped crying, but her face took on a set, hard look. She felt that work, relentless, determined work was the only thing left for her now. Long hours of unremitting labour, that Nelson's film might be done in time.

At her flat she forced herself to eat some sandwiches and swallow a glass of champagne, then directly her bags were packed she set off for Hatfield.

Outside the Studio gates stood a newsvendor selling evening papers. He carried a placard that caught her eye. It read:

Lord Gavin Fortescue's tight mouth creased into a satisfied smile as he studied a copy of that same paper, in his room at Claridge's. He was well pleased with the result of the second long cable which he had despatched to his agent for transmission to Vitelma, when he had received news of Nelson Druce's voluntary surrender two nights before.

20

Vitelma Loveday takes a Hand

Hinckman's cigar had gone out, but he did not re-light it or take another. He chewed and gnawed at the end he held between his teeth while he strode restlessly up and down.

Lord Gavin sat hunched in his arm-chair, his small fingers playing a light tattoo upon the table at his side.

'You seem worried, my friend,' he said softly.

Hinckman came to a sudden halt, and swinging round faced the little man. 'Waal!' he snapped, 'I guess you wouldn't be sitting so pretty if you had a charge of complicity in attempted murder up against you. We're in England, too, remember— they treat these things different to what we do back home— the fools don't understand who I am.'

Lord Gavin shrugged his frail shoulders. 'My dear man, surely you are not worried about that, you know quite well that they will never be able to bring home this charge against you. It is only an excuse for postponing Druce's deportation.'

'I know, I know, but take a look at the news sheets. It's not the English ones I mind, it's those rags in the States. They're making a regular hoo-ha 'bout the Combine. Talk of invoking the anti-trust laws an' hell knows what. That don't suit our book at all.'

'Your fears are quite unfounded, Hinckman. You may rest assured that my legal advisers went very carefully into the question of the anti-trust laws before I sailed for the States, and they are not apt to make mistakes.'

'Maybe, but what about me—these guys are slinging all the mud they know. That don't do no good to a man in my position. They're saying I'm every sort of Bolshevik unhung. I've cabled my attorneys to sue one sheet for libel.'

'Then you have acted very unwisely. You will call more attention to those very matters which you wish to keep quiet. This sort of thing is unpleasant for you at the moment, of course. It is a clever move on the part of Drefus & Drefus to stir the Press up in order to get public sympathy for young Druce, but it will blow over, particularly when he is released.'

'You figure the girl will play?'

'Certainly she will—providing Vitelma Loveday is properly coached. How did she take it when you talked the matter over with her last night?'

'So, so. I met her off the boat-train and dined her at the Carlton, but she's that thick-headed I could have hit her, that's why I figured it 'ud be best for you to put her wise today.'

'Have you any further news from Hatfield?'

'Nope. I guess the kid's pretty near through with her film, but there's nothing fresh.'

'Is there no possible means of wrecking it?'

'Not a hope, she's got every sort of protection short of the military—my birds can't get near the place.'

'Well, after all what does it matter if she does make her film as long as we secure the projector?'

'That's so—all the same, I wish Druce had never invented the darned thing. You can bet it's rumours 'bout that keeps Issey sitting on the fence. If he wasn't sitting tight to hear what comes of the "Z" he'd have been in our pocket a month back, an' the Combine floated by this time.'

'My dear Hinckman, what you say is perfectly true, but the fact remains that Druce did invent this thing, and it is actually in operation. It is vitally necessary therefore that we should obtain possession of the patent. Let us be thankful that we ascertained through the young man in Drefus's office that he had made it over to the girl. At least we know where we are, and with this woman Loveday's help I am certain we shall get it. Once we have that our battle is won.'

'Sure—an' I'll say it was a mighty fine idea of yours to get the Loveday over. The Bamborough kid would never have trusted me in the deal.'

The house telephone at Lord Gavin's side tinkled. He picked it up quickly. 'Yes, yes, certainly—show her up at once.' He replaced the receiver. 'That is Miss Loveday,' he added to Hinckman.

'O.K., you'd best do most of the talking, I said my piece last night.'

Lord Gavin nodded. 'I think I shall be able to persuade her of her own best interests,' he said softly.

A minute afterwards a page showed Vitelma into Lord Gavin's room. The voyage had done her good, and she was looking if possible more lovely than ever.

'Say, kid, you're lookin' fine,' Hinckman greeted her. 'Meet Lord Gavin Fortescue.'

Vitelma put out her slender hand and smiled her well-advertised smile, although for the moment she was a little taken aback by the strange ill-proportioned figure of Lord Gavin. His body seemed so tiny compared to his massive head, but as his pale eyes bored into Vitelma's she felt at once the force of his personality.

He bowed her to a chair and began at once. 'Miss Loveday, I cannot say how deeply I feel for you in your terrible situation, it is most gallant of you to have come all the way to England in the hope of getting your fiancé released.'

'Sure,' said Vitelma. 'It's just awful, an' I haven't figured yet just what I can do. It was friends in Hollywood put me up to makin' that statement to the Press. I reckon they thought it 'ud be good publicity.'

'Of course.' Lord Gavin smiled—he knew perfectly well who had advised her, they had acted on his instructions. 'I feel sure, however,' he went on smoothly, 'that now you are here, you would wish to do everything in your power.'

'I'll say I do. Isn't he my fiancé?'

'Certainly, and we wish to help you. Now on the night of the crime, I understand that you visited Druce's home, but you did not find him there?'

'That's so.'

'But when you were a few hundred yards down the road on your way back to Hollywood, you recognised his car, and you stopped your own.'

'Oh, no. I didn't do that.'

'No, of that I am aware. In actual fact you drove out to a road house about twenty miles distant and spent the evening dancing.'

Vitelma's blue eyes opened wide. 'Now how in the world would you know that?'

Lord Gavin smiled. 'No matter. It happens that I do know. Now let us go back a little. Had you met Nelson Druce on the road what would you have done?'

'How can I say? Maybe we'd have spent the evening at the Druce home. Maybe I'd have taken him dancing.'

'Exactly. Now, nobody could blame a woman for telling a few untruths in order to save her lover's life. I suggest, therefore, that you should tell the police that you met Druce and went with him to this road house. That will provide him with an alibi.'

'Well, I'm certainly willing to say that—but will they believe me? What about the folks at the road house an' the fellow I was dancing with most of all night?'

'That,' said Lord Gavin slowly, 'is where we can assist you. Mr. Hinckman has been in communication with the young man you refer to—he is willing to swear that he danced with you once or twice, but that Nelson Druce brought you there and took you away again, and that Druce was with you most of the evening. We have also, what I believe you term "squared"

199

the hall-porter and two of the waiters. The evidence of these people, in support of your own, should prove conclusive.'

'You don't say! Well, that's fine. I guess you're a little won-der,' Vitelma added archly.

Lord Gavin winced, but he went on in his quiet, musical voice: 'There is, however, one little favour which we must ask in return for our assistance, and of course you are quite correct in assuming that your word would not be accepted alone.'

Vitelma eyed him narrowly, then she laughed. 'Say—I thought there was a catch in it somewhere.'

'There is, and one which concerns you vitally. You are aware, I think, that Nelson Druce has formed an attachment to an-other woman while he has been in England?'

'I certainly am. That sly cat of a Bamborough girl has been hitting it up with Nelson. I had a hunch that she was a bit gooey about him back in Hollywood.'

'Yes. Now I wonder if you are aware how serious this attachment is?'

'What exactly do you mean?'

'You know about Nelson Druce's invention, the "Z" Pro-jector?'

'Sure. I know about that.'

'Well—Nelson Druce is so deeply interested in Miss Bam-borough that he has made over the whole of the patents for the invention to her absolutely.'

'Well, now! Can you beat that?'

'You're not goin' to let her get away with that, are you, kid?' Hinckman put in.

Vitelma's beautiful face took on an ugly look. 'I certainly am not,' she snapped.

'That's the stuff,' Hinckman applauded.

Lord Gavin nodded. 'To do so would be quite absurd,' he said mildly. 'I would suggest therefore that you should see Miss Bamborough and put the position to her. Tell her that you are able and willing to save your fiancé, and that you will do so, but she must make over the rights of the "Z" Projector to you.'

Vitelma looked puzzled. 'I don't get that,' she said, with a shake of her golden head. 'Avril Bamborough's gotten this thing off Nelson an' it's worth good money, I guess—why would she be fool enough to hand over? Nelson's my fiancé, not hers.'

'That is true, but I happen to have had some experience of women of Miss Bamborough's type, and I have reason to suppose that she is very attached to Nelson Druce. To save him she would be willing to do many things.'

'I guess you're all wrong—she'd be an awful mutt if she did.'

'Possibly,' Lord Gavin smiled, 'but I think she will, and I trust you will accept my opinion upon this interesting point in female psychology.'

'I don't take much stock in sy-cology,' Vitelma smiled, 'but it don't put me in too good a light. Am I to stand there an' say—I won't help Nelson out unless she hands over?'

'That is the attitude which you must adopt, not a very pleasant one, I fear, but necessary, and if you like I will provide you with a suitable excuse for the position which you are going to take up. Tell her that you are afraid Nelson might throw you over and marry her, since she possesses his invention. You wish to hold it yourself as security for his good faith.'

'Sure,' drawled Vitelma, 'that's an idea, but just supposing he's bats about her and throws me down—marries her in any case, projector or no—where do I get off then?'

'Clever kid,' Hinckman nodded, 'but don't you worry, that's where I join the party. You just do as we say—land us the "Z" Projector, an' if Nelson Druce don't marry yer, I'll sign you for a first class star contract with Trans-Continental Electric— or the Combine, as I figure it'll be then.'

Vitelma turned to him quickly. 'Land *you* the projector. I guess this is the first we've heard of that.'

Lord Gavin smiled at her. 'I am sure you will realise, Miss Loveday, that we do not ask anything unfair. This is the small favour which I mentioned in the first place. You will sign an undertaking now to turn the "Z" Projector over to us, should it at any time come into you possession.'

'What for should I do that?'

'We have to meet our expenses, Miss Loveday. The—er— fellow with whom you danced upon the night of the murder requires a very considerable sum. The hall-porter and the waiters also have to be provided for, you could hardly expect us to meet these obligations out of our own pockets. The "Z" Projector is our price.'

'And say I turn you down?'

'It's you who'll be the mutt if you do,' Hinckman spoke sharply. 'What sort of life d'you figure to have—Nelson Druce don't cut no ice as a husband behind the bars—an' you're goin' to let the other girl get away with his invention. You'll be back in Detroit sweating yer wits how to fix some old man to do the marriage stuff. You can't do a thing without us, an' that's flat. Be sensible an' do as you're told. If you do—you'll get Nelson as a free man an' I guess he's got a pretty fat wad somewhere. Or at worst you get a slap-up contract with me.'

'There's another little point that we might mention,' Lord Gavin added. 'If we assist you in clearing Druce, the police will at once assume that his confession was false and only made with a view to shielding Miss Bamborough. She will be re-arrested, and extradition will follow. She will eventually get off, of course, upon the plea of self-defence, but she will first have to face several very unpleasant months in an American prison. May I suggest that you would regard that as a not un-suitable punishment for a woman who has endeavoured to take you fiancé from you?'

'That goes with me,' said Vitelma slowly. 'I guess I'll do it—but won't she see that part about being rearrested herself? She'd be stark crazy to agree.'

'Sometimes,' Lord Gavin murmured, 'people do become crazy, and I am rather banking on the belief that Miss Bamborough is suffering from this type of madness now. I think you will find that she will agree.'

'An' I get Nelson as a free man, or the contract.' Vitelma stood up. 'Well, that's O.K. by me.'

'I am glad that you are so sensible, Miss Loveday.' Lord Gavin made a little bow as he rose from his chair. 'This is the agreement regarding the projector, and this—a document em-bodying our promise to you about your contract in the event of Nelson Druce refusing to keep his word with you. It becomes operative only when the patents are handed over to us, of course. If you will sign the first, Hinckman will sign the second.' He handed her a pen.

Vitelma scrawled her name in large round letters, placed the other paper which Hinckman had given to her in her bag, and turned to Lord Gavin. 'When'll I have my little talk with Avril Bamborough?'

'As soon as it can be arranged. Mr. Hinckman proposes to lend you his cottage down in Surrey for the interview. You will not, of course, mention to her that we are in any way interested.'

'For why?' asked Vitelma suspiciously.

'I don't think we need to go into that. It is to your interest in every way to bring this business to a satisfactory conclusion. If you were to mention Mr. Hinckman's name you might prejudice your chances very seriously; please accept my assurance of that. You may be certain that Miss Bamborough will prove quite willing to enter into arrangements with Nelson Druces's fiancée that she would not agree to with anybody else. You have the right to make proposals to her which she would not listen to from any other source—therefore it is important that she should believe you to speak for yourself alone.'

'Yes, I suppose that's so, but why can't we meet in Town?'

'This is an important interview, Miss Loveday. It would be best if you met in some place where there is no possibility of your being disturbed. You can say that you have taken this cottage for your stay in England in order to avoid the Press.'

'O.K. When's it to be?'

'That we are about to arrange.' Lord Gavin picked up the telephone. He asked for Ronnie's room, and spoke to his aide-de-camp. A moment or two later Ronnie joined them.

'Hello, chaps.' He looked round. 'Hullo, Miss Loveday. I see from the papers you're going to get poor old Nelson off.'

She smiled. 'I certainly hope so, Mr. Sheringham.'

'Listen,' said Lord Gavin. 'I wish you to telephone to Avril Bamborough, she is certain to be at Hatfield. You will say that Miss Loveday arrived in England last night, that you have seen her today, and that she is very anxious to meet Miss Bamborough to discuss methods of procuring Nelson Druce's release. You will add that Miss Loveday has taken a quiet cottage down in Surrey—in order to avoid as far as possible the attentions of the Press. Ask if Miss Bamborough could see Miss Loveday at her cottage this evening and offer to run her over yourself in your car. Impress upon her that the matter is urgent and on no account mention that Miss Loveday is here with Hinckman and myself.'

Ronnie obediently put through a call to Hatfield, and a few moments later he was speaking to Avril. In his cheerful, airy way he said or implied all that Lord Gavin had told him to say. He listened for a moment in silence, evidently Avril was making up her mind at the other end of the line, then he quickly clapped his hand over the transmitter.

'She's scared,' he said. 'There won't be any funny business, will there—this is a fair deal, eh?'

Lord Gavin nodded quickly.

Ronnie nodded, too, and laughed into the transmitter. 'What nonsense—of course not. I'll take you there and bring you back myself. . . . Rather! I shall be there all the time. . . . No, I don't know what her scheme is but she wants your help. . . . Splendid. I'll come for you then at about six o'clock.'

He put down the telephone. 'Well, that's fixed up.'

'Thank you, my dear boy. Now I want one word with Hinckman on another matter, so perhaps you would take Miss Loveday down to the lounge for a cocktail.' Lord Gavin turned to Vitelma. 'You will excuse me, I hope, not offering you something here. I shall not detain Mr. Hinckman for more than a few moments and then he will take you down to Cutmill in his car. May I wish you the best of good fortune in your interview?'

'That's real kind of you, Lord Fortescue.' Vitelma extended her slim hand once more. She smiled at Hinckman. 'See-yer-later, big boy,' then she left the room with Ronnie.

Hinckman lit a fresh cigar. 'You certainly got her set the way you wanted.'

'Yes.' Lord Gavin nodded his massive head. 'It now remains

with you. Keep the Loveday woman up to it on your way down, and impress upon her how necessary it is for her to appear to be acting entirely on her own. The Bamborough girl would never give up that patent if she had any idea that it was coming to us.'

'Sure. I'll see to that, and tonight's the night all right; once we get that projector—I guess we're through.'

'Yes.' Lord Gavin's pale eyes glittered. 'We shall have achieved the greatest victory that modern commerce has ever known.'

'There's only one snag. . . . Just supposin' the Bamborough kid does refuse to play?'

Lord Gavin's pale eyes held Hinckman's with a firm glance. He tapped the table for a moment with his small pudgy fingers and the sinister note crept into his soft voice as he replied: 'This is your opportunity—if she refuses you must see that she never returns from the cottage at Cutmill.'

21

The Cottage on the Common

At a little after eight o'clock that evening Ronnie was driving Avril through the by-roads that lie between Guildford and Cut-mill. The car was one which he had purchased recently from a friend of his who was a dealer. Ronnie, in funds, or in prospect of funds, was never without a car. He drove with apparent recklessness, but actually he had an extraordinarily sure control of his wheel. He loved speed in any form and his nerve was quite perfect.

They had had sandwiches and sherry in Guildford, since it was impossible to say how long the meeting would last; Avril hoped that it might be brief. She rated herself for a fool, but nevertheless she could not throw off a miserable and unjustified feeling of guilt at the prospect of meeting Nelson's fiancée. She wondered if Vitelma had ever received Nelson's letter asking for his freedom. It might be cowardly, but she could not help hoping that Vitelma had not, perhaps it was still somewhere out upon the Atlantic chasing her back to England. It would be hateful and so incredibly degrading if the beautiful blonde accused her of alienating Nelson's affections. She was determined to leave again at once if any signs of a squabble on those lines arose. In fact, she would never have agreed to meet Vitelma had it not been for that bold announcement in the papers a fortnight before, when it was stated that the film star was definitely coming to England to get her fiancée off.

Avril had puzzled again and again as to how Vitelma proposed to set about it. She herself knew that Nelson had shot Angelo Donelli, beyond a shadow of doubt. How, then, could the other girl prove his innocence? And now tonight, she was wondering what possible part she was to be asked to play—the question proved beyond her, but directly Ronnie had spoken to her on the telephome she had decided that it was up to her to meet Vitelma and hear what she had to say. No possible chance must be neglected that might lead to Nelson's release.

Avril had taken off her hat and let the cool breeze blow through her hair. Her cheeks were pale and there were dark lines under her eyes from sleeplessness, and overwork. The film was done at last, thank goodness, and she had no doubt whatever of its ultimate success.

Titchcock had thrown himself into the thing with even more than his accustomed vigour, and the cast had supported her nobly. Again and again she had had shots repeated when they were nearly good enough, but not quite perfect. It was by far the best work that she had ever done, despite the fact that she had worked at fever-pitch and under a frightful nervous strain during its making. It was now in the hands of the continuity men and finishers. Arrangements had been made for the Première to take place at the Rivoli three nights hence. That would be on the very night before Vandelstein's money became due. The margin of time would be terribly narrow, but it had been utterly impossible to get the film finished under the fortnight, and once the public had seen the projector at work, it was hoped that they might be able to raise a loan upon it in the City on the morning after the Première. Invitations were to be issued to the most distinguished people in London society, and it was believed that Royalty would be present. The first announcement of this great new triumph in the film world was appearing in the papers that night.

The small car hurtled round corners, and up and down the little slopes in the narrow, winding lanes. It was not the same road that Avril and Nelson had taken on the night of the fire, but so near it that had Avril known the same clumps of pines upon the little moorland knolls could be seen from both.

They ran swiftly down a short hill, across a dip where in the day-time there was visible on each side a little stream curving and eddying between the willows, veered to the right and up the opposite slope, where the headlights flashed for a moment upon a red post-box nailed to a telegraph pole, then on the top of the rise Ronnie brought the car to a halt.

'Is that it?' Avril looked doubtfully at a labourer's cottage, abutting on the road to her right.

Ronnie laughed as he backed the car. 'Lord, no! It's a bit bigger than that, and about three hundred yards down the track.' He drove the car onto the grass as he spoke. Open common lay upon the left, and after they had passed the garden of the cottage near the road, to the right as well. Avril could see the heath on either side, with the fronds of the high bracken glowing in the headlights, and dark patches of gorse here and there. Wheelmarks on the grassy track showed plainly that other cars had passed that way.

'This can't be much fun in winter,' Avril remarked, as they bumped along.

'No, a car would soon get stuck—but it's a summer place, that's all; very quiet and peaceful, isn't it?' The car came to a jerky halt.

Avril could see the cottage now, it lay upon their right, low and dark, with lights only in the room at the far end. The garden sloped towards the alder woods, through which must run the stream that they had passed upon the road, to the left the open moorland continued and beyond the cottage the tree-trunks of a silver birch wood were visible in the summer twilight.

Ronnie sounded his horn twice, and then got out. 'I'd better go first,' he said, 'I know the way.'

He unlatched the wicket gate and led her down a tiled path that ran along the side of the building. It was then that Avril saw it to be three cottages knocked into one. At the corner he turned and entered a small loggia. It looked towards the sloping garden, there were two terraces and a little lawn, white steps gleamed in the light from the window, leading down to the brook. In the still evening air the gurgling of the waters came plainly to the ear.

Ronnie pushed the house-door that led into the sheltered loggia. 'Anybody at home?' he called.

'Come right in.' It was Vitelma's voice. Avril unconsciously squared her shoulders as she followed Ronnie into the narrow hall and down a short passage to the right.

They entered a pleasant lofty room, with wide windows looking out onto the woods. There was a large open fire-place on the left of the door, and the old beams above it had been allowed to remain. They supported the upper rooms which jutted out over the fire-place, having something of the effect of an enclosed minstrels' gallery—but Avril was not looking at the room, she was studying Vitelma.

The fair girl stood up. 'It's nice of you to come, Miss Bamborough. Come right in and sit down.' She showed no animosity.

'Thank you,' Avril smiled. 'Your message came as a surprise, but I shall be only too pleased to help you in any way I can about Nelson.' Mentally, she gave a little sigh of relief, his name had been mentioned, at least that fence was over.

'That's nice of you, I felt sure I could count of your assistance. Seen much of Nelson lately?'

'I have not seen him during the last fortnight.'

'Oh, before they put him behind the bars, I mean.'

'Once or twice only—since I returned to England.'

'Is that so? . . . You sure are some fast worker.'

Avril flushed. 'I don't know what you mean,' she said quickly.

'I'll say you know all right—but let's not go into that now; keep the party clean, as we say in the States.'

'I should much prefer to do so.'

'I guess you would. Well, then, this is what I figure to do. Nelson shot that little wop all right and we both know it. If I say he was with me all evening—how's that go with you?'

'Yes, if you can prove it. I'm afraid they will not accept your word alone.'

'Of course they won't. I'm wise to that, but I bin fixin' things, squared an old boy friend, the hall-porter, and two waiters at a road house twenty miles outside Hollywood to say Nelson was there dancing with me all night. I guess with their backing, my story ought to get over.'

'Yes,' said Avril, a sudden light of hope showing in her eyes. 'Yes, if you can count on them I really think there is a chance.'

'Well, what d'you say?'

'What do I say?—I think it's splendid, and most awfully clever of you.'

'But are you game to play up?'

'Certainly I am.'

'Do you realise just what it means, Miss Bamborough? They'll sure pick on you again, it'll be terrible unpleasant, and I guess your only line'll be to say you gave Angelo his in self-defence.'

'Yes—I realise that.'

'An' you'll go through with it?'

'Yes.'

An unwilling admiration showed in Vitelma's eyes. 'Well, I'll sure hand it to you for guts,' she said. 'Seems to me you must be mighty sweet on him.'

'I think we might leave that out,' said Avril coldly.

'I'm willin'. I guess I can look after Nelson when I'm with him, even if there are other dames about.'

Avril had a very different opinion as far as Nelson and herself were concerned, but she thought it best to allow Miss Loveday to continue in her armour of conceit.

'Now there's another thing,' Vitelma went on. 'Jus' a littl' matter of a present Nelson made to you—when you got him all het up.'

'I'm afraid I don't understand, he has never made me a present in his life, except for the things he gave me when he shipped me off to England.'

Vitelma nodded. 'So that's how he got away with it, was it? He's got brains all right, has Nelson, but I suppose you don't figure that the sole rights on the "Z" Projector is any sort of gift?'

Avril sat forward suddenly. 'What do you mean? The "Z" Projector has nothing to do with this.'

'You're not denying by any chance that he did pass it over, are you?'

'No. I am holding it at his wish.'

'That's O.K. then. But as Nelson's fiancée, I guess I'm the proper person to keep my fist on any little thing like that, that's knocking round, while he's behind the bars.'

'That might be so in an ordinary case,' Avril agreed, 'but not in this. Nelson made over to me the rights of the "Z" Projector for a specific purpose connected with his business. I consider myself entirely as his trustee—that is all.'

'Then you're not prepared to hand over?'

'No. I'm sorry but I can't. Of course, at any time Nelson wishes to have these patents back I am quite willing to give them to him, or, for that matter, I will agree to hand them over to anybody else if it is on his instructions, but I should need to receive those instructions from him by word of mouth. No written document would satisfy me.'

'Now wait a minute, Miss Bamborough, what's going to happen when Nelson comes out?'

'I'm sure I don't know,' Avril parried a little faintly.

Vitelma leaned forward, looking straight into her face. 'D'you think he's going to marry you?'

'I don't know,' repeated Avril in an even lower voice.

'No, but I guess you got your own idea. Now, say he throws me down—though why he should God knows, Nelson Druce isn't all that wonderful—but say he does—what happens then?'

'I don't know,' Avril repeated once more.

'You don't know, kiddo, well, I'll tell you—Vitelma Loveday has to get back to work, an' that's all about it. But if Vitelma's got the "Z" Projector Nelson'll get over his fit of the bats and come through the marriage lines—d'you get me?'

'Yes, I do.' Avril spoke quickly. 'You want to force him to marry you whether he wishes to or not. Now look here, I'll be frank with you, I love him, I make no excuses for that, none whatever, but I do and I'm willing to pass several months in an American prison in order to save him. I'm doing more, all my life I shall be branded as a woman who killed a man, whatever the excuse may be—while all you're doing is a little mild lying in a witness box. Well, then, let's start fair. God knows you're attractive enough, you ought to be able to keep a man, and you'll have the enormous advantage of being with him all the time I'm in prison—let him make up his own mind, you'll be with him and I shan't, but I don't care; let him choose for himself when I come out.'

'Nothing doin'.' Vitelma shook her head firmly.

'You're afraid,' Avril taunted her. 'You're afraid—you don't love him, you don't care a straw for him, you're after his money and position, and he doesn't love you, that's why you're frightened . . . you know that you can't hold him.'

Vitelma kept her temper remarkably well in the circumstances. She only laughed and nodded her golden head. 'Well, baby, you have got it badly, and that's a fact. Nothin' doin', my dear. Nothin' doin' at all, you're just going to be a good kid and hand over that "Z" Projector.'

'I'm sorry, that is quite impossible, unless it is Nelson's own wish.'

'Nelson's wish! Now, kid, don't try an' pull that stuff—you sure want to keep it for yourself. What good 'ud the projector be to Nelson if he gets fifteen years?'

Avril's face went a shade paler. 'You—you can't mean that

211

you're going to let the question of the projector interfere with your saving him.'

'I certainly do.'

'What—having it in your power to procure his release, you'd deliberately sit still and let him be sentenced because I won't hand over this miserable invention?'

'That's so.' Vitelma looked away quickly, she did not like this particular part of her rôle one little bit.

'It's impossible,' gasped Avril. 'I never did believe you loved him, never—but this is beyond belief. I could understand if you really minded perjuring yourself, but it's not that—you're bargaining, haggling, trying to make capital out of your fiancé's misfortune.'

'Maybe,' Vitelma answered doggedly. 'I got to look after myself, ain't I? You seem pretty certain you've taken him away from me—all right, why should you have it all your own way? You let up in the "Z", and we'll see who gets Nelson later.'

'But don't you understand that I can't. It isn't mine.'

'Now that's a lie.'

'It's in my name, but I couldn't possibly make it over to you without Nelson's consent.'

'It's bein' in your name's what matters. See here.' Vitelma drew a paper from her bag. 'I've had a letter all typed out ready; you just be sensible and sign on the dotted line.'

Avril's mind was in a turmoil. One thing at least stood out clearly. She need have no further scruples about having come between Nelson and Vitelma. The girl simply did not care a straw for him, she was prepared to sell him for what she could get. It was horrible, but as Avril thought about it she realised that Vitelma was only behaving in a way which might be expected of her and taking steps to protect herself. Her life had been one long struggle to stardom from the gutters of Detroit. When she saw her rich lover slipping through her fingers, it was natural that she should try every means to save something from the wreck. Avril would have been only too willing to sign away the 'Z' Projector if she could save Nelson, but she knew how bitterly he would feel about it, she must allow him to choose for himself. The thing was not hers to give away.

'No,' she said. 'It's quite out of the question—but if there is any other way. It seems that this has turned into a business discussion now. If it is a question of securing your future in the event of Nelson not marrying you, I am willing to do anything I can. I am not rich in the American sense, but I could settle quite a decent sum on you.'

Vitelma shook her head. 'Nothin' doin', kiddo, it's the "Z" I want.'

Avril rose to her feet. 'Well, I'm sorry. The only thing I can suggest is that I should see Nelson tomorrow. If he's willing, I'll do it, of course.'

'That ain't no good. You know Nelson, he's pig-headed as hell. I guess he'd rather go behind the bars than do what he don't want. It's up to you to save him in spite of himself, that's how I see it.'

Avril knew just how right Vitelma was. She felt instinctively that Vitelma would hold the possession of the projector over him as a threat. If he refused to marry her, she would sell it to the Combine. Nelson would see that himself, and he would never agree. 'No,' she said. 'No—I can't possibly do it.'

'Is that so?' came a man's sharp voice. One of the three tiny doors in the minstrels' gallery above their heads had been thrown open, and looking up with a start Avril saw Hinckman frowning down upon her.

'Ronnie, quick!' She rushed for the door into the passage just below the place where Hinckman was crouching, realising with a sudden terror that she had been trapped.

The door opened at her touch, but on the other side stood a man who quietly raised an automatic to the level of her chest. She could not see his face, he wore a leather helmet and motor goggles. With his free hand he roughly pushed her back.

'Take me away,' she cried to Ronnie. 'Take me away—you promised.'

Ronnie was looking uncomfortable. He had sat silent, quietly smoking, his feet upon a chair, throughout her interview with Vitelma. He stood up slowly now, running his hand through his curly hair. 'Look here, Avril,' he said. 'You've no

213

need to worry—nobody's going to hurt you, but why don't you sign this wretched thing? Really it would be best for everybody, you know.'

'I won't, I won't,' Avril protested fiercely.

Hinckman's heavy tread could be heard coming down an unseen staircase from the room above. He pushed past the man in the passage and joined them. The man came in, still carrying his automatic. He closed the door behind him and leant against it.

'Now see here,' said Hinckman sharply. 'I guess you've caused us too much trouble by half, an' I'm through with you. You'll sign that paper right now, and no monkeying.'

Avril shook her head wildly. 'I won't sign, I refuse.' She turned fiercely on Vitelma. 'You were lying—the whole thing was a plant. You didn't want this thing to protect yourself with Nelson, you were going to turn it over right away to his enemies; the very thought of you makes me sick. How could any woman be so vile.'

Hinckman gripped her by the wrist and forced her down into a chair by the table. 'Cut out the talk—and sign, or it'll be the worse for you.'

She struggled wildly to free her arm. 'I won't,' she screamed. 'I won't—let go, you're hurting!'

He gave her wrist a sharp twist, the pain was agonising.

'Oh!' she screamed. 'Help! Ronnie, you can't let him do this.'

Ronnie's face had gone a shade paler under the brown tan that he still retained from his stay in Hollywood. He stood with his back to the fireplace, his hands in his pockets.

'Look here,' he stared at Hinckman, 'I've had enough of this. It was understood that there should be no funny business. She signs of her own free will or I take her back to Hatfield.'

'Sez you,' growled Hinckman.

'Says me,' Ronnie's voice had become suddenly sharp.

'An' who the thunderin' hell are you, anyhow? I've got this damned cutie where I want her now, an' she don't leave this house before she's signed. Get that?' Hinckman's face had turned deep red, his eyes were half closed, and his

214

chin jutted forward. Suddenly it seemed as though his well-tailored clothes became ill-fitting on his body. He was no longer the millionaire business man, but the primitive, dangerous half-breed of the Western mining camp where force was law and death the portion of the vanquished.

Ronnie's blue eyes had gone hard and glittering. 'Let her go—d'you hear, and quick about it.' His voice had all the quiet authority that he had inherited from his long line of ancestors. . . . Men who had landed with the hardy Normans and held commands at Cressy, Agincourt, Poitiers.

'Lupus.' Hinckman's sharp order rang out to the man at the door. 'Get that guy!'

But Ronnie was too quick. His brown hand closed upon a whisky bottle, and with all the strength of his broad shoulders he brought it crashing down on the man's head. The fellow dropped where he stood, his automatic clattering to the floor. Then Ronnie went for Hinckman with the ugliest weapon in the world, the jagged end of the broken bottle, the neck still clutched tightly in his hand.

Hinckman dropped Avril's wrist and leaped to the other side of the table. Vitelma screamed. Avril was only just in time to save the lamp. If it had gone over the whole place would have been on fire in a few seconds. She picked it up for safety, holding it to light the combatants in their grim fight.

The two men glared at each other across the table, both crouched ready to spring. Ronnie made a sudden dash, lunging at Hinckman's face with the jagged bottle. Hinckman dodged, slipping to the other side of the table again. Vitelma stood there screaming, her hands above her head. Hinckman pushed her roughly and she fell, gasping for breath, upon a small settee.

Suddenly Hinckman stepped backwards towards the door, he slipped in the blood that was pouring from his gunman's head, fell to his knees, but his hand found the automatic. Ronnie rushed in upon him Hinckman took the jagged bottle upon his upraised arm; he gave a sharp cry of pain as the glass cut into his flesh. Then came the crash of shots. He fired

215

twice, point-blank, into Ronnie's body. With a choking gasp Ronnie crashed forward in a heap.

Avril was horror struck—there was nothing she could do to help him, she must try to save herself, but she was embarrassed with the lamp. She set it down with trembling hands and dashed for the big window, but Hinckman was on his feet. Just as she reached the sill his fingers closed upon her hair. As he jerked her backwards she screamed with pain. Struggling wildly he dragged her across the room, over the two bodies, and out into the passage. Then he unlocked a door. In the faint light she saw some cellar steps, next second he had flung her down them, and turned the key quickly in the lock.

22

The Horror of the Marsh

To Avril, it seemed a long time that she lay dazed and stupified, where she had fallen on the stone floor of the cellar.

She was brusied and shaken, her head was aching atrociously, her clothes were torn, and her hair hung in disorder about her face.

Slowly the full horror of the situation began to penetrate her mind. She had been trapped into coming to the cottage for this meeting with Vitelma. Ronnie could not have known, of course, at least he must have realised that Hinckman would be there, but not that he would use force. Now Ronnie was dead or dying, only a miracle could have saved him from those bullets fired at close range straight into his body, so she was left powerless in Hinckman's clutches.

He would come back presently, she supposed, and try to force her into signing that agreement. He might torture her. He seemed quite capable of it, her wrist ached dully where he had twisted it, and every time she moved, a sharp pain ran up her arm.

She picked herself up and sat down on the cellar steps, wondering vaguely if there were any means of escape. The place was pitch-dark, there was not even a ray of light under the cellar door.

After a little rest she decided to explore, and standing up, moved slowly forward with her hand upon the wall. She had only gone a few steps when she stumbled and nearly fell over some knobby thing that sounded, as it moved, like a lump of coal. She felt about in the region of her feet and soon decided that it must be the coal cellar in which she was imprisoned. That gave her some little hope, there must be some opening in the roof through which the coal was shot in. If she could find it and it was not too high up out of her reach, she stood some chance of getting out. She began to climb up the stack of coal, its apex should surely be near the place where it had been shot in. The coal slithered and tumbled beneath her feet, making a terrific din in the small confined space. She feared every moment that Hinckman must hear it in the room above, but there was no sound from overhead.

Scrambling breathlessly to the top of the pile, she bumped her head. A little thrill of hope ran through her. The roof must be immediately above, in fact, she could not stand upright. She felt about but could discover nothing except joists and beams, the cracks between them she assumed to be the joining of the floor-boards. Presently she found a crack that ran crossways to the others, and then her fingers fumbled on a rusty hinge. There was a trap-door, then, if only she could open it?

She felt about again and found another hinge, then the crack along the other end and a bolt holding the trap firmly shut. She wriggled back the bolt and pressed upwards with her hands. The trap-door gave very slightly, enough to show a pale ray of light for a moment and let in a breath of cold, damp air—it must open into the garden.

She pressed again, but as she did so the heap of coal gave beneath her feet and she nearly caught her fingers. The door seemed to be a terrific weight. She struggled manfully, but every time she got it a few inches open, the lumps of coal slid from under her and she found that she was losing height. Then she had an idea. She hunted round for a small, flat piece of coal and next time she got the trap open, she wedged it so that it could not shut again. After that things improved, it gave her a faint, steady light to work by. She jammed the opening with more lumps of coal, gradually getting them further back along the sides towards the hinges, until at last the front was raised enough for her to crawl through.

It was a struggle, and she was terrified that the wedges of coal might slip. If that happened she would be caught by the heavy trap, but with an effort she wriggled through and stood free, breathing the cool air of the garden.

For a moment she was undecided. Ronnie's car must be on the other side of the house. Could she get the engine going and be away before they caught her? She thought of the rough, bumpy track, and decided that it would be best not to risk it. If she crossed the brook at the bottom of the garden, she could get through the woods and strike the road a few hundred yards further back, stop the first car she met, and hurry for the police at Guildford.

She skirted the side of the house carefully. Lights were still burning in the big lounge. She stooped below the level of the sill as she crept past the window, then she reached the lawn, the soft turf deadened her footsteps and she ran swiftly down towards the stream.

A fence lay along the bottom of the garden with a small gate leading to the woods. She unlatched it carefully. Immediately beyond it was the brook, plainly visible in the starlight; it was about three feet wide. Somewhere among the feathery alder trees a nightingale, belated in its migratory passage, was singing.

Avril jumped. She landed with one foot on the soggy ground the other side, one foot in the water. When she lifted her foot out of the brook her leg was wet to the calf and her shoe covered with black mud, but that did not trouble her. She must reach the police at Guildford at the very earliest moment. She stumbled forward through the low-growing trees, but the green moss was deceptive. At her next step she was ankle-deep in bog! She drew it out quickly, with a sucking sound, leaving her shoe behind. From nowhere, it seemed, water had filled the hole where her foot had been a moment before. She looked about her for safer ground and saw a great tussock of coarse grass between the trees. She jumped and landed on it, clutching a frail alder stem to steady herself. In the faint light she could see other tussocks just ahead. She jumped again and landed on the next, there were three more in succession, then they seemed to stop. She was nervous now, the fair green ground was treacherous; beyond the last tuft of grass she could just make out a fan of reeds and the wood seemed to come to an end—that was a sure indication of a real morass. To her left the ground seemed to rise a little, that should be safer although it led away from the road. Between her and the higher ground she could make out several hummocks. They were not coarse grass such as she was standing on, but had a mossy look and seemed a darker shade of green. In no place were they more than two feet apart. She should be able to use them as stepping-stones; the nearest would be the most difficult to reach, it was a good five feet away. She balanced herself carefully and sprang —the hummock gave under her like an airy sponge, she had sufficient impetus to get her second foot on the next, but it sank right in, the tussock disappeared like a pricked balloon and the ice-cold mud closed round her leg up to the calf.

She seized a slender alder branch, which gave under her weight, and struggled to free her leg, but her other foot was now in the deadly grip of the morass. She pulled and jerked frantically, her front leg was now in up to the knee—the branch snapped and she fell forward, wildly clutching at another tree. The sudden wrench freed her other foot, it came out with an oozy plop, but she had no time to place it carefully, and being already off her balance it came to rest beside the first. With a wicked gurgle the green slime closed about that too.

Avril was frightened now, every story that she had read of people who were trapped in marshes and quicksands to suffer a terrible death came back to her. Yet surely this bog could not be of any depth? That safe tussock of grass that she had left was not more than ten feet away—she was scarcely further from the stream—and beyond lay the safety of the sloping garden. She could see the lights of the house clearly through the low branches of the alders, and yet she dared not call for help, Hinckman was there, how he would triumph in her recapture. At worst she would have to remain there, a prisoner, till the morning.

She ceased to struggle, hoping that she would not sink further in, and endeavoured to support her weight a little with the aid of two more frail stems of alders, but the oozing slime was already well past both her knees, the cold of it was chilling her feet and legs.

For half an hour that seemed like a whole night, she remained quite still. She tried to deceive herself, but she knew that the mud was gaining on her. Then for a moment her nerve broke and she began another frantic struggle to get free. The green slime made little sucking noises as she fought, it almost seemed as if this terrible soulless enemy were conscious, and chuckling with a foul delight as it drew her further into its cold embrace. When with a sobbing breath she ceased to fight once more she was engulfed up to her hips.

Avril's heart thudded in her chest, her breath came in little gasps. She was frightened now that she might lose her life unless she called for help. How ghastly it would be to die, choking and screaming, as the mud crept up over her neck and face. She stayed rigid for a while, the icy cold was numbing her limbs, and she was afraid that she would soon have cramp in one leg. She remembered reading somewhere that the proper thing in such a situation was to fling yourself forward on your face and crawl. You stood a greater chance by distributing the weight of you body over the soft ground, but it was too late to think of that. She was sunk in the mire now up to her waist, she *could* not throw herself forward!

The nightingale still sang his songs some distance to the left, while she stood shivering, half-embedded in the slimy ooze. Within a few feet of her great golden kingcups showed faintly in the pale light. About the place brooded all the quiet serenity of an English summer night.

Thirty miles away lay the greatest city in the world, with its eight million inhabitants, its theatres, churches, palaces, and restaurants, all those miles upon miles of stone and brick that man has made as a sure shield against the dangers and treachery of nature—while here, in the marshy glade, the scene remained unaltered since the Ancient Britons set their snares for moorhen in the marsh and the Roman Legions passed that way.

Since her last struggle it seemed that she was sinking much more rapidly, and the cramp which she had feared, seized her right leg—she could feel no trace of bottom to the bog. It was no use to struggle any more, she was so far in that she could hardly move her limbs, and every motion gave rise to that evil, persistent sucking. She must shout for help, that was the only thing to do, and *now*, before it was too late. Bitterly she accepted her defeat and called lustily for Hinckman.

For a moment there was no reply and she had a sudden awful fear that he and Vitelma might have abandoned the cottage after the shooting. She called again, louder, choking back her sobs of rage, and then she saw him against the lighted windows coming down the garden path.

'Well, where you got to?' he cried, pausing at the little gate on the other side of the brook.

'I'm here,' said Avril between her sobs. 'Stuck in this wretched bog.'

'You don't say!' he drawled. 'Stay put, I'll fetch a torch.'

It seemed that he was away for ages, and she could feel the mud pressing in below her breasts. At last he returned and shone the light in among the trees.

He laughed when he saw her. 'Well, I'll say you're in a jam.'

'Help me out,' called Avril.

'Sure, I'll get a ladder.' He walked quietly back to the house.

Once more it seemed an eternity before he came down the garden path, dragging a long ladder behind him. With a sigh of relief, Avril saw him place it in position across the stream. The end of the ladder reached within a few feet of her. He picked up a coil of rope and walked across to her side of the brook, then he paused, shining his torch full upon her.

'Now, kid,' he said sharply. 'What happens if I get you out of here.'

'What do you mean?' Avril parried.

'Do you sign that damned paper or don't you?'

'No,' said Avril with an effort.

'O.K.' He turned away abruptly. 'Then I guess you stay put for keeps.'

'Come back,' she called. 'Come back.'

He stopped, turning to look over his shoulder. 'Waal?'

Avril endeavoured to bargain. 'What about Nelson Druce?' she said.

'What about him?'

'If I sign will Vitelma do all she said?'

'Yep—I guess so.'

'All right—I'll sign.'

He came back then to her end of the ladder and threw her the rope. 'Best knot it round your shoulders, kid—you'll take some shifting.'

She wrapped the end twice round her body, under the arms and then tied it firmly. 'All set,' he called, and began to pull.

Hinckman was a strong man, but the task was quite beyond him. The mud sucked and gurgled as Avril fought to get free, but the bog refused to give her up. After some minutes of vain struggling Hinckman threw down the rope with a grunt. 'Hang on, kid. I'd best get help.'

He walked up the garden path bellowing some foreign name that Avril could not catch, then he stood mopping his face with a large red handkerchief. A small dark man came trotting out from the back of the house.

'All l'or things pack, boss. All leady in auto,' Avril heard him say, and she saw that he was an Oriental in the neat dark clothes of a valet.

'O.K. Is Black Eye still at the far end of the trail?'

'Yep, Boss—he watchin' road like you said.'

'Go get him, an' make it snappy; best get Wally, too.'

222

The small man trotted off into the darkness, returning a few moments later with two other men, one dressed in a chauffeur's uniform, the other in similar kit to the man Ronnie had knocked out with the bottle. All four of them set to work on the job of dragging Avril out of the marsh.

It was a long and painful business; had it not been for the resourceful Oriental Avril's flesh would have been cut to ribbons. He fetched towels and cushions from the house with which he padded the rope where it went under her arms and round her back, then they all hauled together for the firm ground on the other side of the brook.

Slowly, reluctantly the marsh gave up its prisoner, and with a last great plop. as her legs came free, Avril found herself being dragged face downward along the ladder. She yelled to them to stop and then fainted from pain and exhaustion.

When she came to, she was in the sitting-room again, stretched out on the sofa. Vitelma was pouring brandy down her throat and stroking back her hair. Hinckman was leaning back up against one of the old oak beams that supported the false minstrels' gallery, a freshly lit cigar in his mouth. The others had disappeared.

Avril sat up with a shiver. She was covered with mire from head to foot and her lower limbs seemed frozen. Hinckman stepped over to her.

'Come on,' he said harshly. 'Let's get through with this. I wanta get away outa this place.'

'You let her be,' snapped Vitelma. 'Can't you see the poor kids all in. I guess you've done enough rough stuff to last you a piece.'

'Think I wanta stay in this place all night?' He gripped Avril by the arm and jerked her to her feet, then scowled at Vitelma. 'You go hit the car, an' make it snappy. Give Wally the wire to have all ready when I come. Now beat it.'

For a second Vitelma wavered. Her blue eyes were full of an angry rebellion, but Hinckman was in far too dangerous a mood to be crossed with impunity. His eyes were red and bloodshot, all his veneer of urbanity had disappeared. Vitelma had never seen him like this before and she was scared. She

223

half believed that the fight with Ronnie had turned his brain.

'O.K.,' she said sullenly, then to Avril as she left the room: 'Get it over quick, kid, then slip upstairs an' take a hot bath. I guess you'd better sleep here tonight—or you'll get yer death of pneumonia. I'll do my end about Nelson. Don't you worry.'

Hinckman supported Avril to the table and plumped her down in a chair. He dipped a pen in the ink and thrust it into her hand. 'Now get busy,' he said tersely.

Her numbed fingers could hardly hold the pen, but she scrawled her name at the bottom of the paper and then flung it down with a little sob of bitterness at her defeat. She let her head fall forward on her arms and burst into tears afresh.

'Can that!' said Hinckman fiercely. 'It don't cut no ice with me.' He blotted the paper quickly and threw it into an open attaché case that stood upon a nearby chair. Then he stooped swiftly and picked Avril up in his arms.

She lay there unresisting as he carried her out into the garden, thinking he meant to take her to the car. Her heart almost stopped beating as she realised that he had turned down the path towards the stream.

'Where are you taking me?' she cried.

'Where you came from,' he snapped.

'You can't—you can't,' she gasped.

'I certainly can. It's your own fool fault. If you'd signed in the first place I wouldn't have to. Think I'm going to leave you sitting pretty to put the police on me for shooting young Sheringham?—not on your life.'

'Help!' screamed Avril. 'Help!' The thought of being left to die in that terrible marsh sent her mad with terror. She fought and struggled to wriggle from his grip with every ounce of her remaining strength—but it was useless.

He strode across the ladder to the far bank of the stream and with a terrific heave of his massive shoulders flung her—a whirling heap—back into the bog.

23

Ronnie Sheringham cashes in his Writs

Nelson Druce lay upon the narrow bed in his cell at Brixton. He had been trying to read, but had given up the attempt some time before. He turned restlessly from side to side.

He had resigned himself to a long sentence of imprisonment —he saw no escape from that He knew that every artifice would be used by the capable Mr. Drefus to take advantage of the law's delays and so put off his trial, but the result must be inevitable. As far as he was able during the last fortnight he had put out of his mind the terrible experience in an American prison that awaited him. Time enough to face that horror, with what resolution he could muster, when the day arrived; but the very fact of what lay before him had made him more doggedly determined than ever to smash the Combine first. He was living from day to day in that one hope.

There were just four days to go now before Vandelstein's money became due. Avril would do everything that was humanly possible he knew to complete the film and get it exhibited by that time. He had learned from Drefus that progress at Hatfield was considered satisfactory. They had hoped to complete by today, but Nelson knew that some days at least would have to elapse before the film could be ready for exhibition, and even then it was no matter of the audience who witnessed it simply pouring money into a hat. Enormous sums would be involved and lengthy legal documents had to be drawn up before he would actually receive the money in his bank and be able to pay Issey Vandelstein. It would be a desperate race against time, and here he was cooped up in prison, unable to help in any way.

During these days of agonising suspense his only comfort had been the thought of Avril—that sweet, wonderful woman who was fighting his battle for him. But he cared not think of her too much, that way lay madness. Too think of Avril was to think of those fifteen terrible years in prison that he must go through. That was unbearable enough in any case, but knowing that she loved him made it a thousand times worse, for it meant the added torture of their compulsory separation.

How bitterly he regretted the shooting of Angelo Donelli. He had done it in the mad rage following his father's death. If he had only turned his whole attention to the Combine first, then later he could have dealt with the Italian. Perhaps it might even have been possible to bring the assassination home to him in the proper way, or trace his history and get him upon some other charge for his shootings in the past. Chicago gunmen were not always loyal, as Nelson knew, and doubtless Angelo had his enemies. He was too fond of women to remain without. It was pretty certain that at some time or other he had filched some girl off a confederate. Time and money might have unearthed many things to his ultimate ruin. Nelson did not regret that Angelo was dead for one second, only that he had not brought about his death in some other way.

The big key grated in the lock of Nelson's cell and his warder entered.

'You're wanted,' he said briefly. 'Good thing you're not undressed yet. Come along, please, and bring your hat.'

Nelson got to his feet and preceded the man down the long corridor, wondering what in the world could have happened. The order to bring his hat obviously meant that he was to leave the prison, but why, at this hour of the night? Perhaps they were transferring him to some other prison, but what an extraordinary hour to choose for such a purpose. He saw by his watch that it was after ten o'clock.

He was led out into the yard and locked into a cell inside a prison van. 'Say, what's going on?' he asked the warder who sat with him in the Black Maria.

The man shook his head. 'Don't know, not my business, and you're not supposed to talk. Still, there's no 'arm in me telling you you're being took to the Yard,' and that was all the information Nelson could get out of him.

At Scotland Yard Nelson was taken at once to a room at the top of the building. A big, burly, red-faced man with a crop of ginger curls was talking in a low voice to Captain Rudd of the American Detective Service. The big man turned to Nelson, his sharp blue eyes running quickly over him.

'So this is Druce. Got your note-book, Gartside?' He addressed a tall, lean Inspector who had entered from an adjoining room.

'Yes, sir.'

'Right, then we'd best get inside. Mr. Druce, I'm Superintendent Marrofat; there's some fresh evidence in your case, but the man wouldn't make a statement unless you were present, that's why we brought you up from Brixton. Come this way, please.'

Wondering more than ever what could have happened. Nelson followed Rudd and the Superintendent into the next room, the Inspector brought up the rear.

It was a small, white-painted bedroom, and Ronnie Sheringham lay there on the bed with his eyes closed. On a chair at his side sat a man in civilian clothes, evidently a doctor. At the foot of the bed stood a hospital nurse.

'How is he, Doc?' asked the Superintendent.

'Pretty bad, but I reckon he'll last out tomorrow.'

Ronnie opened his eyes, his face was deathly white, absolutely drained of blood, but he made a feeble movement to rise, and smiled as he saw Nelson Druce.

'Hullo, Druce,' he said, in a weak voice. 'Glad they got you here so soon. I'm afraid I'm for it.'

'I'm sorry,' said Nelson quietly. 'What happened? Have you had an accident?'

Ronnie shook his head feebly. The doctor raised him a little on his pillows, he coughed and the nurse wiped his lips with a piece of lint. Upon it showed a trickle of blood. Ronnie looked round at the little group of faces.

'Ready, chaps?' he asked.

The Inspector had his note-book open upon his knee. He nodded.

'Right. Well, I'm done for, I'll be dead tomorrow, so that's that, otherwise I would never make this statement, but as a

227

dying man it's up to me to tell the truth.' He paused and looked at Captain Rudd.

'You remember me in Hollywood. You remember that I dined with Avril Bamborough the night Donelli was shot?'

'That's so,' said the American.

'You remember I said that I was the first to reach her room after the shot?'

'Yep.'

'Well, I never left her, only for a few minutes to fetch something from my own room. When I came back she was fighting with that wop. It was I who shot him, d'you understand?'

'So you say,' drawled Captain Rudd.

'That's the truth. Her yarn about another man breaking in was to cover me. The chap was seen running through the garden may have been anybody—nobody saw him climb down from her room—there was no other man. I was with her in the room when the house detective came. I should have thought you would have guessed. I'd been seeing her every day. It was plain enough that I was in love with her.'

Captain Rudd nodded. 'Yep, that fits all right. I guess I oughta have spotted that—but where's Druce come in?'

'He doesn't, nobody would ever have thought of him, if he hadn't fallen in love with Avril Bamborough too. Then like a mug, when you arrested her, he went and made a false confession to get her off. You would have laughed at him and never let yourself be taken in by that—if it hadn't been that Donelli was supposed to have killed his father the night before, and you haven't even got proof of that.'

'That's a fact—we got nothing on him, except motive—but I will say that seemed pretty clear. Whose was the gun?'

'Mine, of course, I always carry one in the States, chap has to if the police can't make it safe.' A gleam of Ronnie's old humour showed in his eyes, as he delivered this last thrust. He sank back on his pillows, white and exhausted.

'Well, I guess that lets you out, Druce.' Captain Rudd looked at the pale, drawn face of the young man at his side.

Nelson was almost stunned by this strange confession, which lifted the guilt from his shoulders. He could hardly believe it to be really true. He drew a hand across his forehead and muttered thickly: 'Yes, it lets me out all right. I guess that's true.'

'Now, Mr. Sheringham,' the Superintendent leaned forward, 'we'd like to know how you came to arrive at the Yard with a couple of bullets in you, and darn near dead.'

Ronnie opened his eyes again. 'Better give me another shot, doctor, I feel—beastly weak.'

The doctor picked up the hypodermic which lay ready in its bath of spirit, on a table by the bed. He fitted it together and gave the injection in the upper arm.

Ronnie closed his eyes once more and lay quite still for a few moments, then he spoke again, his voice coming stronger than before. 'Chap named Hinckman shot me.'

'Where was this?' asked Marrofat.

'Place called the Cottage on the Common, near Cutmill, in Surrey.'

'When?'

'About half-past eight.'

'Was there a quarrel?'

Ronnie nodded.

'What about?'

'Same girl—Avril Bamborough—but it was over business this time.'

'Give us what particulars you can.'

'She has the rights on a patent. It was Druce's invention to begin with. Hinckman's the head of an American syndicate, they want this thing pretty badly—it means a lot to them. There's a girl called Vitelma Loveday—she's Druce's fiancée—and they've got her over from America, she had some scheme to get him off. I arranged a meeting between her and Avril Bamborough—drove Avril there myself from Hatfield this evening. Vitelma was at the cottage—Avril didn't know Hinckman was there. Druce's fiancée offered to get him off if Avril would hand over the patent—but she wouldn't—then the trouble began.' Ronnie paused for breath, he choked again,

229

and the nurse carefully wiped the blood from his lips. He lay still for a moment.

'Don't hurry yourself,' said the Superintendent.

'All right,' Ronnie answered feebly. 'Well, up to that time Avril didn't know Vitelma was acting for the Combine, but when she wouldn't sign Hinckman came in with one of his gunmen. They tried to force her, but I couldn't stand for that.'

'What happened?'

'There was a scrap,' Ronnie grinned suddenly. 'I ousted the gunman, cracked a bottle over his head, then I got busy on Hinckman with the broken end—but I was unlucky—he got the other chap's gun off the floor—and shot me—I faded out after that.'

Superintendent Marrofat stretched out his large hand for the telephone. 'Squad call,' he said sharply. 'Three cars and issue automatics.' He turned back to Ronnie. 'How did you manage to get away?'

'I came to about ten minutes later, I suppose, it couldn't have been much more. I was lying on the floor of an out-house, with the body of the fellow I'd done in. I crawled out and managed to reach my car, then drove straight here.'

'God! you've got some pluck.'

'I'd have passed out before I got here, if I'd stopped to see a doctor on the way,' Ronnie said weakly.

'What happened to Avril?' Nelson's voice was filled with tense anxiety.

'Don't know. Didn't see her after I was shot. I expect she's still there.'

Nelson jumped to his feet. 'Look here—I just hate to leave you, Sheringham. like this, but anything might happen to her now—if she's alone with Hinckman.'

'I know—don't worry about me. The place is just past Shackleford—about a mile, there's a dip, and as you go up the far side you'll see a red letter-box nailed to a tree—then—there's a workman's cottage on the other side, it's behind that, down a—a track, about three hundred yards from the road.'

The Superintendent and the Inspector were already near the door, Marrofat looked at Nelson Druce.

'I'm afraid we can't take you, sir—it's against regulations, you're still under arrest.'

'But I must go,' Nelson cried. 'I simply must, and I've been cleared.'

'We can't release you at this time of night, there's formalities to go through. That'll be tomorrow morning.'

'Now, listen,' Nelson pleaded. 'I give you my word I won't try an' escape, for God's sake take me along.'

Superintendent Marrofat looked sympathetic. Druce's terrible anxiety was plain to all. 'Well, it's up to Captain Rudd,' he said briefly, 'you're his prisoner—not ours—we're only holding you for safe custody. If he takes responsibility, I'm willing.'

'Sure,' Captain Rudd nodded. 'I ain't got nothin' on Mr. Druce—let's go get these guys.'

Nelson gave a sigh of relief. 'That's great of you, Captain.' Then he stepped over to Ronnie's bed and took his hand. 'Sheringham, I guess you know what I feel—I can't say . . .'

Ronnie stopped him with a warning look. 'You've got nothing to thank me for,' he said, 'except a couple of weeks in Brixton. I'm sorry about that—but I wouldn't have let you go to the chair.' His blue eyes gave the ghost of a smile. 'Still, if you feel that way about it you might be a good chap and clear up my bills—will you?—they're only a few hundreds—nothing to you—and I always meant to pay them some time. If you like to put it against this evening—count it as—man's time.'

'Sure. Of course I will.' Nelson pressed his hand, he felt a brute leaving him, but there was Avril. Feeling suddenly sick at the thought of what might have happened to her, he tore himself away.

A few minutes later the shrill sirens of the squad cars, setting out upon their night dash down into Surrey, came clearly to the little bedroom high above the Thames Embankment.

Ronnie turned feebly to the doctor. 'Well, that's that,' he said; and then after a moment, 'Wasn't it Charles the Second who apologised for being a long time dying? He—he was a great chap, Charles the Second. . . . I hate dying—but—but after all it's better than cancer at sixty, isn't it? and I've had a damn fine time.'

His lips twitched in a smile. 'Terribly sorry, doctor—if—if —I keep you waiting—now.'

24

The Fight in the Woods

The long, low police cars dashed out of the yard, Nelson was in the back of the foremost, with Superintendent Marrofat and Captain Rudd. Inspector Gartside sat beside the driver. The others were filled with members of the flying squad.

With amazing speed they flashed through the streets of south-west London. The theatres were just coming out, so the amount of traffic was considerable, but in an almost magic manner the blocks of taxis and private cars seemed to dissolve in front of them. There was no fuss or excitement, no policemen on point duty brought his hand to the salute. Senior officers in private clothes are never publicly recognised by the force, but every man knew the special number on Superintendent Marrofat's big car. With that amazing efficiency of which the outward signs are only a few quiet signals, almost imperceptible to the general public, the traffic was held or diverted, and the squad cars raced unchecked through open streets. Every man on duty knew that the flying squad were going forth to battle.

They were through Hammersmith and across Barnes Common almost before Nelson realised that they had cleared Greater London. Up the rise past Sandown Park, now innocent of its crowd of racegoers, through Esher and sleeping Chobham, out into the open country beyond. Past Foxwarren, with its private Zoo shrouded in darkness, the lake at Wisley a shimmer of pale light under the stars. On through the pine-woods with a deafening roar, then the outskirts of Guildford. Here again the police had been warned by wireless from Scotland Yard, belated motorists had been held or side-tracked at the first long blast upon the sirens of the racing cars. They tore down the steep cobbled hill of the old Cavalier city, swerved to the right, and up the rise past the station into the open country once more.

The Superintendent had wasted no time. He asked Nelson for particulars regarding Hinckman directly they had swung through the gates of Scotland Yard.

Nelson related all he knew or suspected of the gigantic conspiracy to control the Film Industry of the whole world, which had begun in Hollywood nearly three months before. He found that the Superintendent was already aware of Avril's belief that John Bamborough's death was deliberate murder, and was well informed about the fire at Frensham and the case which was being brought against Hinckman for attempted murder of the watchmen. Captain Rudd also proved well up in these affairs, and in addition, had considerable knowledge of the happenings on the other side of the Atlantic. Both were now convinced that this proposed Combine, headed by the Trans-Continental Electric magnate, was no wild figment of the imagination, but a definite menace, to accomplish which the leaders were prepared to go to any lengths.

With luck they should find Hinckman still at the cottage, but it was unlikely that he would be alone. It seemed probable that Ronnie Sheringham had accounted for one of the gangsters who had killed John Bamborough, but there was the other. He might be lurking there somewhere, and Hinckman was not the man to go about unaccompanied, there were probably servants who could be trusted to help him in a scrap. It looked as if there would be trouble when they reached their destination. As they rushed through Guildford they fell to thinking of the approaching fight. The Superintendent was profoundly thankful that he had ordered automatics to be issued to his men.

Nelson was thinking of Avril. She was there alone. She had been a witness to the shooting of Ronnie—after that, would

Hinckman let her go? Nelson prayed desperately that in the confusion of the moment, he might, but he doubted it; and he dared not dwell on what might happen to her.

Hinckman would be desperate now, Nelson knew. No longer the calm, forceful big business man, but turned by sheer force of circumstances into a hardened criminal. His decision to kill Barton Druce had led him, from that fatal night, into a web of intrigue which had compelled him to adopt one unscrupulous measure after another, unless he was prepared to witness the complete collapse of his vast plans. Lately he had even abandoned reasonable precautions. Tonight he had come out from behind his screen of gunmen and killed Ronnie with his own hand, while at least two witnesses were present. If he had been driven to such desperate measures he might murder Avril, in order to close her mouth. Nelson felt the perspiration break out under his scalp. All the relief which he should have been feeling at his miraculous release from prison was swamped by his terrible anxiety for her.

The narrower lanes necessitated more careful driving, but every member of the police who is allotted to a squad car wheel is picked from hundreds for his skill and nerve. The headlights blazed upon an ever-changing prospect of hedgerows and green trees as they took the bends and rises with almost breakneck speed. The towers of Charterhouse were left unseen in the darkness to their left, and a few minutes later they came to a halt upon the open common, some hundred yards beyond the red letter-box nailed to a tree-trunk. It was barely fifty minutes since they had left Scotland Yard.

They tumbled out upon the road almost before the cars had stopped. Marrofat and Gartside held a quick consultation in the darkness.

'This'll be the track,' said the big man. 'I'll take that, the house is about three hundred yards on, so they say. Take the men in the second car up the road, Gartside, and come in from the north. Captain Rudd,' he paid his brother officer from overseas the compliment of giving him a separate command, 'take the lot in the third car, across the heath and come in from the back. All drivers but one come with me.'

As he spoke a shrill whistle sounded out of the bracken, close to the road. 'Hello!' he added, 'they're on the look-out, that's a pity, we may have to use our pistols. Don't shoot, though, unless they shoot at us.'

An automatic cracked from the place where they had heard the whistle, the bullet sped harmlessly over their heads.

'Swine!' cried Marrofat. 'We'll learn 'em—come on, boys,' and without any thought of cover, he set off running down the track.

Nelson dashed after him, he had all he could do to keep up with the Superintendent. The big man was amazingly agile despite his bulk.

A dark figure was racing on ahead of them, the sentinel had left his cover in the bracken, Nelson thought, and even as the idea came to his mind, the man turned quickly in his tracks and fired. One of the police chauffeurs stopped the bullet. He swore loudly but ran on. 'Blighter got me in the arm,' he gasped.

Two cars were standing near the house, Hinckman's big Daimler and a small two-seater. A spurt of fire came from behind the large car, Wally, the chauffeur, had joined in. The other man had reached him, and together they bolted for the house.

'Stop there, you,' roared the Superintendent, 'we're police officers. Stop, I say.'

Neither of the men paid any attention. A sudden crash of shots came from the moor. Gartside's men had opened fire from the other side. . . . The chauffeur pitched and tumbled, they caught a glimpse of his cap as he fell before a lighted window. The other man ran on and gained the house.

A spurt of fire came from the window before which the chauffeur had fallen. For one second they saw the yellow face of the Oriental and then the light went out. The police driver who had been hit before, gasped and fell, he had stopped a second bullet.

Marrofat came to a halt before the fence and crouched quickly in the ditch. He fired three times in rapid succession into the window where the light had been. There was the splintering sound of flying glass, and then shots in return.

A burst of firing came from the other side of the house and then two clear single shots in reply; Captain Rudd had brought his men into action. The Superintendent put his whistle to his lips and blew two short shrill blasts. At his signal the squad men leapt out of the bracken and rushed the house from all sides.

After that pandemonium broke loose. The Superintendent threw his whole weight against the kitchen door, it gave like matchboard. The yellow man was there crouching in a corner. His pistol blazed, but the Superintendent ducked, and one of his men fired from over his shoulder. The Oriental choked and fell forward in a heap, blood streaming from his mouth. They pulled his body aside and rushed into the passage. Rudd was there, having forced an entrance at the back.

'Hot lot, ain't they?' gasped the little, tubby American. 'We gave one guy his, guess it was the bird in them bushes.' His face was streaming with perspiration, but he seemed in his element.

'I'll take upstairs, you take down,' bellowed Marrofat. squeezing his way up the narrow stairs. Nelson hesitated, the lights were on in the downstairs rooms, perhaps the Superintendent was giving his American colleague the honours of the battle. He decided to follow Rudd, who was already running down the passage to the end room.

Rudd burst the door of the sitting-room open with a rush, two deafening reports followed close upon one another, Hinckman stood, broad and massive, at the far end of the room, a smoking automatic clutched in his hand, his face grey and set. The first bullet had taken the American detective in the shoulder, and as he fell backward, the second sang past Nelson's head. Nelson caught a glimpse of Vitelma, wide-eyed and terrified, crouching upon the floor near the fire-place. He realised with growing terror that Avril was nowhere to be seen. Next second he had charged Hinckman.

The automatic flashed again, its shattering explosion sounding like a shell burst in the confined space of the room. The

236

bullet missed Nelson but hit the man who followed him. With his free hand Hinckman snatched up the lamp and flung it at Nelson's head. It caught him on the shoulder, knocking him sideways, he tripped and fell across a chair. In a second the paraffin was streaming across the carpet, a wide sheet of leaping flame. Marrofat had dashed down the stairs and was in the doorway, his pistol barked twice, and the shots crashed through the window. As Nelson picked himself up, he saw Hinckman spring from the window seat into the garden, apparently unhurt.

The flames were spreading rapidly, in a few seconds the armchairs were blazing, and a fierce crackling started as they seized hungrily on the old oak beams.

Rudd sat cursing in the doorway, where he had fallen, clutching his bleeding shoulder. He thrust his automatic into Nelson's hand. 'Go get him, boy,' he gasped. 'He's sure your meat.' He seized the collar of the wounded man who had entered the room behind Nelson, and staggering to his feet began to drag him into the passage away from the flames.

Marrofat bellowed sharp orders to the remaining men. Two dashed back through the kitchen and two through the side door on to the loggia, in order that Hinckman might be cut off if he tried to double back round the house. Nelson, with Rudd's automatic, had disappeared through the window, after Hinckman. Marrofat followed with mighty, crashing steps, like some elephant gone mad.

A rattle of shots sounded from the direction of the cars outside the gate. It was the wounded chauffeur, who, unnoticed, had crawled to the two-seater. He had got the engine going, and was off down the grassy track, bumping and swerving. Gartside was after him with all his troop. A back tyre burst with a loud report as it was hit, a bullet clanged upon the mudguard, another shaved the man's head as he stooped over his wheel and shattered the windscreen. The flying glass caught him in the face, and the car swerved off the track, coming to a jerky halt. Gartside had leapt upon the running-board, thrusting his pistol in the driver's face. The man put his hands above his head, then they fell weakly to his sides, as he collapsed from loss of blood.

Nelson and Marrofat stumbled and slipped as they dashed over the uneven ground. Shouts were coming from all directions, as they sought for Hinckman.

'He went this way.'

'No, he didn't—he's over there.'

'There he is—there he is.'

Someone blazed into a dark bush.

'Don't fire,' shouted someone else and Gartside's men dashed round the corner.

'Spread out,' bellowed Marrofat. 'Spread out, I say—don't bunch like that.'

'There! There he goes!' It was a voice on Nelson's right. He looked quickly in that direction, a dark shape was moving swiftly through the trees.

'Help!' came a cry. 'Oh, help!' from somewhere at the bottom of the garden. It was Avril's voice. He shouted in reply:

'Avril—Avril—where are you?'

'Here—in the marsh—Oh! quickly—please!'

In his excitement he had lost sight of Hinckman. So, it seemed, had the men who had just sighted him. Another burst cf firing sounded from far out on the left. Hinckman could not have moved so quickly. In the darkness Gartside's men were mistaking the low bushes of the common for crouching forms.

'Help!' came Avril's voice again. 'Help!'

Nelson ran swiftly towards the stream, he tripped and fell, sprawling full length in a great clump of St. John's wort, his gun went off in his hand, the shot echoing through the trees, the automatic was dashed from his grasp. Suddenly a figure rose beside him and a pistol exploded nearly in his face, the flash of it dazed and blinded him as a voice cried in surprise:

'Hullo, Druce! By God, I'd like to give you yours—your girl-friend's drowning in the pond.'

The automatic barked again, but Nelson had jerked himself

238

aside. With a sudden turn he had Hinckman by the legs and brought him crashing to the ground.

The two men fought and struggled desperately, each striving to get his hands upon the other's throat. Hinckman had dropped his gun. They slithered from the cluster of St. John's wort and rolled over and over down the sloping lawn. A sudden bump and they landed on the lower ground below the second terrace, Hinckman on top. For the moment every breath of wind had been driven out of Nelson's body.

The flames were leaping now about the gables of the house, dense smoke was pouring from the windows.

'Where the hell are you? Can't you speak?' Marrofat was roaring from near the house. He had dashed back with another man when Nelson's gun had exploded as he fell, but the fight was hidden from him by the dip of the terrace, although the remainder of garden and the terrace were lit up by the fire as bright as day.

'Help!' came Avril's voice again. 'Oh, help!'

Nelson knew that she must be within a few feet of him, but he was locked in Hinckman's fierce embrace. With all his strength he kicked out and at the same time twisted. Hinckman slipped out from on top of him and they rolled the remaining few feet towards the stream, bringing up sharply against the fence.

'There they are! There they are!' shouted a chorus of excited voices, and the squad men began to run towards them from all directions. In the bright light Hinckman saw them clearly, he wrenched himself free of Nelson's clutch, and staggered to his feet. His face was damp and ashen as he leapt the fence, landing in the middle of the brook. Somebody fired as he floundered up the other bank and crashed through the low branches of the trees.

'Don't fire. Don't fire,' yelled Nelson. He was terrified that Avril would be hit.

Her voice came clearly now. 'Here he is. Here—don't shoot or you'll hit me.' Nelson stumbled to his knees, by the light of the flames he saw the ladder by the gate and ran towards it. Marrofat and the others were pounding down the slope.

Wide-eyed and haggard Hinckman was plunging through the marsh, his feet sinking deeper at every step he took, but with superhuman strength, the terror of death upon him, he wrenched them free. He stumbled upon Avril where he had left her, she was now half-buried in the mud. Nelson was out upon the far end of the ladder, the padded rope that Hinckman had used for her temporary rescue clutched in his hand. He flung it to her and she caught at it.

Hinckman was within two feet of her, he clung precariously to an armful of alder shoots, balancing by one foot upon a hummock of coarse grass. As Avril reached out and drew the padded rope towards her it seemed for one moment that he was about to snatch at it himself. It was the one certain way to safety out of that morass, but behind it lay Nelson and the police.

The glare from the burning house was now so strong that the light penetrated far into the marshy glade, throwing weird shadows from the stunted trees and high tussocks, upon the treacherous moss; lighting the little rivulets of water that filtered to the brook and glimmering upon the stagnant pools where the bog lay green and slimy, in its most dangerous form.

Hinckman looked wildly round, seeking a way to safety. In the strange, unearthly light he saw the higher ground that Avril had tried to reach. He jumped and landed, both feet in the ooze, but his hands and elbows upon the firmer earth, his fingers dug into the coarse grass, and with a terrific heave he pulled himself onto the little ridge.

Avril had got the rope about her body, Nelson had commandeered a couple of the squad men to help. With one strong pull they dragged her free, onto the far end of the ladder.

Marrofat stood upon the garden bank of the brook straining his eyes into the flickering, deceptive shadows of the woods.

'There he is!' he cried, raising his pistol. 'There he is!' and as Nelson stooped to pick Avril up he caught a glimpse of Hinckman's crouching figure running along the low strip of firm land.

The Superintendent fired twice, but Hickman ran on,

bounding from side to side through the alder trees. Suddenly there was a splash and a low cry. They could not see him now but knew that he had landed in another patch of bog.

Nelson was carrying Avril up to the house, of which even the further end was blazing now. The place was a roaring furnace. Gartside assisted him to get her into Hinckman's car. Her teeth were chattering and her limbs like ice, but her eyes were bright, and not with fever. Nelson was there—how, she did not yet know—but he was there beside her, and she held his hand in hers, while they wrapped every rug they could find about her and forced brandy down her throat.

Faintly above the roar and crackle of the flames the squad men could be heard calling to each other as they searched for Hinckman. After that one cry all trace of him had been lost. Could he have been swallowed up so suddenly by the bog? Was he out there in the darkness of the marsh, sinking by inches, yet determined not to call for help—or had he escaped to the further side? The detectives dared not penetrate far into that treacherous morass, and after half an hour the search was given up as hopeless. Marrofat left two men on duty and came to the door of Hinckman's Daimler. Avril was seated in the back—Nelson before her, endeavouring to restore some warmth to her small feet.

With commendable discretion the Superintendent allotted a police chauffeur to the car, and closing the door left them to be driven back to London alone.

As the car jolted along the track towards the road Avril snuggled down, her head upon his shoulders—but after a moment she looked up with a little frown.

'Nelson, I'm still worried about that wretched paper that they made me sign.'

He laughed. 'You needn't be, my sweet—don't I keep telling you it must have gone up in smoke with the rest of the outfit half an hour ago?'

'Well!' she wriggled down again, 'if you're quite certain— kiss me!'

And he did.

25

Armistice

After her terrible experience in the marsh, Avril narrowly escaped a breakdown, but Nelson's constant presence and the knowledge that he was free proved sufficient to stave it off.

Three nights later her doctor agreed that she was recovered enough to attend the Première of the Super Film that she had worked so desperately hard to finish, and before it Nelson dined quietly with her at her flat.

There were dark hollows still beneath her eyes, but her face was flushed with happiness as they sat together at the little table, and while they drank their coffee one of her hands slipped into Nelson's firm clasp.

Only one shadow remained to mar the joy of his miraculous release: Issey Vandelstein's ten-million-dollar loan was due for repayment at midday next day, and Nelson found by enquiries in the city that it would be utterly impossible to raise so enormous a sum on the projector at such short notice.

He had cabled Hollywood for a postponement, but the reply from the Mozart office had been definite:

'Vandelstein still in sanatorium—not attending business—date of repayment must stand.'

For the tenth time they were discussing the situation.

'After all,' Avril argued. 'Hinckman's dead.'

'Sure,' he agreed.

Avril gave a little shudder. 'It's horrible, darling, to think of him choking and gasping in that relentless slime.'

'I know, but he was right out among the reeds where the marsh turns to watery bog—must have tumbled slap into it, and gone under in a couple of minutes.'

'Those minutes must have been ages, Nelson—still, he's dead and the whole thing hinged on him. Surely the Combine will drop to pieces after tonight?'

'I'm not so certain. Maybe there's another big boy in the

background somewhere, an' anyhow there's the rest of the bunch—Stillman, McTavish and the rest. They'll not throw their hand in now—this thing's gone too far.'

'What do you think Vandelstein will do?'

'He'll sure close down on me. Then he'll have control of Pacific Players and his own outfit. I'll bet he's fixed a price with the Combine already—they'd pay anything to get him in. They'll have eight out of the big ten then an' they'll go to flotation right away. It'll only be a matter of months before they have world control.'

'Well, darling, at least we have the "Z", we'll make our own little pictures at Hatfield and take theatres to exhibit. They'll be so different to the others that everybody will flock to see them—so we'll be small, but independent—just like Star Artists.'

Nelson laughed as he reached out for her other hand.

'Damn the old projector—I've sure got you, an' that's all that matters. Come on, let's beat it to your masterpiece!'

The Rivoli was packed from floor to ceiling; the grand circle and the stalls crowded with celebrities. A Royal Prince would honour the production with his presence, and everyone was eager to see the first fruits of this new invention which, it was said, would revolutionise the whole film industry.

The clever Mr. Drefus was there, and Superintendent Marrofat resplendent in evening dress, but beyond these two and Avril, Nelson and Titchcock, no member of the gay and careless audience knew the grim history that lay behind the making of the film they were to see.

Avril was greeted on every side by a host of friends who had not seen her since her return from America. It was her first appearance in public since her uncle's death, and she would not have been present had it not been such a very special occasion.

The great house darkened and the show began. A carefully selected comedy was put on the screen and then the news. The lights went up again while late-comers were shown to their seats, and the band struck up 'God Save the King'. His Royal Highness had arrived.

Avril made her curtsey and Nelson was presented as the

243

inventor of this new technique. The Prince graciously suggested that they should join his party, and Avril was seated on his right with Nelson on her other side. Then the big film began.

It was a success from the beginning. The new lenses had the effect of making the artists on the screen stand out with a clarity which the most expert photography had never been able to give before. It almost seemed that the actors had depth and body, so that their moving shadows came to life upon the screen. The only thing which could approach the new discovery for reality were those illusions which have been presented on a darkened stage by a complicated arrangement of mirrors; but here instead of lasting only for one silent moment, the film ran through all its scenes while the actors lived and talked.

Avril had played her part marvellously. It almost seemed as if the high tension to which she had been subjected during the whole production had served to give her new artistic force.

As she saw the result of her many hours' hard work unrolled through the space of seventy minutes, she felt herself that she had created a masterpiece. Titchcock was beaming as he saw his greatest creation come to life. Nelson sat silent through it all—the amazing realism of the photography was no new thing to him, but he felt that he owed a very great debt to Avril and Titchcock who had enabled him to present his invention to the world in so perfect a production.

When at last the film was over the applause was loud and prolonged, there could be no possible doubt about the verdict of the public. His Royal Highness was full of pleasant compliments and insisted that a private presentation should be given for their Majesties at an early date.

Immediately the Prince and his party had left the theatre Avril and Nelson were surrounded by their friends in the foyer —snowed under by congratulations on every side. Nelson was afraid that it would prove too much for Avril after her recent strain, and between handshakes he was trying to find a way for them to escape. Suddenly he gripped her arm.

'What is it, sweet?' she whispered.

'Issey!—Issey Vandelstein! Here in London.' Nelson pointed.

'Darling, so it is!'

They looked towards the little Jew. He was standing quietly on the edge of the crowd evidently biding his time to get near them. He caught Nelson's eye, and his gold teeth flashed in a grin of recognition. Nelson beckoned and Vandelstein edged towards them through the crush.

'Good evenin', Mister Druce.' He extended a warm hand. 'Ven the folks is gone Ai'll be vatin' for a vord afore you go.'

'No time like the present, Issey—come right along.' Nelson took Avril's arm and they shouldered their way through the admiring throng towards the manager's office.

Once inside Nelson smiled at Vandelstein. 'Now, Issey, let's hear you say your piece about the film. I'm mighty glad you chose London for a sanatorium—the straight stuff from a man like you is worth hearing.'

'It was fine, Mister Druce—fine! Ven yer goin' to start vorking der new projector in Hollywood, eh?'

'That all depends,' said Nelson cautiously.

'Vell, if yer vantin' any financial help. Mister Druce, vat's the matter with Issey Vandelstein? Ai don't vish yer no ill vill.'

'I'll say that's real kind of you, Issey.'

' 'Taint kind—it's business. Ain't I got ten million dollars comin' in ter-morrer—vhy vouldn't Ai put it in a good thing ven I see one?'

'You mean the money you loaned me on my Pacific stock?'
'Sure.'

'Then how about a deal right now, Issey? I formed a company this afternoon to market the projector. Miss Bamborough's in it—she's Hatfield now—an' I'm figuring to let in Uncle Andy and the Jung people on the ground floor. How about coming in, too?'

'Vell, vhy not?'

'Tell you what I'll do. Call it a day on the Pacific loan an' I'll allot you a fourth of all the shares in the Projector Company.

245

Now that's generous an' you know it, you'll see your money back time and again—but there's conditions.'

Vandelstein's eyes narrowed. 'Vat's der conditions, Mister Druce?'

'That you sign an undertaking not to part with any portion of your stock, an' that's to be binding on your heirs for the next fifty years. Top of that the Company'll give you full use of the projector in you own concern, but Mozarts must remain independent. They're to keep out of this rotten Combine for good and all.'

The little Jew spread out his hands. 'Vell, Mozarts is Mozarts, ain't it?'

'Sure—now what do you say?'

'Vell, Ai never vant no combines, and I vish yer all der luck in der vorld.'

Ten minutes later Mr. Vandelstein and Nelson Druce exchanged letters of agreement.

Nelson's eyes were bright with joy and excitement. He could hardly contain himself until Issey had left the office, then he seized Avril round the waist. 'Darling—isn't it just too marvellous—what gigantic, stupendous luck Issey turning up in London. Pacific's ours again, for keeps this time. Hatfield's ours and Jung, and Issey's tied to keep outside the Combine. Give me six months working the "Z" Projector and I'll smash them yet.'

But Avril was not listening. A moment before a commissionaire had handed her a thick envelope marked urgent. She had opened it at once and quickly scanned the few carefully penned lines. Her face had grown white and scared—she caught at Nelson's sleeve and thrust the paper in front of him.

'What can this mean?' she asked, with an anxious frown. 'Oh, Nelson, what can it mean?'

He took the thick sheet of paper from her and read:

'Lord Gavin Fortescue presents his compliments to Miss Avril Bamborough and Mr. Nelson Druce, and requests the honour of their company for supper tonight at Claridges Hotel. Should Miss Bamborough and Mr. Druce have prior engagements Lord Gavin Fortesque hopes that they will make their excuses to their friends and give him the preference, since by so doing they will have the opportunity of meeting the real owner of the "Z" Projector.'

Nelson looked up with a puzzled frown. 'I sure don't like it, honey, not one little bit.'

'Shall we—had we better go?' Avril asked nervously.

'I guess so—best know the worst if there's going to be trouble. If we only knew for certain that paper'd been destroyed or sunk with Hinckman in that bog!'

'Perhaps Hinckman got away after all.'

'No, he couldn't have—I saw the place with Marrofat in daylight after—he could never have got across.'

'Then the thing I signed must have gone down with him, or else burnt in the cottage.'

'That's so, honey. Anyway, we'd best go and see what all this is about.' As he spoke Nelson took her arm and led her out into the vestibule.

On the way to Claridge's Avril leaned her head on Nelson's shoulder as they sat together in the back of her car.

'What *does* it mean, sweet?' she murmured. 'What *can* it mean?'

'It's got me beat, dearest,' Nelson confessed, 'but I wish you'd let me take you home to bed—I'll go see this bird later.'

'No, darling, no. We're in this thing together. I wouldn't be happy to let you go alone. But there can't be anything in it, surely? It's someone who's gone mad—or some joke?'

'Wish I could be sure of that,' Nelson answered uneasily. 'When you were staying over in Hollywood there was some swell with a name like that at the Garden Palace. Ronnie Sheringham knew all about him—twin brother to some Duke or other—got a kink in his brain because he didn't inherit, so I heard. Now, I wonder? . . .'

'What, dearest?'

'Well, you know I've had a hunch for some time that there was a bigger man than Hinckman behind this Combine. If this is the man who was in Hollywood when the trouble started it is just possible that he is the bird.'

'But what can he mean by the "real" owner of the "Z" Pro-

247

jector, Nelson? If there is anything in it the whole of your wonderful triumph tonight goes for nothing.'

'I know, honey, I know—an' it's a whole heap worse than that—we'll be wiped out altogether. But there can't be anything in it—there just can't.'

For the rest of the journey they sat silent, both a prey to a new and terrible anxiety.

When they arrived at Claridge's they were shown up at once to Lord Gavin's room. Both endeavoured to conceal their surprise at the queer little figure that greeted them. Avril thought that she had never seen such a strange clever face, it reminded her of those marble heads of the Cæsars in the British Museum; strong—powerful—full of determination, but soulless and blank about the eyes.

Nelson found something almost repulsive in the small but perfect body out of all proportion to the massive head.

'I am delighted at the honour you do me,' Lord Gavin bowed, 'particularly as your evening must have been a tiring one. Even success is apt to take its toll of energy. Permit me to offer you some refreshment.' He waved his hand in the direction of a side table upon which stood caviare and fresh toast, a variety of things in aspic, and a beautiful array of fresh fruit— nectarines, raspberries and a golden Canteloupe.

Nelson motioned his offer aside. 'Very nice of you, Lord Gavin, I'm sure, but the last few days Miss Bamborough's been far from well—I guess she'd be in bed now it it weren't for the rather curious wording of your invitation. If you don't mind we'll get right down to that.'

'Indeed yes, I know quite well to what you refer. However, you will join me in a glass of wine. I can recommend the Steinberg Cabinet, a very fine example of that famous vineyard— but perhaps youth prefers champagne?'

Avril smiled, the little man seemed so anxious that they should partake of something. 'One glass of champagne,' she said, 'and just the tiniest morsel of caviare, if you insist.'

'I'll take a glass of Hock,' said Nelson, a little unwillingly. 'Now let's get down to business.'

'Ah, business—a most distressing word,' Lord Gavin murmured. 'Nevertheless I must thank business for the pleasure of receiving you tonight.' He helped them carefully and sipped appreciatively at his Hock.

'You mentioned something about the real ownership of the "Z" Projector.' Nelson kept anxiously to the point. 'Now what precisely did you mean?'

'I will answer your question by another. Were you aware—before tonight—that I was interested in the film industry?'

'I certainly was not.'

'Exactly—I thought as much. Well, I am, and to a very considerable extent. I own majority holdings in Reno Films, Alpha Talkies and Ubiquitous.'

Nelson's brows darkened. 'Then you'll be the man behind the Combine?'

'That is so,' Lord Gavin assented gently. He was feeling in a particularly good temper tonight, and he held all the trump cards in his hand.

'It was a great conception,' he went on smoothly, 'a very great conception indeed, but, unfortunatley, my poor friend Hinckman lost his head—and with it, I understand, his life. That entails a few alterations in my plan. Perhaps it would have been better for all concerned if you and I had done business together before, Mr. Druce. Things might have panned out very differently.'

'We shouldn't have,' said Nelson sharply.

'Indeed?' Lord Gavin's eyes glittered suddenly. 'And yet, young man, we are about to do business together now!'

'I doubt it.'

'We shall see—let us review the situation. Upon my side I have Trans-Continental Electric, Klein Brothers, Stillman Comedies, Reno Films, Alpha Talkies, and Ubiquitous. Do you think you can stand up against such a combination?'

Nelson gave a short laugh. 'Stand up and win,' he said firmly.

'I see. In that case I take it you would not be prepared to join the Combine, even if I offered you the great position at its head which Hinckman has left vacant?'

'You can. Just how far you're concerned in the murder of

my old man an' Miss Bamborough's uncle I can't say, but there's one thing I do know. This Combine's a dangerous menace to the whole industry and I'll spend my last dime to smash the darn thing up.'

'Dear me, what vehemence—but no matter, I have the answer to my question. And now, my young friend, perhaps you will tell me why you are so certain that you will succeed?'

Nelson leaned forward, his eyes hard and gleaming: 'Because you'll never be able to float the Combine—that's why! Vandelstein has given me an undertaking tonight to stand out. You'll never get him now—and you'll never get Star Artists or World Wide. You've got no pull in Europe either; Jung and Hatfield both remain independent and so shall I. There's too much weight against you—an' every one of your companies has landed itself with enormous commitments trying to pull this thing off. In six months I'll have rebuilt the Pacific Studios on new and better lines out of the insurance money that's coming to me—and when all your companies are down and out the profits on the new projector will send Pacific stock soaring to the skies!'

Lord Gavin nodded. 'My congratulations, Mr. Druce, you are a most intelligent young man. You have forecast with complete accuracy the position as I foresee it myself. Unfortunately I have failed to secure the margin of supremacy which I have always considered necessary to the successful formation of a Combine, and I must pay the price of my defeat. I am sure it will interest you to know that I have decided against the flotation of a Combine.'

'Is that so?—well, I'll say it's a darn good job.' Nelson did not seek to disguise his dislike of Lord Gavin's personality.

'You think so?' The little man smiled. 'Well, that is my decision, and I think we are agreed as to its result. The other companies must stand on their own. Their shares will fall in an alarming manner whilst yours will rise by leaps and bounds.'

'Well, I guess that serves you right.'

Lord Gavin shrugged his narrow shoulders. 'Let us not engage in personalities, my young friend. The point is this: I have said that I must pay the price of my defeat—I am willing to do so. Those vast profits which I foresaw will never mature now, but—I have expended capital. I propose to take no further interest in the film industry—but I mean to retire with honour from the field!—my capital must come back to me.'

'If you've dropped money, I'll say that's your look-out.' Nelson frowned. 'Anyhow, I don't get what you're driving at.'

'Simply this. You will remain in the industry and will therefore have an opportunity of reorganising certain companies if they come under your control—work which I have neither the patience not the expert knowledge to undertake. I propose therefore that we should do a little exchange. You will make over your holding of Pacific stock to me—the rise in value which is certain to take place will enable me to get back the money which I had expended—and I will make over to you my entire holdings in Reno's, Alpha, and Ubiquitous.'

'You're mad!' exclaimed Nelson, utterly dumbfounded by the quiet assurance with which this sinister little man put up such an absurd and outrageous proposition. 'You're clean dippy!—why should I?'

'Ah!' Lord Gavin quietly sipped his Hock. 'That is where the "Z" Projector comes in. You made the rights over to Miss Bamborough, did you not?'

'Well, what if I did?'

'And she, since your release from prison, has made them over again to you?'

'That's so.'

A sudden tenseness seemed to come into the atmosphere of the curtained room. Lord Gavin's pale eyes held Nelson's steadily.

'Are you aware that Miss Bamborough made those rights over to Miss Loveday some days ago, and therefore had no power to return them to you?'

Nelson's mouth suddenly went dry. 'Yes,' he said anxiously, 'but I thought . . . '

'You thought that the document had been burnt, eh?'

'Yep, or gone into the marsh in Hinckman's pocket.'

251

'Well, you were mistaken,' Lord Gavin purred. 'Miss Loveday had the sense to secure it when the police broke in.'

'Vitelma?'

'Yes—and in the confusion she managed to evade capture, although I gather that the poor girl spent a most uncomfortable night. The gorse bushes of our English Commons are apt to play havoc with silk stockings and a tender skin.'

'Where is she now?' asked Nelson angrily.

'In Spain, I think. I made it my special care that she should leave the country with all expedition. That was the least I could do when she came to ask my assistance to escape the attentions of the police.'

'By it, you mean, by handing over this thing which they forced Miss Bamborough to sign.'

'As you wish,' Lord Gavin shrugged, 'the point is immaterial, what matters is that Miss Bamborough made the "Z" Projector over to Miss Loveday, who in turn made it over to the Trans-Continental Electric—and that I hold both these documents.'

Nelson was thinking quickly. He had signed the articles of a Company to market the projector only that afternoon—worse, he had sold a quarter share to Issey Vandelstein that evening. Both were fraudulent transactions, and he realised that he had placed himself in a terrible position.

'Well, what do you figure to do?' he asked bitterly.

'I have a choice,' Lord Gavin answered slowly, 'strictly speaking, Trans-Continental Electric own the projector now. By handing over these papers I could save them from bankruptcy, and for that they might be willing to pay me a very handsome sum. On the other hand, Hinckman is dead, and I might have some little difficulty in obtaining the money from his successors—particularly in view of the fact that the patent is legally theirs already.'

'That's so?'

'However, there is an alternative. None but ourselves know the existence of these papers. If I destroy them your title to the projector will be once more indisputable, and your own Corporation will reap the benefit of your invention.'

Nelson gave a grim little laugh. 'Sure—I get you. You mean to soak Trans-Continental Electric who have the legal right to it, or else soak me whose moral property it has been all the time—well, what's your price?'

'Merely this little exchange of shares which will enable me to participate in your good fortune.'

'Say I refuse?'

Lord Gavin shrugged again. 'You would be a very foolish young man if you did. Apart from any question of a Combine the company which owns the projector will have the whip hand of the rest. You will be bankrupt in six months if you reject my offer, and I shall find ways to make the other people pay. I wish to save myself trouble—that is all.'

For a moment Nelson sat with his head buried in his hands, then he looked up again. 'O.K. I'll do it,' he said slowly.

'You can't, Nelson—you can't,' cried Avril, 'don't let him have his way—that signature of mine was obtained by force, it's not legal—let's fight it in the courts!'

'No.' Nelson shook his head. 'I'll do it.'

'Thank you.' Lord Gavin stood up. 'I felt sure that you would see the good sense of agreeing to my wishes. The papers are already prepared here on my desk.'

Nelson scrutinised each paper carefully, and then with seeming unwillingness, he signed. Lord Gavin took the papers one by one and blotted them carefully, then retaining his own, he returned the others to Nelson. After which he unlocked a drawer and produced the two original documents that had been signed by Avril and Vitelma.

'Would you kindly examine these?' he asked affably.

'Thanks,' said Nelson briefly. 'Yes, they're O.K.'

'Good, then let us destroy them and drink another glass of wine to our new partnership.' As he spoke Lord Gavin threw the papers on the fire, where they burned merrily.

Nelson accepted another glass of Hock, then he said slowly:

'Let's just get the new position clear, Lord Gavin. I control Reno's. Alpha, and Ubiquitous, while you control Pacific. Is that so?'

'Exactly. You see, my young friend, how modest I have been.'

'You certainly have,' Nelson laughed suddenly.

Lord Gavin glanced up sharply. 'What do you mean?'

Nelson drank up his Steinberg Cabinet and set down the glass. 'Only that you've made the most colossal bloomer. The "Z" Projector doesn't belong to the Pacific Corporation. It never did. It's my own private pigeon an' it's a separate company. Pacific's don't benefit one cent; you may think you're cute, Lord Gavin, but this time you've been properly stung.'

The wrinkles in Lord Gavin's broad face suddenly seemed to deepen, for a second he glanced at the fireplace where the vital papers were now blackened ash, and as he did so the hand that held his glass trembled so that he spilled his wine.

'That is not true,' he stammered thickly.

'It certainly is.' Nelson took Avril's arm. 'And now, since there's no more to be said. I guess we'll be getting along.'

'Wait—wait one moment.' Lord Gavin eased the collar at his neck. 'I haven't finished—you can't do that with me, young man.'

Avril became afraid. Lord Gavin's pale blue eyes had suddenly filled with fierce burning malevolence. The little table on which he leaned shook as he stood before them, trembling with rage.

'And why?' asked Nelson calmly.

'I know too much.' The words came in a hoarse whisper, almost a snarl. 'What of the murder of Angelo Donelli?—you did it! Yes, you!' Lord Gavin pointed an accusing finger.

Nelson passed his tongue quickly over his dry lips. 'No,' he said. 'No. Ronnie Sheringham confessed to that.'

Lord Gavin laughed, it was a weird, terrifying sound. 'That's what he told the police—yes, but it's not true. I know!—I was there. He was with *me* when the shot was fired—with me in my sitting-room nearby. He went along the corridor. . . . I took the balcony. . . . I saw you, a handkerchief over your face. . . . I saw her too!' His pale eyes gleamed at Avril.

She shrank away. How right he was, she knew. That small, child-like figure behind the curtains on the balcony with the queer, big head. . . . The figure that had stood peering in and then vanished so silently when she turned away to open the door to Ronnie.

Nelson mopped his face. He had thought that he was clear of that nightmare for good. Was it all to be dragged up again now with this terrible new evidence? A man who had been present and out of malice was prepared to swear to his identity. It was too ghastly—but he would not give in.

'I'll fight,' he gasped, 'they won't belive you.'

'You can't,' cried Avril, 'Nelson—please. Think what it means to both of us if we lose.'

'They will believe,' Lord Gavin whispered hoarsely, 'you forget that a man was seen running through the garden—that will support my evidence.'

'I'll fight,' said Nelson doggedly,' I won't give in, I'll stand my trial and expose every transaction of the Combine. You sheltered Vitelma from the police . . . they'll get you in that at least. I'll spend every penny I've got tracing those other murders. Thing's come to light . . . I'll get you yet!'

With sudden resolution he turned towards the door, drawing Avril with him.

'Wait,' gasped Lord Gavin, 'wait!'

They paused in the entrance of the doorway.

Lord Gavin sank into a chair, his massive head shaking as though he were stricken with palsy. 'I ask an armistice,' he croaked, glaring at Nelson from beneath his brows.

'Well?'

'Give me one month to sell,' came the soft whisper, 'a month to sell while you remain inactive . . . time to unload my shares upon the market . . . give me that and I will give you a letter freeing you for good . . . a statement to Miss Bamborough that I cannot help her trace the murderer because I was asleep in bed. . . . No one would ever believe my story after . . . if I give you that!'

'I'll deal,' said Nelson harshly, 'now write.'

With trembling hand Lord Gavin wrote the letter, dating it a fortnight previously.

Nelson gave a sigh of relief as he took it and placed it

carefully in his pocket. The 'Z' Projector was now his for good —he had control of three great corporations, and by selling a portion of their stock he would be able to buy his Pacific shares in again as Lord Gavin released them on the market. The menace of the Combine was over, and the death of Angelo Donelli could be buried for ever. He smiled suddenly as he took Avril's hand, and the little wrinkles that she loved came round his eyes.

'You can have three months if you like,' he said. 'Next week we're going on our honeymoon.'

If you would like a complete list of Arrow books please send a postcard to
P.O. Box 29, Douglas, Isle of Man, Great Britain.